Death of a Clown © 2012 by Heather Haven

The Wives of Bath Press
223 Vincent Drive
Mountain View, CA 94041

http:// www.thewivesofbath.com

Cover Art © 2013 by Dawné Dominique
Edited by Baird Nuckolls
Layout and book production by
Heather Haven and Baird Nuckolls

Print ISBN 13: 978-0-9884086-3-0
eBook ISBN 13: 978-0-9884086-4-7

Dedication

This book is dedicated to my mother, Mary Lee, known as Jerull Dean during her stint as a performer at Ringling Brothers and Barnum and Bailey Circus. While many exciting things happened to her in her youth, murder was never one of them! I thank her for letting me borrow her persona as a springboard for this story. She is, frankly, a wonderful person.

Acknowledgments

Along the lines of it takes a village to write a book, I would like to thank all the people who have helped bring this work to life. That would be Baird Nuckolls, my literary partner, for all her wise words, hard work, and strong support; Ellen Sussman, author and teacher; and the writer friends I am fortunate to know, including Elizabeth, Katy, Tracy, Maggie, Ginger, Sid, and many others my wanting mind cannot remember. Finally, thanks to my husband, Norman, for making the effort possible. You are all wonderful.

Death of a Clown

A Noir Mystery

Chapter One
7:30 a.m., Sunday, July 5ᵗʰ 1942

I didn't wake up this morning thinking about my past or a little boy's face that sometimes makes me cry in my sleep. No, it's a typical day and all I'm thinking about is the act.

I push out into space and up toward the canvas sky, the trapeze and I as one. It's exhilarating, the closest thing to flying I'd ever known. The fatigue from yesterday's Fourth of July parade and two shows turn into wings. I am more than an eagle. I am free.

The trapeze begins its arc back to the center of the ring and I throw myself over backward, catching either side of the bar with flexed feet. I swing like that for several moments, my long, blue-black curls falling loose from the snood and sweeping the air. I arch my back, reaching up from behind to grab the bar with my hands, then release my feet. The momentum swings me up and over. I land straddling the thin metal bar with my abdomen and find my balance.

Then comes the pose; legs straight out, ankles crossed, toes pointed, arms outstretched. I have a well toned body, and I know it looks good. Back and forth I go, smiling the grand, Big Top smile. Tin Foot, my web sitter and friend, applauds from forty feet below for a trick that goes perfectly.

The air, so silent you can hear the rub of rigging on metal, is pierced by a discordant, blood-curdling scream. It goes on and on, like an air raid siren. Only a siren has no pathos behind it, just sheer pitch and volume. This sound is one of the basest of human agonies, pure horror that comes from the soul.

Shock vibrates through my body and I topple over the thin bar, losing concentration, out of control, falling. Even with the safety net sixty-feet below, if I land wrong I could break my neck. I snatch at the bar with my left hand and hang beneath, swaying from side to side. The shrill scream stops as suddenly as it starts, shrouding the Big Top in a split second of uncanny silence. A low, anguished wail rises again into its long siren of death. I let go of the bar and lay horizontally on the air, my body speeding toward the ground. With practiced timing, I reach palm down for the webbing just as I hit the net. While my walk to the edge is fast and efficient, there is no styling for the audience, just a dead run toward the screeching voice.

Tin Foot, even with his limp, is right behind me. We throw aside the tent flap and run out, ignoring the light rainfall. I struggle to stay on my feet in the ever-deepening ruts and potholes of the muddy, narrow pathway.

Sandwiched in between the main and dressing tents, dozens of iron-barred wagons are kept, pulled in and out daily for the shows. Against the darkened sky and glossy wet from the rain, the six-by-eight foot cages seem to jump out at us as Tin and I dart by. Flashes of color - red, blue, yellow, purple, and orange – sparkle with the circus name in flourishes of gold.

Inside the cages exotic animals react to the screams. Gargantua the Gorilla grunts and pounds on his bars, big cats growl, bears rumble low and threateningly. The shrill laughter of hyenas slice through the air. The screams grow louder as we near the only green and gold wagon which houses Old Kirby, an ancient but beloved lion. There we stop, transfixed by the sight of the lion, silent and huddled in a corner, staring at the shrieking woman. The young girl lies sprawled on the steps directly outside Old Kirby's wide-open cage door, a figure grasped in her arms.

I recognize the wailing sixteen-year old assistant knife thrower but not the man, whose face is hidden in the shadows. I look for signs of a struggle, clawing, blood, something. There's nothing. In confusion, I reach out for the girl's shoulder.

"Catalena, what happened?"

She slaps at me so savagely, I stumble backwards.

"Go away," Catalena hisses.

I turn to Tin Foot, who comes forward. "Come on now, girl," he says. "Let go. Let me see how bad it is."

"He's dead! That's how bad it is." Her voice is hoarse and worn out. She begins to rock him gently, crooning to him in her native Romanian.

I grab her shoulder again but this time hold fast. "Catalena, listen to me. He may not be dead. Maybe we can help. But we won't know unless we can get to him. Now don't fight us."

We lock eyes. I see a flicker of hope come into hers then die. With a mute nod, she releases her hold and sits up, laying a thin hand on the man's breast. Her body sways in an unsung lament.

Tin Foot reaches out and lifts the girl in his massive arms. As he steps away, I get a clearer view of the man lying on the steps. His face is turned to the side, obscured by a fall of light brown hair and broken pieces of straw. I reach with trembling fingers for pulse points at both his wrist and neck and find none.

I brush away the hair to reveal the swollen and lifeless features of Eddie Connors, the youngest of the clowns. Vacant, bulging eyes stare back at me. A protruding tongue along with mottled purple and white skin, create a grotesque image, much like something from a Lon Chaney horror movie.

Breathing hard, I lean against the bars, flashes of a living Eddie running through my mind. He was about twenty, two years younger than I, and only with the circus a short time. He called it his new home.

Above the body, the lion's cage door gapes open. I pull myself together knowing I have to shut it. Old Kirby might be the most gentle and sweet-natured of the big cats, but he is still a wild animal and could be unpredictable, especially in times of stress. More to the point, if Old Kirby wanders out, a panicky townsperson might shoot him.

I move carefully to the other side of the steps and give the barred door a small shove. It swings closed easily on well-oiled hinges, the round staples of the door and cage aligning perfectly. That's when I see the padlock is missing. If I can't find the lock, I'll have to use rope, anything I can get my hands on, to keep the door closed.

Searching in the mud below the steps, I spot it lying on a patch of grass under the shadow of the top step. The heavy lock feels as cold as a block of ice. I look down into its polished surface and see the reflection of my own brown eyes, large and darkened by death. It has tracked me down again. Sometimes you can never be free.

Stretching up, I pass the hinged shackle through the door and iron frame and snap it closed. I pull on the lock several times to make sure it's secure. Whatever happened here, the lock did not come off of its own accord. Backing away from the stairs, I fold my arms about me, trembling not just from the rain and cold but the violent death of a sweet, sweet kid.

Chapter Two
7:45 a.m., Sunday

With such close proximity to the sleeping cars, it's only a matter of time before others show up. Surprisingly, Vince is the first. A short, lumpy man with large ears and a pockmarked face, the general manager of the circus races around a corner, still buttoning his shirt. He's followed closely by three half-dressed roustabouts, the men who erect and dismantle tents, care for the grounds, and handle animals and equipment. One of the many nameless kids who travel with the circus tagged behind.

"What's going on here?" Vince holds his side, gasping for breath. "What's happened? Who's been screaming?" His gaze jerks from Tin Foot to Catalena and then back.

I answer before Tin Foot can speak. "It's Eddie Connors. There's been an accident." Vince looks beyond Tin Foot, and sees me for the first time.

I point at the clown's body on the steps. "He's dead."

His eyes follow my gesture and he comes around to my side of the wagon.

"Holy Toledo." Vince stands gaping, unable to move. Then he rouses himself and begins to pace, looking from one shaken roustabout to the other. "What do we do? This has never happened before. What do we do?"

"Send for the police, Vince," I say, but either he doesn't hear or is ignoring me.

I decide to keep my mouth shut, at least for the moment. I know a thing or two about what to do at times like this, having previously been a private investigator for a short time with the Brinks Detective Agency, but it's something I keep a low profile on around here.

I look past Vince and watch Tin Foot carry Catalena's limp body under the awning of the nearby panther's wagon to get out of the rain. She lies against my giant friend's chest, eyes looking at nothing, breathing rapid and shallow. She needs to be brought to the First Aid Tent as soon as possible. I go over, take off my thin sweater and drape what little there is of it around her.

A stunned and shivering group of people still in their nightwear begin to gather in the rain, uncertain of what to do. One of the First of Mays lets out a small scream and weeps uncontrollably, clasping at her face. I hear soothing murmurs directed at this girl, still among the living. No one is murmuring much to Eddie.

I know Catalena needs help, but I was the one to find Eddie and I feel responsible for carrying through; that's my style. I don't want to leave the crime scene in Vince's useless hands. Then I notice Margie pressing her way through the crowd. Six-feet tall in bare feet, with henna-dyed golden hair, she tends to stand out.

"Margie," I call out. "Over here."

"What's the skinny, Jeri? What gives?" Margie asks, a bit bleary-eyed from sleep or maybe her current lover, a newly hired trumpet player. "Somebody hurt?"

I grab her hand and pull her closer to me.

"That young clown, Eddie, is dead," I whisper. I throw a glance over to Catalena but she is beyond hearing my voice or anyone else's.

"Dead?" Margie stutters. "What happened?"

"Will you help Tin take Catalena to the First Aid Tent? She found Eddie."

"Poor kid," Margie looks in sympathy at the young girl curled up in Tin Foot's arms. When her large green eyes come back at me, they're filled with questions.

"Listen," I say before she can speak, "I'll tell you about it later."

"You'd better spill like a milk jug when I see you."

"I promise. And throw your robe over her while you're at it," I say. "I think she's gone into shock. We need to keep her warm."

"Sure, sure. But jeesh, I don't have much on under this," Margie murmurs.

"Take it off, anyway. Give the guys a thrill."

"I usually charge for this," Margie quips but strips off her heavy, chenille bathrobe, revealing a sheer, black-lace nightgown underneath. Margie throws the robe over the girl.

I touch Tin Foot on the shoulder and bring him back from wherever he's gone in his mind. "Take her to Doc's tent, so he can look at her. Margie will go with you."

"Whatever you say, Jeri."

"It's going to be okay, sweetheart," I hear Margie say to Catalena as I stroke her cheek.

"Go on." Margie waves me off. "Don't get a case of Italian Catholic guilt, Toots. We've got her. She'll be all right."

I shoot her a grateful look and turn back to Old Kirby's wagon. Roustabouts wander around almost tripping over one another while Vince swipes at his face with a bulky, wrinkled handkerchief. Whether the moisture is due to the light rain or nervous sweat, I can't tell; probably a little of both. He might be good at the every day running of the circus but he's often thrown by an unexpected situation or crisis. I've wondered more than once how he got the job. I guess it's slim pickings, what with the war.

I feel anger boiling up inside me as I watch him. He needs to do something, take charge. I step up, about to let him have it, when Vince shouts for quiet. The restless crowd settles down and looks at him expectantly. He turns to the boy trailing behind him, eager to be useful.

"You! With the red hair. Go wake up Boss Man. You know his sleeper car?" The boy nods, cheeks red from excitement. "Tell him there's been a terrible accident and he's got to come to the big cat wagons right away."

"Yes, sir." The boy turns to run.

"Wait a minute, kid." Vince hesitates. The boy stops in his tracks, awaiting further instructions.

"Don't say a *terrible* accident. That might scare him. Just say, 'there's been an accident.' Got that?"

"Yes, sir. I'm to tell Mr. Tony that there's been an accident and he's to come to the big cat wagons right away," the boy repeats.

"Yes, that's it," Vince says, wiping at his face again with the soggy cloth. "Hurry up now."

The boy takes off, with Vince and the roustabouts watching him, unwilling or unable to turn their eyes back to the lifeless man on the steps of the wooden carriage.

I go to the edge of Old Kirby's wagon directly behind Vince. Out of his line of vision, I scrutinize the clown's body.

Judging from Eddie's face, I'm pretty sure he'd been strangled but with the shirt collar, tie and jacket, I can't see much of his neck. I lean in, almost touching his face with my nose, and get a whiff of Old Spice After Shave Lotion. I twist, straining to see down inside his shirt. There lies a half-inch, flat wire, pulled so tightly it's imbedded in the skin, all except below his right ear. Small, random driblets of dried blood blotch his skin, but not enough to have bled through the shirt.

"Move out of the way, Jeri, so I can see what's happened."

I straighten up and turn to find Doc Williams standing directly behind me. In one hand he carries his medical bag. Though there is a steady sprinkling of rain, the other hand clutches a closed, thin black umbrella, emphasizing the doctor's own bony frame.

I step aside and let him take my place, realizing I never once considered calling the circus doctor for Eddie. No one had. We knew he was dead from the first moment we saw him.

"What a shame. So young," Doc says. "Hmm. His skin is cold to the touch," he mutters, "but it's chilly this morning.

It's going to be hard to know how long he's been dead until there's an autopsy." He pulls back the shirt collar staring at the bit of wire revealed below the clown's ear.

"Looks like he was strangled. Too bad it happened in Old Kirby's wagon. Circus folks are already superstitious about the color green."

I don't say anything. He seems to be talking more to himself than to me.

"Jeri, did you know this boy?" Doc asks, suddenly aware of me. "He never came to see me, but I heard good things about him. He seemed like a nice young man."

I finally speak. "He was." I feel my throat constrict and take a deep breath. It will be less painful to concentrate on what's happened rather than the boy himself.

"Doc, I don't think it happened here. I mean, not here at Old Kirby's cage," I say. "And by the way, Catalena Baboescu found him and she's pretty broken up. Margie and Tin Foot have taken her to your tent."

"As soon as I finish, I'll go look at her." Doc shakes his head. "Although, I don't see that I can do much here." He turns to me. "Why did you say that? About it not happening here?" Doc's hand rakes his unshaved chin.

I look at the slight man with the watery blue eyes. He is clever in so many ways. I know that. Didn't he come up with that tin big toe for Tin Foot, enabling him to perform and walk with only a slight limp? Doc has done other things and not just for the humans, either. Just the other day he made a sling for the mother chimpanzee to carry her newborn in when she'd hurt her arm and couldn't hold the baby. And yet in some ways Doc can be almost myopic. The obvious can elude him when least expected.

I lean into him, not wanting to be overheard. "The straw and mud on the back of his shoes and legs, for one thing," I say, pointing to the clown's feet. "Plus look at the drag marks in the mud." He follows my hand movements with startled eyes. "They begin back that way. The rain's going to wipe them out soon, if it keeps up like this."

The rustle of the crowd stops any reply on the doctor's lips. We turn to see Boss Man, Tony Phillips, arrive. He is tall, elegant, and soft spoken, with an outer shell which belies the shrewd, power house of the inner man. James and Harry North, known as the Brothers, are heirs to the Big Top. They travel with the circus but are rarely seen. The Brothers prefer to stay in the background, leaving the day-to-day running to Tony and his assistant, Vince.

Boss Man keeps his distance but studies the sight on the steps of Old Kirby's wagon. "Jesus Christ. This is bad," he says. On the heels of his words, the rain changes abruptly from light to heavy. He glances up at the sky and tugs at the brim of his Panama straw hat to shield his face.

"Get those awnings down!" he shouts to Vince. "Can't you see it's raining? These animals can take the cold but they can't take the wet, too. You know that."

"Yes sir, Tony," Vince says, visibly relieved to give over authority. Turning to the roustabouts standing nearby, Vince barks out orders. "Didn't you hear the Boss Man? Get those awnings down right now!"

Several men hustle, lowering rolled up canvas on either long side of each wagon.

The animals taken care of, Tony nears Old Kirby's wagon and stands in front of Eddie. His usual tanned face wears a grim pallor and his David Niven mustache twitches on one side.

Tony and I are friends of a sort, getting to know one another due to his involvement with my other best friend, Doris. I have respect for him, even like him, but find dealing with his bouts of self-centeredness and mood swings difficult. Doris chooses to ignore his moodiness and her southern charm tends to bring out the best in him, as it does with everybody. Besides, she loves him. That forgives a lot.

Tony turns to me. "Are you the one who found him?"

"To be exact, Catalena found him," I say. "Tin and I heard her screams and came to help. There's a wire around his neck. He's been strangled."

"You didn't touch anything, did you? Not just him. You didn't touch anything in or around the cage, did you?"

"Of course not," I reply, a little sharper than I intend. "Wait a minute. The cage door was open. I closed it. Other than picking up the lock and putting it back on the door, I didn't touch him or anything else."

"Good," he answers. "No point in giving the local authorities even more to grouse about. There's going to be hell to pay for this as it is. They always feel they have to put up with enough when a circus is in town, never mind a murder," he adds, staring down at the body.

My eyes well up at the thought of Eddie's murder being no more than a nuisance to the town of Springfield. I fasten my gaze on the clown whose final mask is one of terror and death.

Tony looks at me. "I'm sorry, Jeri. That sounded more callous than I meant." He blows out a deep sigh, revealing the stress he's trying not to show. "I guess we shouldn't touch anything here."

"Sure we should," answers Doc, who walks up behind us. "Won't do to have Old Kirby get pneumonia. Get the other side, Jeri," he orders.

Doc and I go to opposite sides and release the cords. Both awnings drop in one fluid movement, rain tapping softly against the fabric.

Tony turns away from the scene, yanks the collar up on his trench coat and reaches into his pocket for several coins. He motions to the red-headed boy who had fetched him, loitering two paces behind ever since.

"Here, son. Take these nickels and drive my car to that soda fountain back near Five Points, the one with the public telephone. The keys are in the ignition. You know how to drive, son?"

The boy nods.

"How old are you?" Tony asks, staring at the boy.

"Sixteen, sir." The boy gulps.

"What's your name?" asks Tony.

"Wally, sir."

"You look more like thirteen or fourteen to me but okay, Wally. Call the sheriff and tell him to get here as quick as he can. Then you turn around and drive right back."

"Yes, sir," Wally says, swelling with pride at being given such an important assignment.

"And hurry up," Tony shouts to the boy's disappearing back. He turns to the general manager. "Vince, you'd better go wake up one of the cat hands, make it Harold, and get him over here to keep an eye on the lion until the sheriff arrives. Then find out how old that Wally youngster really is. We don't need to get in Dutch with social services again." He looks at the wagon again.

"Have one of your boys stay with the wagon 'til someone in authority gets here. I've got to go and let the Brothers know about this."

"Right away, Boss Man," says Vince, as he takes off in a run, forgetting to assign one of the roustabouts the task of staying put. Tony's eyes follow him with a look of exasperation.

"I'll stay, Tony," I say, coming up to his side. "Kirby and I are old friends."

He looks over at me and mouths a 'thank you, Jeri.'

"I'd better go see about Catalena," the doctor says, unfurling his umbrella in the downpour. "There's nothing more I can do here."

Tony turns to the crowd. "Everybody get inside and out of the rain. This man can't be hurt anymore," He adds, "and like Doc says, it won't do for the rest of us to get
pneumonia." He ushers people toward the big tent as he speaks.

At the other side of the wagon, I flip the lowered canvas awning over my head, hoping not to get any wetter than I already am. I reach a soothing hand in between the bars to the panting lion, overlooked in the tragedy, who is suffering himself from the shock of what has happened.

Old Kirby is a long time favorite of mine and in his prime, a magnificent animal. Now over eighteen years old, silver flecks the gold of his muzzle and mane. He endures rheumatism and tooth loss but his one-time nobility is still apparent. Though Old Kirby is no longer able to perform many tricks, he's trotted out at the end of the act by the lion tamer's assistant, posing on a red stand emblazoned with a gold star, and roars on cue.

Last year, when the assistant sprained her ankle, I stepped in to help for a few days and discovered this fine example of a wild, predatory animal was just an old sweetie. I have to laugh when his mere size and regal bearing brings gasps from the audience.

He reaches over and licks my hand with his enormous tongue, maybe in gratitude.

"It's okay, Kirby. You relax now. It'll be okay." I whisper again and again, stroking his chest and the shoulder leaning against the bars.

His labored breathing lessens, as does the rain, becoming deep and steady. Still, he never takes his eyes off the body lying on the platform on the other side of the bars. Neither do I.

I lean against the bars, with images of a living Eddie flashing through my mind. He'd been with the circus only a short time and always rescuing things. Went from house to house in Poughkeepsie to find a home for the stray dog he found by the railroad tracks. Last month he spotted a parakeet in a tree and talked it down to his fingertips. None of us that share cars are allowed to have pets or anything personal other than one trunk, but Eddie had coaxed the North Brothers into letting him keep the bird as the clown mascot, saying it didn't take up much space. Everybody chipped in to buy it a cage with all the fixings. Eddie was the type of guy who made it his business to save things. Too bad nobody saved him.

I look down at Eddie, a sheen covering my eyes. His left hand is balled up in a fist. I'm wondering if there might be something inside that fist, but my eye catches movement on the other side of the far awning. I can tell it's not the wind, but a slow-moving figure, brushing against the wet cloth. Old Kirby notices, too, his ears pricking, breaths becoming shallow and disconnected again.

As I open my mouth to ask who it is, a man's sadistic laugh freezes the words in my throat. I clutch at Kirby's mane. Beyond the expanse of the lowered awning, a black boot kicks viciously at the dead man's exposed legs, not once but several times. Horrified, I let out an involuntary gasp. The sound hangs in the humid air, almost as if it's a living thing.

I sense hesitation on the man's part; he isn't sure what he's heard. Seizing the opportunity, I hurl back the flap and run out into the cold drizzle. The man breaks into a run back in the direction from which he came.

I try to move faster but muddy earth churns like butter, grabbing at my feet and ankles. Rounding a corner, I hit a small patch of grass and the slick mound sends my feet out from under me. My right hip crashes into the iron hitch of the wagon, which hurts like hell. By the time I right myself and hobble to the other side, the man is gone.

Trembling in the rain, I rub my bruised hip, my breath coming in shallow, staccato waves, much the same as Old Kirby's. Maybe the lion felt earlier what I'm feeling now. It's like the very air we breathe is gone, commandeered by someone or something else. Evil stalks the circus. And even a gentle old lion knows it.

Chapter Three
8:15 a.m., Sunday

Harold, the senior lion handler, half dressed under a flapping black mackintosh raincoat, huffs toward me brandishing a whip and looking like a youthful Ichabod Crane. At his hip is a gun, presumably loaded with blanks-- the standard rule being that you want to control the cats, not kill them.

I call to him, "Harold! Did you see anyone running away?"

He screeches to a stop. "Did I have fun on the Great White Way?" he shouts back, mystified. "I was never on the Great White Way. I come from Nebraska. Nebraska!" he hollers again for emphasis.

Like most men in the circus, Harold is 4-F. Other than being partially deaf, he is fairly young and healthy. He has an old-fashioned hearing aid, shaped like a horn. He uses it when his wife insists but most of the time we just scream at him. Even the big cats learned to roar a little louder.

I grab his arm, make him look into my face and hope he'll read my lips. "No, no, Harold. Did you see anyone running in the opposite direction just now?"

"Oh!" he lowers his voice in comprehension. "No, there warn't nobody I could see," Harold answers, then raises his voice again as he sees what lies behind me. "Great Caesar's ghost! Who is that and what have they done to Old Kirby?"

"One of the clowns," I shout. "Eddie Connors. He's dead."

"In Old Kirby's wagon?" he asks, appalled. He goes to the other side of the wagon. "Look at my boy!" he says, focusing on the lion and reaching through the bars with both arms.

Old Kirby comes to life. He stands up, brushing his massive forehead against the man's upper arm, like a house cat. Harold coos softly to the animal, ignoring the nearby calamity.

I watch them and feel I'm free to go. Then it hits me, something that's been nagging at me all along. I race over to Harold and grab the sleeve of his mack to gain his attention.

"Harold! Where's the guard?"

"What?" he bellows.

"The guard!" I yell. "Who was guarding the animals last night?"

Now Harold stares at me. I can see his not-so-swift mind working. "Coke. It was Coke and Aspirin last night. Where is he?" He releases the lion, swivels on his heels, and looks about him.

"Coke!" he roars into the stratosphere. "Where are you, you son of a bitch? You left my cats alone and look what happened."

"Harold!" I grab him again. "We need to find him. He should be here. You start at the back end of the wagons and I'll take the front." I can see Harold's reluctance to leave the lion. "Old Kirby will be all right for a moment. This won't take long."

Harold shakes his head, thin, wispy hair blowing in the wind. "No, I'm not going anywhere. I'm staying right here. It serves Coke right, leaving my cats like that. He's off on one of his snorts with his cocaine tainted bottles of Coke he thinks we don't know about." He turns to the lion. "Old Kirby needs me. Don't you, boy?"

"But something must have happened --"

"No!" Harold interrupts. "My place is here with Kirby." He leans his head into the bars and the large cat licks his face.

I'm wasting precious time. "Okay. I'll do it myself," I say through chattering teeth. Harold turns around and looks me up and down for the first time. I'm still dressed in my black rehearsal leotard and flesh-colored tights, drenched to the skin.

"You'd better take this, sister. You ain't dressed for this weather," he says. He rips off his battered mackintosh, handing it over.

"Thanks." I shrug gratefully into the warmth of the coat. "I'll be as quick as I can. If anybody else comes, send them to help me."

Tossing a mental coin in my head, I hurry to the back of the line of wagons, checking behind bales of tarp-covered hay, large hauling tractors and other equipment. Coke is under the fifth wagon belonging to two sleeping tiger cubs. He lies half-hidden under the straw, curled up in a fetal position. If it hadn't been for the broken coke bottle by one of the wheels, I would've missed him.

I scream for help and crawl under the wagon, clawing at the soupy ground. Whitey Parks, head bull man and a guy I'm too crazy about for my own good, hears me and comes running, blond hair slicked down by the rain, cobalt blue eyes alert and anxious.

"My God, Jeri," he says, grabbing on to my shoulder. "Jeri, are you all right? Are you hurt?"

"It's not me. It's Coke."

He focuses on me trying to pull Coke free of the muck and mud, takes over, and plucks a limp Coke out by himself. I guess pushing a bunch of elephants around gives you the strength of ten men.

The two of us are breathing hard and covered in mud, Coke looking half-dead between us, when Harold shows up. The cat handler must have heard my screams and something in the sound of them made him leave Old Kirby and come running. He crouches beside us, expelling fear with every breath.

"Harold," I yell, "Go get Doc!"

"Tell him to get here right away with a stretcher," Whitey adds.

Wordless, Harold gets up and runs, sliding in the mud. Out in the rain, the blood and mud covering Coke's head flows in rivulets down his still face. Hysteria lobs at my throat but I fight it back and find Coke's pulse, weak though it is.

Whitey takes off his jacket and throws it over Coke's wet chest and torso. Whitey looks at me, eyes searching mine.

"What the hell's going on, Jeri?" He reaches out to touch my face but sees the mud covering his hand and pulls back. "You're sure you're okay?"

I nod and notice the rain streaming down both sides of his face then fall from his jaw line. Whitey Parks is one of the handsomest men I've ever seen in my life, with a rugged face yet patrician at the same time, tanned and impressive. It's an image that comes to me when I least expect it.

I give him a quick rundown, while I pull Coke's unconscious body closer to me. I try to shield him from the downpour and share some of my body warmth.

I finish off by saying, "I think Coke got in the way, Whitey, of whoever killed Eddie."

"What's keeping Doc?" Whitey looks around him. "Coke's too still for my liking."

"I know. I hope that doesn't mean..." I break off when I see Doc Williams, Harold and two of other roustabouts carrying a stretcher running toward us.

"Over here, Doc!" I call out.

"Hurry up," Whitey says.

The doctor kneels down on the other side of Coke and feels for a pulse. "He's still with us." He glances at Whitey and then at me, his voice low. "Jesus, this feels like I'm on the front lines again, one casualty after another. What's going on?" he says, parroting Whitey's question. His gaze stays on me as if I might have an answer.

"I don't know," I say, shaking my head.

He gives an abrupt nod and turns to the roustabouts, "Let's get him inside. Be careful putting him onto the stretcher. Mind his head."

After the men lift Coke onto the stretcher, Doc looks at Whitey and me. "You two want to come with me? You look like you could use a stiff drink. At least, get out of the rain. What about you, Harold?"

Harold shakes his head and turns back in the direction of Old Kirby's wagon. I glance over my shoulder. He's fiddling with his gun as he strides, maybe exchanging the blanks for the bullets he always carries in the back of his belt. I know that's what I'd be doing.

"Doc, I need to check on my bulls," Whitey says, meaning the fifty-one female elephants in his charge. They're called bulls but there's never a male among them, too undependable.

"I don't want to take any chances with them until I know what's going on." Whitey turns to me. "Are you going to be all right, Jeri?"

I nod, trying to hide the involuntary shivering. "You go do what you need to do," I say.

With a curt nod toward Doc, he takes off in a near run for the Bull Tent, his muddy jacket forgotten in the rush. I snatch it from the ground, heave myself up, and trudge after the doctor and stretcher. The rain washes mud and straw from my body, while the wind bites at my face and hands. I shiver as much from fear as the cold and wet.

I trail behind Doc but change my mind about going to the First Aid Tent. I don't want a drink and I can get out of the rain just as easily in the car I share with the other girls. Besides, it's not just the mud and debris I want to wash off, but some of the horror. And I need to think. With a quick goodbye, I head for the sleeping cars, wondering what or who will be next.

Chapter Four
8:30 a.m., Sunday

The fourteenth sleeper car, the one with the words 'Ballet Broads' written on the side in large, red letters, has been my home for two years. Pronounced Bally Broads, it's the official nickname for the railway car that holds the seventy ensemble female performers. Another nickname is the 'Virgin Car.' Take your pick; they're only words.

The typical ensemble car sleeps seventy male or female performers in two rows of upper and lower berths, on either side of a center aisle. Then there's the attendant, who takes care of his or her charges. The workers and roustabouts' cars sleep one-hundred and four in rows of three berths, crowded but doable. Bathrooms and showers are at each end.

Single men and women are always separated but married couples, families and specialty acts are given individual compartments for privacy. I haven't had a private moment in two years except late at night, when I pull the heavy, ringed curtains closed around my berth and tuck the ends under the mattress, shutting out the rest of the world. That's when I read my books and think about my future.

With one foot on the lower stair, I'm about to climb the steps to the car, when I hear a woman's voice calling to me, a voice dripping with fake camaraderie and a not so hidden agenda. I take a deep breath and turn to see Rosie O'Reilly walking toward me. A contemptuous smirk crosses her face, only to be replaced by an insincere smile when she catches me looking at her.

Without makeup, Rosie is a plain girl, about my height, five-foot four, with light brown hair and washed-out hazel eyes but a trim, well-proportioned figure. She's wearing a stylish trench coat and matching hat, the khaki color adding to the drabness of her skin tones.

As a featured performer, Rosie is a rung or two higher than me and jealously guards her status. She still likes to think of me as a First of May, the circus version of a chorus girl, but I've risen up through the ranks and have become one of George Balendron's personal favorites. Balendron and his wife, Zolina, are touring with the circus as guest artists this year, he as the choreographer of Dance of the Elephants, a production number starring fifty elephants and chorus girls, and Zolina as its lead performer. Besides Zolina, I'm the only one with formal ballet training and I'm also pretty athletic. Balendron often singles me out for the execution of difficult or important tricks, riding the head of Topsy, my assigned elephant for the year. Zolina is all for it, as she isn't that comfortable around the big, grey darlings. They take some getting used to.

The Dance of the Elephants is a major coup for the Big Top, touted about in all the newspapers and newsreels. After months of Florida rehearsals, the "classical" ballet premiered at Madison Square Garden on the first of May to rave reviews in New York. In Boston and Chicago, the reviews were equally as impressive. We're booked solid and beginning the tour of smaller towns in the mid-west for the rest of the summer and fall, before returning to winter in Sarasota.

This is only my second year with the circus but I'm a major part of this extravaganza, often singled out in each town's newspaper. I'm on my way. Everyone knows it, including Rosie.

There's more to her dislike of me than professional rivalry, though. Whitey Parks, the man I thought might only be my summer-time fling, has become much more. For him, too. A while back, he and Rosie were an item, but it ended quickly, although he won't go into why. I don't think it's so over for her. Lately, I can see Rosie's hostility toward me bubbling right beneath the surface. I keep my distance from her as much as possible, but it's getting harder and harder to do. It's as if she seeks me out, trying to goad me into some kind of altercation.

"What have you been up to, Jeri? You look like something the cat dragged in."

We stand with phony smiles plastered on our faces, Rosie with her hands in her coat pockets, body stiff and unyielding, and me with one foot on the step, staring at one another in the rain. It's silly. I'm the first to break the strained silence.

"Rosie, you might not have heard yet but there's been an accident," I say, "and --"

"You mean that clown's death?" she interrupts. "Oh, sure, I know about it. I know just about everything that goes on around here," she says pointedly. The focus of her pale eyes shifts from me to the mud-spattered bomber jacket in my hand. "So, why don't you tell me what you're doing with Whitey's jacket?" Her face is still graced with the bogus smile but the words are thrown down like a gauntlet at my feet.

I hesitate. I'm really getting sick of pussy-footing around her all the time.

"No, I don't think I will." I turn around and climb onto the platform of the Virgin Car. "But don't worry. I'll give it back to him the next time I see him." That last remark comes off as more of a taunt than I mean it to, but there's no backing down now.

I drape Whitey's jacket over the railing then peel off Harold's mack and shake the loose mud from it. I throw it in a corner outside the entrance way of the car. I can feel Rosie eyes burning into my back. She says nothing more and neither do I, but something had been ratcheted up another notch. Maybe two.

Inside the car, most of the curtained berths are shut tight, meaning the girls inside are asleep. One or two girls are up, staring out of the window of the small hallway, whispering to one another. Saucer eyes and inquisitive expressions greet me; I'm not surprised, considering how much mud is attached to my body.

I put a finger to my lips to shush the girls as I pass by. It's too early to start a conversation with so many still sleeping, so they allow me to wave them off and head for my bunk.

The two upper berths on either side of mine are empty; they belong to my two friends. Margie is with Catalena and Doris often spends the night with Tony in his own private suite. That means I have some breathing time. Unlike the rest of the girls, Margie and Doris would never take a refusal to talk about something like this, no matter what time of day or night.

I open my assigned drawer, one of two side-by-side under the lower bunk, and grab fresh underwear, soap and a towel. With one foot on the small iron bar on the outside of the lower berth, I reach up into my berth for some duds hanging inside on a hook.

Now that this is our second year, we three get upper berths. First of Mays have to make do with lowers. The lower berths are smaller and apt to be jostled by girls passing each other in the narrow aisle day and night. Their outside windows are at eye level, forcing the girls to keep the curtains drawn to avoid prying eyes. Their bunks are dark and depressing. The uppers are larger and the windows can be left open for sun and air, unless one of the clowns is striding by on stilts. Not all that common an occurrence, but it has happened. In truth, nobody likes the lower berths, but tough. That's the pecking order.

Heading to the showers, I pass an assortment of posters taped to the thin wall. *Suspicion* has replaced Joan Fontaine's previous hit, *Rebecca,* and hangs side by side with Errol Flynn's *Footsteps in the Dark.* I straighten the colorful *Loose Lips Might Sink Ships* poster that we are seeing everywhere these days. I think of my three brothers somewhere overseas, then of Lillian's son, Duane, stationed in Italy.

I don't know my brothers all that well, each one being at least a decade older than me and out of the house before I was six. I do feel like I know Duane, though we've never met. Passages of his daily letters, read aloud by his mother, the black woman who takes care of the housekeeping needs of the sleeper, make Duane come alive for me. It's one of life's ironies.

I drop ruined clothes to the bathroom floor, and get into one of the two tiny stalls in the small, metal room. Hot water pours down my face and body for fifteen or twenty minutes before I warm up and my mind starts to work again, helping to shut the emotions off. Once some of the shock goes down the drain along with the straw and mud, I begin to think about Eddie and Catalena.

Putting aside the question of what the hell they were doing at the lion's cage, dead or otherwise, I wonder if they've secretly been an item? She seems such a shy, withdrawn sixteen-year old. I've never thought of her as having a boyfriend or being involved with anyone. Besides, her father guards his two daughters closer than the Yanks guard the coastlines. But it's been my observation that love finds a way.

And Coke? How does he fit in? Is he an innocent bystander or a part of all this? Or is he part of a murder that went wrong on his end?

Chapter Five
9:00 a.m., Sunday

I emerge from the shower, start to dress, and notice my muddied clothes are missing and most of the mess has been cleaned up. Doris glides into the small room. A six-foot, Betty Grable look-a-like, Doris moves through space like the prow of a ship moves through water. Just as graceful and just as powerful. We mere mortals tend to step aside. Whereas, when equally tall Margie sails into a room, we put on our tapping shoes for a rollicking good time. They're both wonderful, fun, and loving. I'm lucky these two elegant beauties are in my life, me a short hoofer from Brooklyn.

I throw on my favorite red pullover sweater and black slacks, and listen to Doris' lilting, South Carolina accent scale up and down the octaves, softening whatever she has to say.

"Jeri darling, I came straight from the First Aid Tent to see how you are. Catalena's son-of-a-bitch father was there talking in that foreign language that sounds like a chicken with its butt on fire. How are you doing, hun? Tell me that."

I smile at her. "Doris, did you clean up after me?"

She throws a towel at me. "I did but don't change the subject. Honey lamb, I rushed right over here when I heard, like the good friend that I am, so don't try my patience."

She inhales a high-pitched, noisy breath, while bringing one manicured hand dramatically to her breasts, covered beautifully by a dark green and white polka-dot dress in the latest look: a low, square neckline, set off by white piping. My fashion plate friend quivers, as blue eyes narrow on mine.

"Tony says you're the one that found the clown's body, you and Tin."

"Yes, we did. It was something I'll never forget." An involuntary shudder runs through me.

"Are you all right, Sugar?" Platinum blonde curls bob up and down on her forehead.

"I'm anything but, Doris. I can't stop seeing Eddie's face."

Doris embraces me, clasping me to her ample bosoms. "You need some breakfast. It won't do for you to starve to death. The rationed ham's all gone but Lillian's fixing you some hot oatmeal --"

"Oh, I wish you hadn't asked her to do that," I interrupt, squeezing her back. "Lillian has enough work around here without you asking her to make me breakfast."

"I didn't ask her," Doris says breaking free. "She said she was going to and you try telling her not to do something she sets her mind at."

"That's true," I say. "Sorry."

"Oh, pish-tosh. Forget it. Isn't it something, though, about Eddie? And, Sugar, you could have knocked me over with a feather. Why would anybody do something like that to him? He was hardly more than a boy, you know?" She sniffs loudly, pulls a matching silk hanky out from inside the depths of her bodice, and blows into it.

"I know." I brush her slender arm with my hand.

For a sliver of a moment, she stares at me over the hanky held against her nose then jerks it away. "Are you thinking of finding out who did it, Jeri? Tell me now, so I can start my worrying about you right away. No point in putting it off."

"No," I say, turning away. "Those days are over; I told you that before. Besides, I'm sure the local authorities are more than able to take care of this. I'm on the sidelines."

"Well, that's a relief." Doris takes a deep breath and fans her face with the hanky. "Now you're sure you're okay? Really?"

I look back into her gorgeous blue eyes and am warmed by the concern in them. "I'm fine, but tell me, did you see Catalena or Coke when you were in the First Aid Tent? Do you know how they are?"

"I didn't see anybody but her rapscallion father, the world famous Constantin Baboescu," she says, striking a theatrical pose. "Then the nurse shooed me out."

"I don't know why you dislike him so much."

"I got my reasons. Besides, he never says anything to anybody. Just stares."

"Maybe he's shy. Not everybody is as open and friendly as you," I say.

"Open and friendly, my Aunt Fanny. You save your sweet talk for the elephants." Doris waggles a red-tipped fingernail at me.

I laugh. "All right, all right. Sorry." It feels good to laugh, but there are more somber things on my mind. "What happened when you were there?"

"The nurse wouldn't say a word to me and Doc was too busy to talk. Margie was inside the room because that child wouldn't let go of her hand, bless her heart."

I'm not sure whose heart Doris is blessing, Catalena or Margie's, but I don't ask. While she fusses with my sweater, straightening the sleeves and collar, Doris rambles on.

"I guess Catalena finds comfort with Margie being there. She has a soothing way of speaking, our Margie, when she doesn't do that thing she calls jive. What the hell does 'shove in your clutch' mean? She says that to me all the time and I don't drive a car. I can't tell what she's saying half the time."

"Neither can I, but it's colorful," I say, freeing myself from her grasp enough to towel dry my hair.

"That poor, unfortunate child, seeing something like that first thing in the morning," Doris clucks, shaking her head.

"I don't think it would be any easier seeing something like that later in the day, Doris. Was the kid sister there? This is all she needs."

"Not that I could tell, but they hustled me out right fast."

I think of thin, little Ioana, barely twelve years old, and not yet over the death of her mother. Everyone likes the two girls, Catalena and Ioana, They're open and sweet. But Constantin Baboescu tends to be a loner, seeking no companionship other than his children. He is known throughout the circus world for his amazing knife throwing act, even though he and his family had only been a part of a small, traveling Romanian Circus previously.

When his Gypsy wife was shot dead by the Gestapo last year in the middle of a performance, he fled with his small family, taking nothing but his precious set of show knives, with their hand-carved ivory handles bearing the initials "C.B." He arrived at Ellis Island to a job offer from the Big Top, where he thrills audiences at every performance.

I've often thought Constantin's withdrawn manner comes from the recent tragedy, plus his inability to speak English well. Doris says no, for reasons never fully explained. Margie is in his corner. Being half-Jewish, she has a soft spot in her heart for any underdog, and he is certainly that.

I come back to the present, folding the towel, and look around the small, metal bathroom. "Doris, thanks for picking up--"

"Don't worry about it, hon," she interrupts. "I threw everything into a big basket outside. I'll get one of the kids to take care of them, if you've got a spare fifty cents."

Doris means the teenage boys that travel with the circus, like the kid Tony sent to phone the sheriff. Their main job is to muck up after the animals. They make extra dough by doing odd jobs, such as bringing buckets of water to the tents in between shows for make-shift showers, when the performers can't get back to the trains.

"Make it a buck, Doris," I say, running a comb through my hair. "Could you tell them to rinse off Harold's mack and give it back to him? It's on the platform at the front of the car.

And so is Whitey's jacket. Ask them to return that, too. The things in the basket can be tossed; they're beyond saving. Thanks."

"Sure, hun. I swear to goodness, Tony is devastated, just devastated by what's happened," Doris says. "He said there's never been a murder under the Big Top before. Course, he's never seen Miss Brassy's Performing Poodles," she drawls. "That act could kill a group of Shriners."

I laugh again, glad for her presence.

Doris studies my face. "You sure you're all right? You look pale. Maybe a little lipstick." She pulls a gold metallic tube from her cleavage, opening it with a click to reveal a deep red color that matches her nails. She aims it at my mouth.

"Not for me," I say, moving my head to avoid her hand. "But you're a sweetie for offering."

She nods, her full lips drawn thin. After using the small, square mirror in the room to apply some of the lipstick to herself, she returns the tube to its hiding place.

"Doris, I need to get to the First Aid tent. See if I can learn anything."

"I saw them load Eddie's body into the ambulance. This is something awful, Jeri."

I nod, handing back her towel. Out into the narrow passageway, I take the few steps back to the sleeping area. Doris follows. Most of the girls are up now, chattering among themselves, staring out the windows on one side of the car. Two police cars and a second ambulance are parked next to the main tent, near the wagons. When the girls see me, the chatter stops.

Before any one of them can ask a question, a male voice hollers up into the car, asking for me by name. I go to the door and see a man wearing a plaid jacket, metal badge glinting just beneath the left side of the collar, and a tattered fedora atop his head. He stands at the bottom of the steps, hopping from one foot to the other.

"You Jerull Deane?" he says when I present myself. He runs my first and last name together as if it were one word. Everybody does. It's my own fault for being such a clever boots. I came up with the name when I signed my first contract with Radio City Music Hall at fifteen years of age. Nobody could talk me out of it, not even Doris or Margie. I've been stuck with Jerull Deane professionally ever since, even at Brinks.

"I'm Jeri, yes."

He removes his hat and stares up at me with somber, mud-grey eyes. "Sheriff Draeger wants to see you. He's in the circus manager's office but I got to take you to the supply tent to wait for him." He turns and twists the hat in his hands as he speaks. No wonder it's broken. "You want to come with me?"

"Sure. Just a minute." The rain has started up again. I reach inside for the yellow mack with my name in it hanging with the others and put on some rubber boots. I don't bother with my still wet hair.

Doris leans into me. "I'll go back to the First Aid tent," she whispers. "Maybe I can find out something from Margie. If I do, I'll come find you. You sure you don't want to eat some oatmeal before you go? It should be ready."

I shake my head and jump down from the train. The deputy puts his hat back on and falls in step with me. I ask him about Coke and Catalena, but he just shrugs his shoulders and walks in silence by my side. He escorts me to the supply tent across the way from Vince's office, a battered, twenty-foot long trailer. When we get to the tent, he reaches over in front of me, grabs the flap and yanks it open. He removes his hat again and looks me square in the face. I move to go inside but his voice stops me cold.

"*Be sober, be vigilant; because your adversary the devil, as a roaring lion, walketh about, seeking whom he may devour.*' Peter, chapter five, verse eight." He goes on, "I don't hold with circuses, young lady. Work of the devil. They should be banned. You should all be ashamed of yourselves."

My jaw drops. I don't know what to say. I take a step forward but turn back.

"*Judge not, that ye be not judged.*" I smile. "I don't know the chapter or verse but I do know it's from the Bible."

He gives me a startled look and walks away. I wonder what I'm in store for with the sheriff, if this is any sample of Springfield's attitude.

It's a tedious hour and a half. Along with Tin Foot, I've been sitting on one of the spare elephant footrests in the storage tent, waiting to be interviewed. The deputy with the mangled hat has been placed outside the tent door and won't let us talk to each other. In silence, we listen to a scratchy recording of "The Boogie Woogie Bugle Boy of Company B" coming from a nearby tent over and over again.

I look at my carrot-topped, titan of a friend and make a face when the Andrew Sisters start their song for the umpteenth time. Dressed in clean but well-worn coveralls, Tin looks back at me, winks and smiles, then returns to a piece of wood he's been whittling since our temporary incarceration.

Despite his lame foot, Tin is an accomplished acrobat and web sitter. Without a sitter who can anticipate what the performer will do on the rope in the air and counter it using his own weight below, most aerialists wouldn't be able to perform safely. It's been my good fortune to be partnered with him since I joined the circus. There was a time when Tin wanted to be more than friends, but I nipped it in the bud. Romance can come and go but a good web-sitter is worth his weight in gold. I have no intention of lousing up a perfect working relationship. Besides, I don't feel electrified by his touch, not like I do with Whitey.

In the beginning, Tin probably liked me because I'd cared enough to ask him his real name. He didn't realize that because I was new, I didn't know one of the major unspoken rules of the circus: never ask someone a question about their past.

I remember saying, "Tin Foot doesn't sound like it would be a name of someone from the Midwest, that's all." I watched his face redden.

"It's not. My real name's Leslie. They only call me Tin Foot 'cause I accidentally shot off my big toe and the two next to it," he'd said. "Doc made me a foot out of tin so I can walk good. I didn't do it on purpose, ma'am, I swear!" he'd added.

"I'm sure you didn't. And don't call me ma'am. It's Jeri. We're working together and we're going to be friends. That doesn't strike me as something you'd do on purpose, shoot off your big toe like that."

"Some people back home are sure I did, to get out of the war and all. Only I didn't want to get out of the war, 'cept now they won't have me," he'd said, looking down at his foot.

I've never seen his naked foot, myself, but one of the girls who'd had a brief fling with him shared details about this false toe made by Doc Williams. Hammered out of tin and hollow inside, it was lined with moleskin and went over the front half of the maimed foot. Tin Foot can slip the contraption on, tying thin leather straps around the back of the heel and ankle to keep it secure. The hollow cavity of the big toe is weighted with sand to give him balance. Clever but simple.

Doc worked out this type of artificial limb after the Great War when iron was at a premium and a lot of young men came in with disfigured feet. The tin doesn't last too long, so he makes Tin a new one every six months or so in his shop at the back of the First Aid Tent.

There's a ruckus at the tent door that makes Tin and I jump. Lillian's voice comes through the fabric, strong and insistent.

"Young man, I want you to stand aside and let me in, because this tray is heavy. I only found out that your sheriff is forcing one of my girls to sit in there with wet hair. She's going to catch her death of cold and it's my job to see that she don't. I got me some hot, fresh brewed coffee in this pot and

I brought enough for you, so if you want some, you'd better do what I'm asking."

"All right," he stutters, "but no talking."

The tent flap flies open and the wide-eyed deputy steps aside to allow the slim, black woman to march inside. A recent widow, Lillian is one of a kind. From Washington D.C., Lillian comes from a Negro family of well educated and proud people. She carries her sense of self-worth with her wherever she goes, and from what I can tell from hearing Duane's letters, so does her son. He was in his freshman year at Howard University when he enlisted in the first all Negro infantry in Italy, recently making corporal. They are not an 'Amos and Andy' family by a long shot.

Lillian has several towels thrown over one arm, plus the tray laden with my hairbrush, hand mirror, hairpins, a thermos of hot coffee, and three mugs. She sets her burden down on a corner table and pours steaming coffee into the mugs.

My hair has dried enough on its own but I am grateful for the brush and pins and snatch them off the tray. Just holding the brush in my hands makes me feel better. Sterling silver and engraved with my initials, it was my big splurge last year in Baltimore to the tune of eight bucks.

While she serves the men hot java and they drink in silence, I brush my hair and pull it back into a chignon. I'm rolling the front of it into curls as Lillian puts a chocolate-colored hand on my forehead, apparently to see if I have a fever. Satisfied I don't, she gathers up the used cups and empty thermos on the tray and leaves, followed out by the deputy. I stow the brush, mirror and leftover pins in one of the large pockets of my mack.

Apparently, Tin Foot was watching me and says, "You gals do that every day?"

The deputy leans inside to shush us again. This is getting tiresome. A few minutes later, he pulls the flap open and looks at me.

"Sheriff wants to see you now." He looks at Tin Foot. "You're next."

Finally, we can get on with this. I hold my mack over my head, and run through the rain, across to the trailer belonging to the manager. Another deputy opens the door and follows me inside. The sheriff, a short, pasty-looking man in a too-tight uniform, is sitting behind Vince's desk. His face wears a five o'clock shadow over his open collar, as if he left home before he had a chance to shave. Tony Phillips sits on the sofa nearby, legs crossed, looking dignified, but tense. Vince stands nervously behind him.

"Hey, little lady! You look just like that gal in the movies, Hedy Lamarr," the sheriff says, waving at me with his hand. "Come on in here, Hedy Lamarr." His voice has a strident quality and he leers at my breasts beneath the open mack.

His face flashes across my mind and I remember him from last year. Always hanging around the back lot, throwing his weight around, making snide remarks, and trying to get fresh with the girls. He was a pest when things were going right. No telling how he'd be now.

Rain thumps on the tin roof of the trailer in a bongo beat. Other than that, there's no other sound. Every light in the room blazes and stale smoke hangs in the air, smelling like it's owned the place for years. It's stifling inside but I shiver, nonetheless. Dropping the mack to my shoulders, I cross my arms over my chest and walk to the desk, disliking Sheriff Draeger more with each step I take.

"My name's not Hedy Lamarr," I reply, facing the smirking man.

"You don't say," the sheriff responds with a grin, as if we're both privy to a small joke. "Okay, so it's not Hedy Lamarr. Maybe it's that other one, Merle Oberon."

He points to an empty folding chair. "Why don't you have a sit down, Merle?" He emphasizes the name by making two syllables out it.

"Actually, it's Miss Jerull Deane," interrupts Tony quietly, before I can say anything. He gets up and comes to my side. "You may call her Miss Deane."

"Whatever you say, Mr. Phillips," he replies in a bootlicking, obedient tone. "Please sit down, Miss Deane. By the way, I meant to tell you, Mr. Phillips," he says, smiling up at Boss Man, "I might just have to shoot that lion. You know, him being a killer and all."

"What?" I explode. "Why, Old Kirby didn't hurt anybody. The man was strangled. There isn't a tooth or claw mark anywhere on him! How could you possibly think --" I stop speaking when I feel the subtle pressure of Tony's hand on my arm.

The Boss returns the sheriff's smile tooth for tooth and says, "Sheriff, I'd like to speak with you privately for just a moment in the other room. If you don't mind."

He gestures to Vince's small bedroom off the office. The sheriff shrugs, gets up and grins at me before he follows Tony. Walking away, they're talking too quietly for me to hear.

I turn to Vince to protest further, but he shakes his head, pulls me out of the chair the arm, and guides me out of earshot of the deputy.

"Don't worry, Jeri," Vince whispers. "Nothing's going to happen to Old Kirby. It's a shakedown, that's all. We get them now and then. This sheriff's that kind of guy. Last year he had a thing about the fire exits."

"A shakedown? By a sheriff?"

"Next you'll be telling me you still believe in the tooth fairy," he mutters then turns away, throwing a smile in the direction of the scowling deputy.

The door to the bedroom opens several minutes later. Tony has a look of resignation on his face and the sheriff is grinning broadly. Draeger returns to his side of the desk, and picks up a stack of papers, taps them on the desk importantly then sits down.

"If you will be seated, Miss Deane, I only have a few questions for you." I sit. His tone is completely different now, respectful, But I can tell he's pleased with himself. "I know you have to get ready for a performance soon, don't you?"

"Well, yes, I -- "

"So I'll be brief," he interrupts. "Did you know this Edward Connors?"

"Just enough to know he was one of the sweetest guys I've ever met. I don't have much to do with the clowns but I liked him a lot. I can't imagine why anyone would --"

"Did you know he was a Conscientious Objector?"

"No, I didn't, but it really wasn't any of my business."

"The war is everybody's business, little lady," the sheriff says in a tone that dares me to refute him. I remain silent. "Heck, I'd be out there fighting myself if they didn't need me here taking care of this town."

I refrain from mentioning that he's probably over the maximum age requirement and considerably out of shape. He smiles at me.

"Now do you know of any reason, other than that, why anybody would want to see him dead?"

"No, no reason. As I said, he was one of the sweetest --"

"Well, thank you, Miss Deane," he says. "That will be all."

"That will be all?" I echo in disbelief. "But what about the drag marks in the mud?" I sputter. "Maybe they've been washed away by now but I saw them. I don't think he was killed in or near the wagon. He was --"

"Why don't you let me concentrate on solving this crime and you concentrate on looking pretty."

"What kind of crack is that? Listen sheriff, Eddie was one of ours. I don't think anyone here is going to be concentrating on much else until we find out who did this. We all want to help as much as possible, right Tony?" I turn to Boss Man, who stands nearby with a grim expression on his face.

"I think we need to let this man do his job," Tony finally says, with a nod toward Sheriff Draeger. He stands tall and distant, avoiding eye contact with anyone, his voice soft, but packed with authority.

"That will be all, Miss Deane." The sheriff rises and looks down at me with narrowing eyes. The interview is over.

I stand and hesitantly move toward the door. When I glance back, all four men are staring at me with closed looks on their faces. Something is going on, something big, but I'll be damned if I know what it is.

Chapter Seven
11:00 a.m., Sunday

A weak sun tries to force itself out between drizzling, gray-streaked clouds. Rain-saturated earth and sawdust mix together with the scent of two thousand assorted animals into a heady but not unpleasant smell. This type of odor can't be masked even though the area is cleaned continually. I wouldn't say you could eat off the ground but since a lot of our animals do, it's kept as sanitary as possible.

I pause for a moment, taking it in, then direct my steps to the First Aid Tent to see how Coke and Catalena are. The light rain stops midway and the sun bears down on me, bringing a muggy and oppressive heat. I take off my mack and sling it over my arm.

When I arrive at the First Aid Tent, a second ambulance is leaving, lights flashing but no sirens. Doc stands in the doorway of the tent writing in a notebook, something I've seen him do countless times. He glances up at me.

"Who was that?" I ask.

"That was Coke but don't be alarmed; he's all right. Let me jot down a few thoughts, as they occur to me." He writes for a few more seconds, then closes the notebook and tucks it in his pants pocket. "He isn't any worse. In fact, he's better, much better. But he was unconscious for a long time and I don't have x-ray equipment here. He should stay in a regular hospital a few days for observation, just in case. Concussions are nothing to take lightly. How are you feeling?" he asks. "You recover yet?"

"A hot shower was all I needed, Doc. How is Catalena? Is Margie still with her?"

He glances around him. "Come on inside," he says and moves toward his office, a back section of the small tent.

We pass three hospital beds on the right; one holds a sleeping Catalena, watched over by the nurse, a plain, chunky woman in her mid-sixties with short salt and pepper hair. The other two beds are empty, although one looks recently vacated. White fabric room dividers stand by each bed, for the patient's privacy.

Behind a row of medical supplies in cabinets, a small portion of the tent is cordoned off with lighter-weight canvas curtains serving as Doc's private office. He brushes back the flap and I follow him inside.

Doc sits down behind a hard used, dark wood desk, one he brought with him from his private practice days. I sit in a straight back chair in front of the desk that is as uncomfortable as it looks. He opens a drawer and takes out a half-empty bottle of Johnnie Walker Red and waves it at me.

"I know it's early in the day but I need this. How about you?"

I shake my head, saying nothing. I've heard rumors about Doc being let go at a county hospital for drinking, but I've never known him to be drunk. Some people would say I've never known him to be sober, either, that he always had a buzz on, the same as Coke. Coke, with his tins of aspirin and black-market Coca-cola he tracks down, bottled before the government banned the use of cocaine in the formula.

Doc retrieves a small, cloudy-looking glass from behind him, pours a fair amount of the amber liquid into it, and downs it in one swallow.

"That's better," he says.

He doesn't look like it's better. He begins to peel the label off the whiskey bottle, in a long tearing motion. He is so intent on it, I don't think he knows the seconds are ticking by.

"Jeri, I've got something to tell you," he finally says. "Something in the strictest of confidence."

I sit up straight, feeling every hair on the back of my neck tingle.

"Of course," he goes on, "I probably shouldn't be telling you this. Probably betraying a patient's confidentiality and all that but I'm going to, anyway." He stops talking and pours himself another shot.

I wait, once again saying nothing. I'm tempted but I learned a lot by working for Brinks in the time that I did. One of the biggest lessons is when someone has something to tell you, keep your mouth shut until they do. Silence is a void most people need to fill.

Doc downs a swig, leans in and barely speaks above a whisper. "A little over an hour ago Catalena suffered a miscarriage."

Whatever I may be expecting, this isn't it.

"Oh, no," I gasp, instantly sorry I've spoken, wondering if the sound of my voice will break the spell. But he doesn't seem to notice. He's concentrating on peeling the label off the bottle again.

"Thank God I sent Margie away when I sensed something was going wrong. Nobody was here when it happened but her family." Doc's voice is so low I have to strain to hear him. "Constantin went wild when he found out, absolutely wild. I've never seen him like that before. I had to get two roustabouts in here to calm him down. He was screaming at the top of his lungs, but I couldn't understand anything he was saying. Fortunately, Catalena was too drugged by that time to hear him and Coke was still out."

"Constantin didn't have any idea she was pregnant? You're sure?"

"None at all. In fact, he made the little girl ask me three times if that's what it was. He still couldn't believe it. Poor Ioana. She was terrified. Her sister lying there, bleeding, her father behaving like a madman. I hated using her for all the questions and answers, putting her in the middle like that.

Sometimes I couldn't understand her through the sobs." A shaky hand pours another drink. He gulps it down. "Jesus, what a life."

I look around me. It's so quiet, it's hard to believe that such a scene took place a short while ago. "Where are they now?"

"Getting ready for the show, I suppose."

"You're kidding." I know the show must go on, but there's a limit. Baboescu doesn't have to perform under these circumstances. Management would never force him.

"He said something about the little girl having to fill in for her big sister. They needed to fit the costume, something like that. Frankly, I just wanted him gone so I could take care of my patients."

He unscrews the cap to the whiskey bottle again, hesitates and puts it back on. Returning the bottle to the drawer, he says. "I've had enough." He stops dead. "I've had enough of everything."

I watch his eyes focus on something behind me or maybe something in the past. I can't tell.

"Shouldn't Catalena be in a hospital instead of here?" I ask, trying to bring him back. "I mean, isn't this serious?"

"I've handled a lot of miscarriages," Doc says in a matter-of-fact tone. "During the Great War. Small villages in France. Women caught in the shooting, bombing, bayoneted just for the hell of it. Losing their babies in the middle of fields or in the bombed out shells of their homes. So many. You stop counting after awhile."

He looks at me with empty eyes. "Don't worry. I'm a good doctor. I know what I'm doing. I could do a D and C in my sleep."

He gets up and paces the small length of the room. I sit, trying to absorb what he's told me.

"Besides, I tried to send her to the hospital, like Coke, just in case. Her father flatly refused. What could I do?" he shrugs. "She's a minor. If her father doesn't want her to go, I can't force it. Said he was too ashamed, something like that. Although, if I see signs of an infection, I'll send her whether he likes it or not. That's why I've got the nurse in there keeping an eye on her."

Doc gazes down at me. "I do what I can, Jeri, but it's never enough. Never enough." He throws himself down and seems to deflate into the chair. I watch him shrink to almost half his size. It's as if his own personal demons are sucking the life from him.

I reach over and touch his hand lightly. "I'm sorry, Doc. I didn't mean I don't think you know what you're doing. You've always done your best and that's more than a lot of us can say."

He gives me a small smile. "You're a caring girl, Jeri, especially for one so young."

"I'm not so young. I've been on my own for ten years, since I'm fourteen."

"I know. You've had a hard life. And still you feel for others. You like to pretend people don't get to you, but they do." He studies my face for a moment. "And you're smart. You could get into trouble being as smart as you are. Be careful."

I'm not sure if that's an observation, a warning or a threat. I decide to let it go.

"Have you told the sheriff yet?" I ask. He shakes his head. "This could change everything, Doc. It could be a motive."

He gets up and paces the small room again. I can tell he's coming to a decision.

"All right, I'll tell the sheriff. I just wanted to give her a little peace. He's already been after me to let him talk to her ever since he got here. I just wanted to give her a little peace," he repeats.

He turns back to me, more like his old self. Maybe the demons are back in check. "It's only a matter of time before the whole circus knows about it, anyway."

"Not from me," I interject.

"No, of course not. That's why I told you. You know how to keep your mouth shut. But there are the others, the nurse, the father, the kid sister, even the girl, herself. Secrets don't last long around here."

I nod in agreement and we smile at one another in a sad, knowing way.

Doc hesitates for a moment, gets up and comes to the other side of the desk. He sits on the edge, looking at me. "I'm one of your biggest admirers, Jeri. I think you know that. I see not just the pretty packaging, but what's inside. You're a good person. You're intelligent. You've got integrity. In some ways, I feel like you're the daughter I never had. That's why I say again, be careful." He leans into me, stressing the last two words. I smell the whiskey on his breath.

Before I can reply, we hear a voice on the other side of the canvas. I'm glad of it. I don't know if it's him talking, or the booze. Either way, it's unsettling. There was mention of a wife once-upon-a-time but what that story is, I don't know. I never ask; he never says. Circus policy.

The nurse calls to him again. "Doctor Williams?"

"Yes, what is it?"

"The patient is stirring. You told me to tell you."

"Yes, I'm coming," he says to the nurse. He turns back to me. "I've got to go. Thanks for listening, Jeri."

"Sure," I say, getting up, feeling achy, feeling tired, feeling otherworldly. "I'll come back after the first show, just to see how Catalena's doing, okay?"

He nods and hurries toward the hospital room in the center of the tent. I wait, then follow him out. As I pass by, Doc is sitting by Catalena's bedside holding her hand and stroking her forehead. He talks to her in a voice that's warm and caring.

Something catches in my throat. Funny what Doc said about me being the daughter he never had. In some ways, I feel like he's the father I've always wanted. I turn away, filled with an overwhelming sadness, coupled with a sense of disloyalty to my own father, no matter what he's done to me.

Chapter Eight
11:30 a.m., Sunday

I step outside to a sun now in full power. Shading my eyes with my hands, I look up to see the flag flying on the Cookhouse, the signal it's open. I'm starving and the Cookhouse reopens at eleven for lunch, so it has to be around that time.

To check, I reach for the lapel watch I always wear. It isn't there. Then it hits me. I left it on my rehearsal clothes, the ones I told Doris to have the kids get rid of. The watch was a gift from two of my older sisters, one of the few I've ever received, and is the only piece of jewelry I wear. To me, it's priceless. I feel panic surging within me, when someone calls out my name.

"Miss Jeri! Miss!" The same gap-toothed, smiling kid from this morning runs up, reddish brown hair glistening with sweat. "I been looking for you everywhere, Miss. I found this on the stuff you was throwing out. Here!" He thrusts a grubby hand at me, turning it over to reveal my lavaliere watch, polished silver glittering in the sun.

I gasp and reach out for it with shaking fingers. "I can't believe it. I just noticed --"

"I gotta get back, miss," he interrupts. "I been looking for ya a long time."

"Oh, here and thank you," I falter, searching my pockets for loose change. "It's Wally, isn't it?"

"Yes, miss," He says, his hands gesturing me away. "But Miss Doris already paid me. 'sides, I knew it meant a lot to you. I never seen you without it." With a flash of another smile, he turns on his heels and dashes off, the boy whose name I only learned this morning.

I gape after my young hero. Talk about timing. To think I didn't realize one of my most precious treasures was missing until moments before his appearance. And he'd been searching for me all the while.

I look down at the lavaliere in my hand, with the small watch hanging from a retractable chain. Above it, ribbons, frozen in silver, come alive in the sun's rays. I put it to my ear, hear the soft ticking, wind it carefully, and pin it in its usual place on my sweater. I check and recheck the catch to make sure it can't fall off. I'm not as on top of things as I'd like to think. Doc is right. I need to be careful.

I join other performers in line at the Cookhouse for a bite before the two o'clock matinee. I ignore snatches of conversation about the recent events, curious eyes riveted on me. I stare straight ahead, not inviting any chit-chat.

There is only one entrance to the Cookhouse but two separate lines. The circus, while liberal in many ways, runs itself on a class system. The artistes never mix with workers, not even for meals. Using one entrance, performers line up on the right and the roustabouts, tent setters, clean-up crews, animal handlers, wardrobe, ticket takers, and other staffers on the left. A canvas wall divides the seating area down the middle. Everyone can hear who is on the far side but no one speaks to the other during meals.

At first, I was uneasy about it but that's the way things run around here. Truthfully, it has its advantages. As an artiste, I'm first in line for everything, treated as if I'm important. The disadvantage might be one of these days a woman will knit my name into an afghan, just like Madame Defarge did. Every time I wear my Marie Antoinette costume in one of the numbers, I think about that and feel a smidgen of fear.

The cafeteria-style food is abundant and filling, with lots of good old American dishes served three times a day. In the circus, room and board is included, so even though you only get a paycheck for the nine-months you work, you can still save money. During our winter hiatus, I teach ballet to little kids who can't afford to pay, solely for the joy of doing it. The Big Top allows me to do that.

I load up with meatloaf, mashed potatoes, string beans and apple pie -- Sunday's fare - and a small carton of milk, and look around for a place to sit. I'd like to sit by myself, but it's family style seating at every meal. We're a friendly lot.

I hear Tin Foot's voice calling to me and stroll over to him. Even seated, he towers above the other performers at the long table; my gentle giant. I slide in on the bench across from him. Tin Foot and I exchange a look, which says 'no talking about any of this now' and chow down. Other than a few furtive glances, no one asks any questions. It's a relief to do something normal, if only for twenty minutes.

On the way over to the wardrobe tent for our costumes, Tin Foot and I drop behind the rest, so we can talk.

"What did the sheriff ask you?" I say.

"Not much. Only if I knew any reason why anyone would want to kill Eddie. I told him no and he said I could leave. I waited for two hours and I saw him for about ten seconds." He shakes his head in disbelief.

I grunt a reply, thinking about the exchange between the sheriff and Tony Phillips when I was there.

"You heard Coke was taken to the local hospital?" Tin asks.

"Yes," I say, still thinking about the sheriff. "Coke's going to be okay, at least, that's what Doc says, but he'll be under observation for a couple of days. I sure would like to talk to him."

"No reason to," the web sitter replies. "I understand he didn't see or hear anything, just felt a whack on the back of the head. Doesn't know a thing."

"Where did you hear that?' I ask sharply, stopping mid-step.

Tin Foot stops walking and turns back to me. "The nurse. She told me when I dropped by to see how the two of them were doing. Why do you sound so surprised?"

"I guess I shouldn't be. I just didn't think..." I break off, not wanting to say my opinion of the nurse's ethics. Doc is right. It's only a matter of time before all the secrets come out. Poor Catalena.

Almost as if he can read my thoughts, Tin says, "So what's the latest on Catalena?"

"Nothing much." I lie easily and walk toward the wardrobe/dressing rooms again. "She's on tranquilizers but Doc said she's going to be fine."

"That's a relief," he says, falling in step with me. "By the way, Whitey was looking for you earlier. Didn't say why but he looked anxious."

His voice doesn't betray anything, but I know how Tin still feels about me – or suspect I know -- so I'm trying to keep a lid on my feelings for Whitey, at least for a while. Having a relationship with Whitey is doable, as far as circus hierarchy goes, which is all in all.

As the head bull man, Whitey lives in a gray area between being a performer and a worker. He's classified as an elephant trainer, but often has to be in the ring during a performance with one of the elephants, especially on a difficult number. Being tall and good-looking, management likes to use him during the shows. He even has a safari costume. His main job, however, is the daily supervision and training of fifty-one elephants and the fifty men that work with them.

Whitey and I got acquainted my first year because of one of the tricks I did with an elephant named Emma. Dressed in a skimpy, spangled jungle outfit, I'd stand in the curve of her uplifted trunk and hold onto a jeweled harness on top of her head with one hand. She'd rear up on her back legs, trunk rounded and high in the air, while I balanced almost upside down in what was considered a glamorous pose. It never ceased to thrill the crowds but it could be dicey. It required a lot of balance and concentration on the elephant's part and sometimes she wasn't in the mood. Whitey stood nearby just in case he was needed.

Thought of as a catch by a lot of the girls, especially with the war on, Whitey is ten years older than me and divorced. I've heard his wife snuck out one night, leaving him for a flyer, but rumors run amok around here and it might not be true. So far, Whitey keeps avoiding the conversation and I don't press it. But if we keep going the way we are, I'll have to soon enough.

"He's worried about you, Jeri, ever since this morning," Tin says, breaking into my thoughts. "I think we're all a little nervous about a killer on the loose." He pauses. "Maybe it was a Townie."

"And if it was, does that make you feel better?"

"I don't know, Jeri. You sure don't want it be one of your own."

"I guess not." We walk on in a moody silence until we come to the large tent entrance and have to go our separate ways.

Before he leaves, Tin reminds me, "Don't forget about Whitey, Jeri."

"I won't. I'll be seeing him once the show starts and I'll let him know I'm all right."

"And are you?" My friend studies my face.

"I thought I was," I say, touching the watch on my shoulder.

Chapter Nine
12:55 p.m., Sunday

Makeup and wardrobe are housed together in one long tent. The men's dressing area is on one side, the women's on the other, and the center is devoted to wardrobe. Each costume has a sewn-in label, denoting the performer's name. All the costumes are crammed on hundreds of portable, steel racks with alphabetical name cards.

How many costumes hang by your name depends on the number of acts you are performing in. I have eleven. I change into three of these costumes during the Spec, which opens the show. The Spec is the teaser or promise of things to come, showing a little bit of all the upcoming acts.

It begins with the ringmaster welcoming the audience to the "The Greatest Show on Earth." He stands on a platform in the center ring, dressed in his "pinks," a costume which is really red and black. He removes his top hat and, with fanfare, waves the circus members in from one large entrance at the back end of the Big Top, divided into two by a red velvet drape.

To thunderous applause and earsplitting calliope music, Topsy opens the show by bounding out from one side of the drape, trumpeting a greeting to the masses. She wears a dazzling pink tutu around her middle. I ride her bejeweled head and am wearing a similar pink spangled getup. We're followed by nine other elephants and girls dressed in the same costumes.

The clowns enter from the other side of the drape. While they do their shtick in the two smaller rings, the ten elephants race around the circumference of the Big Top once, the girls waving to the cheering crowd, then dash out the way we came in. The girls dismount. The elephants are led away and I have less than twenty seconds to change into a lavender costume, reminiscent of Guinevere in Camelot. I leap onto the sidesaddle of a waiting plumed, white horse, grab a lance with an American flag on it, and race back in, circling inside one of the smaller rings. Acrobats, high-wire acts and aerialists have entered by now and are prancing around in the center ring showing promises of things to come. The jugglers are in the other small ring throwing things to one another, bowing and waving to the audience.

The Big Top suddenly goes dark amidst deafening cheers. A pin spot comes up on the ringmaster. With a great deal of pomp and circumstance, he invites the audience to stand and sing the Star Spangled Banner. The lights come up in the bleachers but it remains dark at the back entrance. The crowd rises to its feet, good Americans all. With the Merle Evans Orchestra playing majestically, they begin to sing our national anthem, their forte voices filling the Big Top and surrounding countryside. I get a lump in my throat every time, no matter how often we do this part of the show. America the Beautiful. It's what we're fighting for.

During this time, the performers exit in the gloom, me to a changing station behind the bleachers. The horse is taken away and I change into a much hated forty-five pound, full-length, silver metal, sequined gown, complete with a high, Elizabethan collar and ten-foot train. With the help of two wardrobe people, a body width, red stripe of the American flag is attached to my back shoulders, rolled and tied up like a sleeping bag. Unleashed, it's thirty feet in length and weighted at the bottom.

Side by side with twelve other girls, who are wearing their pieces of the flag, I come out in the dark and with a roustabout's help, climb to the top of one of thirteen rope ladders that have been lowered from forty feet above in front of the red velvet drape. At the end of the song, spotlights hit the thirteen of us, long silver gowns sparkling like nobody's business.

The ringmaster reiterates that the Greatest Show on Earth supports our boys overseas and the American Way. There is a drum roll. The girls and I turn our backs to the audience and as one, pull the cords and drop our hidden, rolled up sections of fabric. Voila! A twenty- by thirty-foot American flag hangs in the Big Top.

While we are in our frozen tableau, twenty elephants are led out and form a circle around the perimeter of the three rings. Holding small American flags in the tip end of their trunks, the big twenty hold their trunks high and turn in circles in place, waving the flags to a cheering, foot-stomping crowd. I suspect the uproar can be heard in the next county.

The first time I was a part of this extravaganza, the sheer volume of the crowd's response almost caused me to lose my footing. Frankly, I think we could go home right after that one, but this is only the beginning of what is truly the greatest show on earth.

I grab five of the eleven of my costumes, take them to my side of the dressing area then go back for the rest. The system is you hang the costumes on your own rack behind your assigned makeup table. You never throw your costumes over a chair, table or anywhere else. If you don't hang them up immediately and the Section Captain catches you - in my case, Margie – you'll be fined. The SC's word is law and never challenged. We are also fined if we smoke, drink or eat in costume, so nobody does that, either. A buck fine coming out of a twenty-five-dollar paycheck is keenly felt, believe me. I was fined once for chewing gum in costume.

Margie can be tough and she shows no favoritism. My pal takes her job seriously and I can see her running this joint one day, the first female Boss Man. She doesn't talk about it much, but she has aspirations.

At the end of each performance, you return the costumes to the racks for cleaning and repair. The wardrobe crew is the best and I always try to do right by them.

I enter the dressing area and find it filled with quiet but tense performers. Hardly anyone talks about Eddie, considered bad luck during a performance, but knowledge of his death crackles in the air like static electricity. Catalena and Coke being hospitalized adds to the unspoken anxiety. In my opinion, it's a lackluster, preoccupied performance but the enthusiastic response from the audience seems genuine enough.

I sneak out into the wings to watch the knife thrower's act instead of reading one of my books, which is what I usually do when I have any sort of break. Constantin comes out brandishing his knives to hefty applause, Ioana trotting behind. The thin twelve-year old girl has been pinned and gaffer taped into her sister's lavender costume. Satin and tulle bunch awkwardly at her chest and thighs, emphasizing what a scrawny little kid she is.

I remember noticing recently Catalena had filled the costume out, bust and hips becoming more rounded. I thought it was the onset of womanhood, but rethinking, it must have been the pregnancy.

Wearing dark coveralls, one of the roustabouts follows Constantin around. He takes Ioana's place handing equipment to Constantin and putting props where they belong. A few of the tricks have been cut but the finale is left intact. After all, it's Constantin Baboescu's signature piece.

With great showmanship, Constantin helps his younger daughter up on a platform and straps her to a giant wheel, skinny arms and legs spread eagle. He struts twenty to twenty-five paces away. The roustabout sets the wheel spinning and Constantin throws over a dozen knives outlining the girl's body. The applause is appreciative and spirited.

The lights go down over the ring, save the turning wheel and Constantin's form. There is a drum roll. The audience becomes as one, straining in their anticipation.

Constantin turns around, his back to the wheel. At arm's length he holds a long, dagger-shaped knife by the tip of the blade. He hesitates dramatically. The wheel continues to spin holding the small girl. He throws the knife backwards over his shoulder and it lands at the top of the girl's head, touching soft, brown curls. The silence is so intense; you can hear the blade cut into the wood of the spinning wheel. The audience is on its feet en masse in deafening applause. I let out a sigh of relief and watch Constantin help Ioana down. He hugs her, kisses the top of her head and displays her to the audience for applause. Like Doc says, 'Jesus, what a life.'

I hurry back to the dressing room to change into my pink ballet costume for the Dance of the Elephants, then dash outside behind the Big Top. All fifty elephants are lined up waiting for their cue, handlers by their sides. Patiently, they stand side by side decked out in their baby pink tutus and sparkling head harnesses with feathers and beads. Fifty elephants with tutus wrapped around their girths is quite a sight, even for a seasoned trouper like me.

I run to my little lady, Topsy, and find Whitey holding onto her harness. He signals for the elephant to raise and bend her leg.

"Sorry I'm late. Where's Sandy?" I say, while I reach up and hop onto Topsy's bent leg, using it as a step.

"He's inside waiting for you," Whitey answers.

Standing on Topsy's leg, I croon to her, "Hey, little girl. It's good to see you again. How's my baby doll?"

I stroke her forehead and grab onto her harness. Half leaping and half pulling myself up, I throw one leg over her head. Whitey makes sure I don't fall. Topsy snorts her greeting to me and I look down at the gorgeous, blonde man by her side.

"Did you get your jacket back?" I ask with a smile.

"Yeah, I got it," Whitey replies, looking at me in a very strange way. He doesn't return my smile. I'm perplexed but have no time to think about it. The lead elephant of our group had started into the arena and the others swivel in turn, grab a tail, and start entering the tent. Away I go.

I hear Whitey's voice calling to me and look over my shoulder in his direction.

"Jeri! I --" He shouts and waves at me. Whitey hesitates, changing his mind about something. "Never mind. It can wait. It's nothing, nothing."

I nod, returning the wave, and turn back to the job at hand. I'll have to find out later whatever Whitey wants or doesn't want.

Inside the Big Top, Zolina heads for the perimeter of the Center Ring astride Modoc, followed by forty-nine other elephants and girls. Topsy's and my place is outside the third ring, where she and I are the featured performers at the beginning and end of the act. Sandy taps his foot waiting for us. His job is to make sure my little girl behaves herself and does all her tricks just as she should. She always does.

With Balendron's clever choreography, the elephants dance to the strains of Igor Stravinsky's ballet music and we're the usual big hit. When it's time for Topsy's and my showpiece, the other elephants leave the Big Top and Topsy strolls to the center ring, me on her head. With great fanfare, I dismount and lie on the ground. Drum roll. Topsy walks over, straddles my body, then lays down on top of me completely covering my body with hers, careful to never put her full weight down. I know she hears the gasps from the audience, same as I, as she lowers her body seemingly to the ground. She stops so close, I can feel the warmth of her skin.

A hush falls over the crowd. They're wondering if I've been crushed to death. On cue, I stick out a hand and wave to them. Wild cheering. After a few seconds, Topsy rises and carefully steps away from me. I stand up and strike a pose, showing one and all I'm fine. The audience goes mad, screaming and cheering.

Now it's time for our piece de resistance. Topsy sits down on her haunches, pulling her front legs upward and into the air. She looks like a large dog begging for a treat. At first shocked, the audience laughs and applauds. I grab onto her left front leg, swing up and sit on it, then hoist myself up by her harness, swing over, and kneel on her forehead. When I get my balance, I stand tall, arms held high in the air. For several seconds my pachyderm partner and I hold our positions, while cheers just about take the roof off. Everyone loves Topsy.

As the applause begins to die down, I hop back down to her left leg and to the ground. Sandy, always nearby, speaks to her with authority, but also kindness and not a small amount of affection. Once when she was sick, he never left her side, staying night and day on the hay next to her. One morning I went by and saw him cuddling as much of her as he could in his arms, both fast asleep. As I say, everyone loves Topsy.

Sandy gives the one-word command to her, as he taps her front end. "Down."

My obedient, little sweetheart lowers her front legs and rises on all fours, shaking herself like a dog. But she's not a dog. She's the largest, most powerful animal on earth, capable of the same kind of mass destruction as one of MacArthur's Sherman tanks. I saw a spooked elephant plow through two feet of solid concrete, coming out the other side with no more than a scratch. You don't forget something like that.

"Up," Sandy says, stroking Topsy's trunk. She curls her trunk up and lowers her head. I climb inside the curl and, lying width-wise, arch my back and strike yet another glamorous pose. To thunderous applause, Topsy carries me out of the tent. Another day; another fifty-cents.

The show nears its end and it's time for the Grand Finale. That's the parade where the various acts, performers and animals prance around the rings reminding the audience of what they've seen during the show. It's a pain in the neck, but the crowds love it.

We change costumes, Margie, Doris and I, laughing and gabbing, as usual. I'm not sure why they adopted me seven years ago when I showed up at Radio City. They were two highly paid showgirls, a few years older than me, and I was a lowly swing dancer, just starting out. The three of us have been inseparable ever since, sharing laughs, hats and shoes along the bumpy road of life.

We joined the circus one freezing November day after reading a casting call in the New York Times. My pals decided that up north was no place to spend another winter and after what happened to me at Brinks, I needed some sunshine.

I needed more than that. Because of me, a little boy was dead. Brinks said it wasn't my fault, but I know better. So we hocked our fur coats, got on a train, and three days later were lounging under the Sarasota sun, along with the oranges and alligators. It was supposed to be for one season but it's been two years and we show no signs of leaving. A new home; a new life.

I stand nude by my makeup table save for my g-string. Doris, sitting beside me, glances over and sees the angry red and purple welt on my hip in a starburst of discoloration.

"Jeri, honey lamb! Who took a bull whip to you?" she cries out.

"Oh, I had a fall earlier today," I say, trying to make light of the incident at Old Kirby's wagon. "I'll be all right." Through the routine of the show, I almost forgot the ugly events of the morning, but with Doris' remark, they all come swimming back.

All the girls look at me, Margie included. She gets up, setting lime green and fuchsia organza sleeves in motion.

Crystalline green stones on her bustier catch the light as she comes over.

"Jer, can you strut your stuff with that? We don't want you getting hurt."

"Oh, please," I say, once again trying to make light of it. "Remember when I broke my arm after I fell off one of the elephants? I worked with a cast for six weeks and never missed a performance. A little bruise isn't going to stop me."

"You're such a trouper, kiddo, they're gonna mount a statue to you." Laughing, Margie adjusts her four-foot high fuchsia headdress, shiny green balls swinging from her movement.

I'm about to reply when the thin curtain to our small section flies open and Rosie steps inside, looking for a fight.

Her face is made up now, broad lines of color accentuating pallid features. She's wearing a shimmering purple-beaded bodice and matching tights. Hair piled on top of her head, several switches included, her look is finished off by a violet-colored ostrich plume, dotted with flashy rhinestones, framing one side of her face. She does up well, as they say. She's also more than a competent performer, a real crowd pleaser, so why she always seems to have a chip on her shoulder, I'll never know.

"Well, look who's slumming," Margie says, turning to the shorter girl. These two have never liked each other. They both want to get some place, but Rosie's a competitive bitch about it.

This time, Rosie ignores Margie but stares bullets at me. "You! What the hell do you mean by leaving the rigging unlatched and hanging in the middle of the air like that? Or are you too stupid like the rest of the grape stompers to learn how to do it right?"

It takes me a second or two to figure out what she was talking about, although, I know right away the crack about 'grape stompers' is a slam at my heritage. Rosie can be the queen of ethnic and racial slurs, when she sets her mind to it.

Being of Irish descent, you'd think she would know better, having her seen her share of bigotry, but apparently not.

I can feel Margie's hackles rise. She shoots me a look and waits, giving me the opportunity to throw on a robe before I reply. I tie the belt in a knot while trying to keep my temper under control, and look at Rosie, who is shaking from anger.

"First of all, I don't appreciate the name calling, so please stop it, at least in front of me."

"Oh, you don't?" Her mouth seems almost deformed by a snarl.

I go on as if she hasn't interrupted me, "Secondly, I'm sorry about not locking the trapeze back in place but when Catalena started screaming I just dropped from the swing and went to help. I realize it should have been re-latched but considering the circumstances--"

"You always have some damned excuse," she interrupts with a sneer. "Like to use your highfalutin words and all that, don't you, you Guinea Grease Ball? Makes you feel important. Well, you're just trash in my book."

"Watch it," Margie says to Rosie through gritted teeth but the warning comes too late.

I slap Rosie's face as hard as I can and stand there, waiting for whatever might come. *Go ahead*, I think, *it's out in the open now. Jump me, pull my hair, kick me, bite me, try something; I'm ready for you.* Nothing.

Her face registers shock and the outline of my handprint glows an angry pink on her cheek. Still nothing. She turns to Margie.

"Did you see that? The Dago bitch slapped me. As the Section Captain, it's your duty to write her up. Report her. I want her thrown out on her ear."

Margie shrugs and saunters away, heading back to her makeup station. She concentrates on an errant curl, her green eyes flashing.

"I don't know what you're talking about, Rosie. I didn't see anybody slap anybody. But I did hear you use foul language. That's a buck fine for each word, you know that. I'm writing you up for a dollar."

"Why, you fucking, kike bitch," Rosie roars.

Margie swivels and stares down at the shorter woman. My friend's heart-shaped face, usually warm and inviting, looked more like cut crystal. An easy 6'4" in her heels, she can be intimidating.

I hold my breath. I've heard one or two people make ethnic slurs at Margie in the past and they've regretted it, big time. Not physically, because Margie's a non-violent girl, but she can use words to hit somebody just as hard as I'd slapped Rosie. Margie decides to go the cash-and-carry route.

"That's three dollars, Toots. Care to make it four? And if you call me one more name, I'll see that you lose your paycheck for a week."

Rosie's head snaps around at the other eight women in the dressing area, who are staring up at her in silence. "Are you all going to sit there and let these two do this to me?"

The women shrug or ignore her, going back to their makeup and hair, except for Doris.

"Land sakes alive, Rosie O'Reilly," my southern friend drawls, "you make more noise than the finals at a Georgia hog calling contest. Now shoo. Go away. We're getting ready for the finale."

Rosie returns her focus to me, fury distorting her face. I glare right back at her.

"You! I'll get even with you for this." She spins back to Margie and Doris. "The three of you! Just you wait! Don't any of you think about turning your back on me."

"Gee, I'm shaking in my boots," retorts Margie.

"There's a wind blowing in here, girls," says Doris, using her most southern, gentile voice. "Or is somebody passing gas? It's hard to tell but I sure enough smell something."

Rosie wheels around to leave, knocking into one of the freestanding changing lights over by the exit. The tall metal pole, topped with three lights aiming left, right and center, teeters and crashes to the ground, glass shattering into the sawdust. Rosie kicks at it and stalks out.

"And that's another two bucks for damaging circus equipment," Margie shouts to her departing figure.

There's a moment's quiet and then collective giggling. A little dazed, I sit down and start putting on my last costume. I'm running late; I'll think about Rosie later.

After ten grueling numbers, where I work hard in the air and on the ground, I get to take a ride during the Grand Finale, dressed up as a Spanish aristocrat inside a howdah. That's sort of a box with a saddle base worn by a camel or elephant. I ride atop a pachyderm named Mabel, known for her prickly disposition. She's willing to walk around in a circle with someone sitting on her back and that's about it.

I step into my last costume, newly made for me. My gown is voluminous and heavy, another one weighing in at forty-plus pounds. Yards of dark blue velvet, embroidered with metallic gold threads and encrusted with pearls encircle the skirt. Shades of blue, red and lavender are woven into a tapestry bodice, as beautiful close up as from a distance. A rhinestone-studded gold crown is covered by a black lace mantilla that flows down my back and along the sides of my face. When I unpin and fluff up my black hair, I feel like an aristocratic Spanish senorita of bygone days.

My contribution to the Grand Finale consists of climbing into the howdah, two times around the Big Top then undress, and go home. Compared to the rest of the show, it's like taking candy from a baby.

Chapter Ten
4:45 p.m., Sunday

It's the end of the first show and I return my costumes to wardrobe. I'm heading out of the wardrobe tent when Vince approaches me from the sidelines. I think he's been waiting for me. There's a damp chill and I look up at the sky. Clouds have returned, dropping the temperature again. I pull my jacket closed and look expectantly at Vince.

"Jeri, got a minute?"

"Sure, Vince. What's up?"

"Boss Man is waiting for you in my office. He wants to speak to you. Right now."

"He does? Why?"

Vince shrugs. "Better ask him. Come on."

I wonder if word had already gotten back to management about my run-in with Rosie. Vince walks me back to the offices and supply tents area, and I prepare myself for the worst.

He knocks on the door of his own trailer, which strikes me as strange. Sounds of a radio playing Glenn Miller's new hit, *Tuxedo Junction*, can be heard through the thin walls. The door flies open and the head chef hovers in the doorframe, carrying an empty food tray. A rotund Parisian, he's dressed in his whites and wearing a chef's hat. He smiles, bowing slightly, and steps aside to let me enter. He continues out and down the steps, muttering something in French, a language I want to learn one of these days.

Vince doesn't come inside but shuts the door behind me. My eyes adjust to the dim lighting and I see Tony seated behind Vince's desk. He's leaning back in the chair, his boot-covered feet crossed at the ankles and resting atop a corner of the small desk. I let out an involuntary gasp at seeing those boots, so like the ones kicking at Eddie's lifeless body only hours before. Tony throws me a questioning look.

I try to cover by saying, "Didn't your mother ever teach you it's bad manner to put your muddy feet on the furniture?"

Almost reflexively he lifts up his legs, swings them around to the floor and leans forward in the chair, a guilty little-boy smile playing on his face. Two round, chrome food warmers rest on the desk, one in front of him and one in front of an empty chair. Napkins, silver cutlery and an uncorked bottle of red wine sit nearby. He lowers the radio and gestures to the empty chair.

"Thanks for coming, Jeri. I took the liberty of ordering in some supper for us. We can eat while we talk." He removes the domed lids to reveal two plates of filet mignons slathered in mushrooms and gravy, baked potatoes and asparagus, steam still rising. If I'm being fired, I'm going out in style.

"So this is how the other half lives," I say. "Cookhouse is serving hamburger tonight."

Tony forces a grin. "Rank hath its privileges. Sit down." He brushes at his David Niven mustache with his fingers, a nervous habit.

I take off my jacket and ease into the chair. As I pick up the white napkin, I study his face. I can see tension and something else tracking across it. Maybe despair. I try to keep the mood light and friendly, even though seeing the boots has really rattled me.

"So judging by this," I say, "you're either trying to seduce me, which I doubt, because there's no fooling around with Doris' man and living to tell about it, or you want something. What is it?"

"I need your help, Jeri. We need your help." He emphasizes the 'we.'

"Okay. I'm listening." I say no more and cut into my meat, waiting for him to go on. He fidgets a bit then picks up the bottle of wine."Wine?"

I shake my head and watch him pour himself a glass. He sets down the bottle but doesn't pick up the glass. Instead, his fingers drift over to a stack of opened telegrams. He pushes the plate of food aside.

"Do you see these, Jeri?"

I nod, again not speaking. He picks them up, fanning them out.

"These are telegrams from towns across the nation. Towns thinking of reneging on their contracts with us after the Associated Press radio bulletins about the murder."

I set down my knife and fork. "You're kidding."

"I wish I were. I heard another news flash on the radio not five minutes ago. I saw it coming this morning, with that sheriff. I thought we were through after the thousand-dollar bribe for saving the lion --"

"A thousand dollars!" I interrupt. "That's more than some performers make in a season. That's outright extortion."

"If it was only the extortion, I would be happy. But the sheriff returned about an hour later with an ultimatum. Apparently, when word reached the city council about what happened, they held an emergency meeting. After rereading the contract, they found that they can cancel our appearance based on a general clause covering citizen safety and the greater good of the people. Should a town be able to prove that the circus jeopardizes public welfare, they can cancel us without fear of breach of contract." He tosses the telegrams back down on the desk. "They were only the first of many to read that clause."

"But how can they hold the circus responsible for Eddie's death? It could have been anybody, even one of the townspeople. Nothing's been proven yet."

"The council and the sheriff are convinced that the murderer is someone on lot." Tony's words are slow and unemotional. "I think so, too."

I look him in the eye. "Agreed. If there'd been a stranger hanging around, someone would have noticed, even at that hour. It is possible it was an outsider but it's a long shot."

It's Tony's turn to nod. "The sheriff is a man with small town prejudices but he isn't stupid. The council has given the sheriff's department seventy-two hours to solve the murder. After that, they shut us down."

I throw my napkin down on the desk. "Three days? I can't believe it."

"What I see happening is the sheriff going through the motions for three days and Springfield canceling our contract. Other towns will follow suit. We're looking at a spotty season, at best."

"What you're saying is we all might be out of a job by next week."

"No," he shakes his head. "You know the North Brothers. They'll keep everyone on salary, whether there's a show or not, for as long as they can. But do you have any idea what it costs to keep the Big Top going? Nineteen hundred people, over two thousand animals at last count. The losses will be astronomical. We might never recover."

"So we're back to 'what do you want from me'?"

He picks up his glass of wine and takes a sip. "I remembered Doris telling me that you worked for Brinks Detective Agency once upon a time and you considered them tops."

"I do."

"I wired them, hoping that they could come here and take over the job the sheriff should be doing."

"Good. Are they coming?"

He sets down his glass, staring at the dancing liquid. "It's this damned war, Jeri. Most of the men joined the service. Brinks has a skeleton crew and no one's free for at least two months. By that time, we could be out of business."

"They didn't have anyone?"

"Well, yes they do. Or did. They had you."

"Me?" My eyebrows shoot up and I stare at him.

"You can read the wire for yourself."

He picks it up and thrusts it into my hand. I read in silence.

"Sorry we can't help. Stop. Overloaded for next two months. Stop. Understand Jeri Deane is with you. Stop. Consider using Deane. Stop. First rate and can handle herself. Stop. Ask about tugboat. Stop. Signed, Brinks Detective Agency."

"What about the tugboat, Jeri?" Tony asks when I look up.

I reflect on something that hasn't come to mind for two and a half years.

"One of the tugboats in New York Harbor was thought to be commanded by a U-boat captain in disguise, getting a count of the ships that come in and out and other important information. I got onboard and found his journal. He went to jail. Capsulated version."

"Simple as that?" he asks with a smile.

"Pretty much."

"So you say. How did you get onboard?"

"Oh, the usual." I smile back. "Girl stranded on a sailboat needing help. It was easy."

"It sounds like it was dangerous."

"I'm surprised Brinks mentioned it. I was told it was national security. I never even told Doris and Margie."

Tony leans toward me. "They say you can handle yourself."

"I could at the time."

"Help us, Jeri."

I shake my head with a determined air. "You're asking me to do something I don't do anymore."

"I'm asking you to save the circus. You can name your price. Within reason, of course."

"It's not the money."

"Don't be ridiculous. You're providing a service. You should be paid for it."

I don't know if he's deliberately misunderstanding me or not. I try again.

"I'm out of that line of work. I don't do private investigating anymore, Tony, not since…" I pause, reluctant to say what happened that caused me to leave Brinks so suddenly. It's not any of his business.

"I don't do private investigating anymore," I repeat. "I'm a performer now," I add, pacing out each word.

He leans in. Now he paces his words. "Jeri, I don't know the reasons you left Brinks and I don't particularly care. You're all I've got. Without you, the circus could close and all these people could be out of a job. Is that what you want?"

He stares at me and I stare at him. My Italian-Catholic guilt comes to the forefront.

"All right, I'll do it. How about a thousand dollars? If it's good enough for Old Kirby, it's good enough for me. That is, if I can pull it off. I'm not saying I can. It's been a while."

"But you'll try?"

I let out trapped air, resigned. "I'll try."

"Thanks, Jeri." His relief is palpable. "I don't know what I would have done if you'd said no."

"Boss Man, in order to do this, I'll need full run of the Big Top. You'll have to open up files to me, tell me things you don't want to, things only you are privy to, even rumors, because we don't have a lot of time."

"I understand." He takes a hard swallow of wine. "One thing I'll say for Vince, he keeps meticulous personnel files on everybody. Some of them are six-inches thick. There isn't much worth knowing about anyone that isn't in them. I think you'll find them interesting."

"I'll also need access to the entire circus, including personal sleeping areas. I may need to poke my head into some unexpected places. Lastly, I'll need somebody else to help me and it can't be you. People pay attention to where you go and what you do."

"No, it can't be me. I'm going to be busy trying to keep this from pulling the Big Top under. How about some of the security boys from the front of the house? Two of them are actually retired policemen."

I mull the idea over. The silence stretches between us but Tony gives me the time to think. "I don't think so; the fewer people that know about this the better. Furthermore, those security guys strike me as pretty hard-nosed. They might not take orders from a woman." I lean back in my chair. "I'm thinking of Tin Foot."

"You trust him that much?" He brushes at his mustache again.

I nod. "If he'll do it, I'll split the fee with him."

"Whatever you say." He reaches behind him into the jacket stretched over the back of the chair, pulls out a small handgun and sets it on the desk in front of me. "You got one of these? For protection?"

I stare at him. "No, that's Chicago you're thinking of. I'm from New York. We use baseball bats."

I laugh at my joke. Tony doesn't. He grimaces, looking down at the gun as though seeing it for the first time. I know what must be going through his mind. Second thoughts.

"This is crazy, Jeri," he finally says. "What am I doing? I must be crazy. I'm not thinking straight. I can't ask a girl to do this. It's too dangerous. It needs a man."

"Hey!" I explode. "Don't think I can't do as good a job as most men, because I can, maybe even better." Anger flares hot within me for the second time today.

"I didn't mean it the way it sounded. It's just that you might be risking your life. There has to be another way."

"Well, when you think of it, let me know. Meanwhile, I'll take the job but not the gun." I pick up the gun and inspect it, feeling the weight. "Nice, though. Good balance."

"I thought you said you don't know how to use one of those things."

"I said I don't have one. I didn't say I don't know how to use it. Besides, if things go the way I plan, whoever it is won't know I'm looking for them until it's over." I check the safety and hand it back. "Be careful with that thing."

Tony returns it to his jacket. "If anything happens to you, Doris will kill me."

"If anything happens to me, I'll help her."

Tony laughs but it ends in a dry cough. "Here are the two master keys that open all the compartments on the train and my chart of who sleeps where. Don't lose it; it's the only one I got."

I take the silver keys and folded chart and put them in a small purse on the belt I always wear around my waist.

"We don't have keys to personal trunks or lockers," Tony says. "Nobody does but the individual. Personnel documents are in there." He gestures to a row of beat up, metal filing cabinets behind him. "Vince keeps those keys somewhere in this drawer." He rummages around in the top drawer of the desk, retrieves a metal ring holding eight to ten small keys, and sets it in front of me.

"You're free to come and go as you please in here or elsewhere, for that matter. Vince knows about this part; he has to, and he's been instructed to keep his mouth shut and to do anything you say."

Tony hesitates then looks at me from beneath hooded eyelids. "About Vince, there's something I should tell you. I found out this morning that Eddie owes – owed - Vince two hundred dollars. Eddie had a gambling problem. A lot of the guys do. Too much time in between shows." He pauses and strokes his mustache again.

I can feel the shock registering on my face. "Two hundred dollars! That's a lot of money for someone who can't have made more than twenty a week. How'd you find out?"

"Vince and I were there when the police found a one-way bus ticket to Salt Lake City in Eddie's pocket. Right after that, one of the clowns brought me a packed suitcase he'd discovered hidden behind Eddie's locker. Vince blew up. He called Eddie a mooching SOB. One word led to another and I dragged it out of him."

"Do the police know?"

"They'd left by that time. Frankly, I don't know what to think about Vince's involvement in this but that's the reason I didn't want him in on the details of our conversation."

"Good call. I want you to get rid of Vince for awhile. Keep him busy doing something else and don't let him back in this office alone. Right now, whether you like it or not, we should consider him a suspect." I pick up the ring of keys and jangle them in my hand. "What happened to the key that hangs on Old Kirby's nail?" I gesture to the wall behind Tony's head that has a row of nails pounded into it more or less at shoulder height. Strips of tape over the nails bear names written in a precise and clear hand. Each nail wears a key except for the one marked 'Old Kirby.'

Tony twists his head around and looks up. "I don't know. Vince must have taken it with him this morning when he went to see about the trouble and still has it. I'll ask him."

"No, don't," I say. "I'll find out when the time is right. Anything else I should know?"

Tony turns to face me again. "I've scheduled a meeting before tonight's show to give everyone a pep talk. I'll make an announcement about what you're doing and that they are to cooperate with you in every way."

"Don't do that, Tony. I think it's better if we keep a lid on my involvement. That's what I meant earlier. Just let me look around on my own without any fanfare. See what I come up with. I need you to do something for me right away, though."

"Name it."

"Ask the sheriff if Eddie had anything clutched inside his left fist. If he did, it might be important."

"I can tell you now. I watched them pry a crumpled snapshot of the Baboescu Family out of his hand. I've got it right here."

"You mean the sheriff didn't keep it as evidence? Did they at least check it for fingerprints?"

He shakes his head. "He handed it to me. I've got it in my wallet. Want it?"

I say yes, trying not to be shocked at the sheriff's lackadaisical ways.

While Tony digs around for the picture in his wallet, he asks, "Realistically, Jeri, how long do you think it will take before the whole circus learns about what we're doing? Two, three days?"

"From what you tell me Tony, that's all we've got, anyway."

He hands me the wrinkled sepia photo and tugs at his mustache again.

"You're going to pull that thing off," I say with a smile.

I take the five-by-seven photo, turning and twisting it in the poor light to see the crumpled images. It's a publicity photo of the Baboescu family posed in full costume. Constantin stands rigid with his arms around Catalena, while

Ioana sits childlike on the ground before the knife throwing spinning wheel. Catalena's features are even and pretty, set off by large, dark eyes. Ioana's face carries the same hook nose as her father, smaller to be sure, but overwhelming her otherwise delicate features.

It occurs to me by the way Ioana is placed in the photo, separated from the other two, that she's probably the least favorite child. Or maybe it's my own face I'm imagining in the photo instead of hers. I put it in my purse for later.

"If I could just make it all go away, Jeri," Tony says, leaning against the back of the chair, his face turned up to the ceiling. "One man dead, another in the hospital with a concussion. And poor Catalena. She seems to be taking Eddie's death harder than anyone."

I say nothing, suspecting that Doc hasn't told Tony the latest about the teenager's condition. No matter how he feels about it, Doc will soon have to. As the man running the Big Top, Boss Man needs to know things like that. But this is Doc's tale to tell.

Tony looks at me. "God, this stinks." He reaches over and finishes off the wine in his glass. "So what now?"

I'm nervous, apprehensive, scared, you name it. But you can't show something like that, another thing I learned at Brinks. If you're calm, the client is calm or, in Tony's case, a bit calmer.

"Now we eat," I say, in my best bon vivant manner. "Or at least, I do. I don't get filet mignon that often. And turn the radio up. I love Glenn Miller."

Chapter Eleven
5:30 p.m., Sunday

I cross the lot, looking for Tin Foot, working out what I'm going to say to him. I avoid going by any place where my two showgirl pals might be. Tony says he's on his way to update Doris and I'm sure she'll turn right around and tell Margie. I don't want to be nearby when they discover I'm the Big Top's new private dick, temporary though it may be.

Doris and Margie helped pick up the pieces when my Brinks days fell apart and this will make them nervous. They tend to treat me like their kid sister, a role I usually love, but that position is apt to get in my way this time.

I'm surprised Doris told Tony about my days with Brinks, although I could tell she hadn't gone into detail, just by the way Tony looked at me with questioning eyes. He wanted to know more, but he was following the "mind your own business" rule of the circus, something I have come to count on.

Then there are those damned boots. Before I let my guard down with Tony, I'll have to check and see just how many men wear the type of boots that are burned in my memory.

Making a quick detour toward the lions' cages, I search for Harold. I find him, as usual, hanging around Old Kirby. He's inside the cage, down on all fours filling up the five-gallon water bowl with fresh water from a hose, and looking more like a grasshopper than a man. Old Kirby is stretched out in a corner of the cage having a cat nap. I reach in and tap Harold on the shoulder to get his attention, unwrap Tony's steak from my napkin, and dangle it in front of him.

"Harold," I shout. "I've got an untouched filet mignon here. It's a shame to see it go to waste. Okay if I give it to Old Kirby?"

Without saying a word, he lifts the meat from my fingers, pulling it inside the cage and examines both sides. "Well," he says with hesitation, "ordinarily I don't let nobody give my cats nothing, but seeing as it's you and it'll just go to waste... Aw, go ahead. It won't do nothing but fill up his back tooth, anyways."

I laugh and trot to the other side of the cage, reach between the bars and drop it in front of the sleeping lion's mouth. Old Kirby's eyes flicker open and his nose twitches. He sits up on his haunches and sniffs the meat, only to lie back down, leaving the food untouched.

"See that?" Harold says, in a worried tone. "He's been like that all day. I don't know what's the matter with my boy. The vet checked him over, got some tests going. Says he looks all right but Kirby's acting peculiar."

"I'm sure it's because of what happened this morning. We're all a little shaken. He'll be all right tomorrow. Try not to worry."

Harold doesn't reply, but shakes his head. He stretches out a long arm and strokes the sleeping cat's mane, ignoring me. I turn to leave.

"Jeri," he calls out. "Thought you'd like to know I found something under the wagon. Meant to give it to Tony but you'll do. Hear you're helping him out."

So word is out already. I have less time than I thought.

He reaches in a corner of the cage, palms a lumpy piece of paper, and thrusts it toward me through the bars.

It looks like a wad of inexpensive notepaper sold in most drugstores, soaked through by rain, now drying into a distorted origami nightmare. Streaks of mud further obliterate the blue inked writing that has almost been washed away by the downpour. I try to force it open but it fights me back, wanting to tear apart in my hands. I stop and look at Harold, who's watching me.

"Sorry about that," he says, his gaunt face animated and thoughtful. "I kept it in here so it could dry out. There ain't much on it that I could rightly tell but in the corner. I thought it might mean something, so I saved it."

I rotate it in my hand and discover Eddie's name, faded and blurred but still readable. "Where exactly did you find this, Harold?"

"Near the left wheel, lying on a patch of grass. As I say, I wouldn't have paid it no never mind, just throwed it away, but I seen Eddie's name."

"Thanks. That was smart thinking."

"You don't get stupid around big cats. They keep you on your toes."

"I'll bet." I hold the paper cupped in my hand, trying to protect it. I'll examine it later. "Who has keys to the big cats' cages besides you?"

He thinks for a moment. "Well, the cat boss, of course, and Vince keeps one hanging in his office. I seen it."

"When was that?"

He shrugs. "Don't know. Last time I was in there. Maybe three, four days past."

"Anyone else?"

"Shouldn't be. Don't pay to have too many people with keys to these here cages. Ain't safe."

I couldn't agree more. "What does the key look like, Harold? I'm just curious."

He gropes in his pocket for a set of keys that jangle when he pulls them out. He picks out a short, squat key with a blunt end from the ring and waves it at me. "This be it, Jeri."

I leave, making a detour to the Virgin Car. Hardly anyone's there, just a couple of girls reading or snoozing in their berths. Going directly into Lillian's small kitchen, I'm relieved to find her gone. I grab a small colander she uses to drain spaghetti, put the wad of paper inside and pass it back and forth under a gentle stream of warm water. Most of the dirt runs off and the warm water makes the paper more pliable. I lift the soggy mess out, wash and dry the colander, put it back, and head for my berth.

Opening the paper without further damage is painstaking work but I manage it. I stretch it out on the glass of my small, sun-streaked window facing the field, where it adheres, and smooth the wrinkles out. I'll check later after the sun dries it to see what, if anything, remains on the paper.

Still on my quest for Tin Foot, I leave the car and pass the post office crowd standing around Pete, a high-wire unicyclist. At the beginning of each season the performers and crew are given the names of towns, dates of appearances, and general post office addresses, with instructions to let people know where mail should be sent.

Pete's been the designated courier for as long as I can remember. Except for Sundays, Pete collects outgoing mail from a central box, drives to the post office in whatever town or city we're in, deposits it and collects the mail.

For this service, everyone chips in ten cents a week, which covers Pete's time, gas and then some. Six days out of seven you can see Pete standing on the same wooden crate, yelling out names in a clear, loud voice. He rarely yells mine.

My sisters write occasionally but I haven't heard from my three brothers stationed overseas for almost a year.

Sometimes I write their wives to see how the boys are doing and they let me know that so far, so good. I used to send my father little tidbits of my life, articles, newspaper clippings, holiday and birthday cards but I never hear back. I stopped writing about six months ago, more of a letting go than giving up. But I still hand Pete my dime every week.

On Mondays, Tuesdays, Thursdays and Fridays, Pete's back with the mailbags around one-thirty. Wednesdays and

Saturdays there's no time to distribute the mail before the first performance, so it's done in between shows, unless there's a street parade, like yesterday. Then the previous day's mail gets handed out the next day. A lot of people get letters and packages two or three times a week or, in the case of Lillian, almost every day.

I see her pacing in the background, an anxious look on her face. Duane writes his mother at least once a day while he's stationed in Italy with the Ninety-Second Infantry Division. Often Lillian reads excerpts to some of her favorite girls, me being one.

Duane is a beautiful writer and wants to go into journalism when he returns to civilian life. His hefty letters are loaded with descriptive, colorful phrases, written whenever he can snatch a minute. He writes about his daily life, nothing war-sensitive, but on the personalities in the unit, the Italian culture, food, countryside and his encounters with civilians. If the mail from overseas is delayed a day or two, Lillian gets his letters in bunches. He's written her every day since he joined up eight months ago. It occurs to me I haven't seen her reading her son's latest letter -- laughing, crying, holding the letter close to her bosom -- for more than a week.

When Pete turns the bag upside down and shakes it, declaring that's all the mail there is for the day, everyone steals a glance in Lillian's direction. I'm afraid she might break down and cry but instead, her face like stone, she turns and walks away. I've never seen such lack of expression. I want to go after her but Lillian's a very private person. She's there for all of us but resists when anyone reaches out to help her. Some people are like that.

"This damned war," I say, parroting Tony's words.

Chapter Twelve
6:15 p.m., Sunday

Tin is sitting on a bale of hay outside the main tent inspecting the ropes he and I will use at the next performance. His eyes squint painfully in the slanting sunlight but this is something he'll never let anybody else do. I realize this is one of the reasons why I chose him. He's not a man who leaves things to chance. Plus, he can charm the quills right off a porcupine when called upon, and every day, I trust him with my life. I'm sure I've made the right choice.

I park myself beside him and get to it, telling him verbatim what Tony and I talked about. I leave nothing out, not even the thousand-dollar reprieve of Old Kirby. A gleam comes into his eyes, after the initial surprise. Tin balks at taking any part of the fee but relents when I tell him there's no other way I'll do it.

"So what's my first assignment?" he asks, putting aside the ropes.

"Find out if Eddie owed anyone else money. Vince might not be the only one. It would be easier for you to do that than me. You ever play poker? I thought you might join in on a game."

"Sure do. Not much entertainment on a farm, Jeri, once you've wrestled some cows to the ground." He winks at me to show he's teasing.

"Is that how you milk them? I wondered." I wink back.

"With six boys on a farm, card games were a way of keeping us out of trouble. At least, that's what Ma and Pop thought."

I jump in saying, "We're not going to do that winking thing again, are we? Because we could be here all day and there's a game going on right now at the Clown tent."

Tin throws his head back laughing, then stands and stretches out his large frame. I glance at his feet.

"Tin, where did you get those boots?" Another pair of what seems to be the guilty boots.

He looks down in surprise. "These? Gus. Boss Man made a deal with him and nearly all the men bought at least one pair. You don't get a chance at handmade boots often, especially at this price. With my toe, I can't wear a regular boot, otherwise."

Gus is the company shoe smith, with a long standing contract with the circus. Every year the performers have a shoe last made of their feet. Gus uses the last to build shoes, shipping them to wherever we are when we need them.

"So that's a bust," I mutter. I get up and brush the hay off the seat of my pants. Looking around to make sure no one else is nearby, I say. "Tin, you've been around the circus longer than me."

"Five years," he answers.

"You didn't get a chance to see what was used to kill Eddie but it was a flat wire, about a quarter of an inch wide, not thin and rounded like this baling wire." I point to one of the wires on the two bales of hay we've been sitting on. "Have you seen anything like what I'm describing on the lot?"

He thinks for a moment, then gives a toss of his head. "I haven't noticed but I'll keep my eyes peeled."

"I think if we find that wire, we'll have a good idea who our killer is. Don't forget your whittling." I pick a chunk of wood and small knife off one of the bales. "Hey, this thing is sharp," I say, touching the slender, four-inch blade.

"Has to be if you want to carve through wood."

I turn the freshly carved piece around in my hand. "What's this going to be, anyway?"

"A cow."

"I might have known."

He laughs and takes the wood and knife from me saying, "I'm nearly done here, so I'll get going. What about you? What are you going to do? We've got about another hour before half-hour call."

"Cracking the whip, eh?" I grin at him, then sober. "I'd like to go through Catalena's things while she's still in the hospital, but without the rest of the family knowing. I'm looking for something in particular."

"Well, there's no time like the present. They're in there, rehearsing." Tin Foot gestures over his shoulder to the Big Top. "I saw him and the little girl go inside about fifteen minutes ago."

I steal a look through the entrance flap to the tent. Constantin is barking something in Romanian to Ioana and the roustabout, who is familiarizing himself with the props. It looks like they're running through the entire act.

Tin leaves and I make a mental note to tell Tony he'll have to cover any losses Tin Foot might incur while gathering information at the card table. I find a private spot behind Albert's cage to study Tony's chart of the compartments. Hardly anyone lingers near the sixteen-foot albino python.

The Baboescu Family has adjoining compartments in the C car housing marrieds and specialty acts. I head for it. I'm not sure what I'll say if anyone questions me about being in there. I figure I'll bluff my way through if anyone asks. It's worked before.

I walk the outside of the car looking in the long line of windows. Most curtains are open, showing empty compartments or people catching a nap in between shows.

Sprinting up the steps at the end of the car, I go inside, as if I'm a woman who belongs. To my relief, the corridor is empty. I hurry over to the Baboescu compartments, fifteen and sixteen, again making sure there's no one around. The chart doesn't give first names of the occupants, so just for the hell of it, I choose sixteen. Inserting one of the two master keys, I go in.

The curtains are drawn and the small room looks dark and cramped. An unmade double bed and a small nightstand holding three books take up the bulk of the floor space. Beside the books, a small bouquet of wild flowers drink from a glass tumbler of water. The flowers give a spot of color to an otherwise gloomy room that smells of stale clothes and sweat. This has to be Constantin's.

Always entranced by books, I run a hand over each one, studying the Romanian words on their binders. I pick up a Bible, realizing it's the first time I've seen one in a foreign language. I read somewhere that the Bible is the most widely published book in the world. I thumb through the sheer, almost translucent pages, coming across a few underlined passages.

One passage draws my attention. Some of the words I vaguely understand, having a similarity to Italian, but I'm not sure. I jot them down on the small pad I carry in my purse for study later, then return the Bible to the stand.

I try the doorknob of the adjoining door but it's locked, and, unfortunately, from the other side. Neither master key work. That means I will have to go back out into the hallway and in through the outside door, a chancy venture. I open the hall door an inch or two and look both ways. No one. I step out quickly and test number sixteen to make sure it has relocked. As I insert the key into fifteen, the corridor door at the far end of the train opens suddenly with a 'blam,' the sound echoing off the steel interior. Charging inside the compartment, I close the door behind me and lean against it, listening hard.

Sounds of a giggling man and woman assault my ears but they pass on by. I hear a compartment door open and close, enveloping the gigglers. Then silence. My heart thumping, I turn and face this small room and see an upper and lower berth. The outside curtains are open. With a swift motion, I close them and look around in the half light.

The lower berth is unmade and filled with dolls and stuffed animals, smelling slightly of lavender. That has to be Ioana's. I grab the side of the upper berth, swing up and into it, and start searching for something in particular.

If girls are the same the world over, I think, Catalena probably keeps a diary. It never interested me but even Margie has one and writes in it daily. She says when she's old she plans on selling it to the highest bidder to pay for her retirement.

Several times I've seen Catalena carrying around a similar small book, red in color, with the same type of lock on it. I want to know what's in that book.

After looking under the pillow, I begin a careful search of the berth itself and locate the diary wedged in between the wall and mattress. I don't think you'd come across it unless you were specifically looking for it. Girls and their secrets. I drop down to the floor, throw the book in the bag at my waist and cross to the door, remembering the curtains at the last minute.

Ioana has a lot on her mind. She might not notice she left them open, but I can't take the chance. I creep over and glance out under the heavy fabric to make sure I won't be seen when I reopen them. I spot Constantin walking by, head down. Ioana isn't with him.

In a panic, I rip the curtains open, turn and run to the compartment door. About to yank it open, I hear the giggling idiots in the hallway again. They stay outside the door for what feels like forever. Their giggles lessen, only to be replaced by the increased sound of thudding boots coming down the hallway.

If that's Constantin – and I'm sure it is -- my only hope is he'll go directly into his compartment and not have any reason to come into this one. The sound of a fiddling key in

the next door's lock allows me to lean against the door in relief. When I hear him inside his room, I open Ioana's door to flee. Just then the adjoining compartment doorknob begins to move back and forth, noisily. Before Constantin realizes it's locked from my side, and comes in from the corridor as I did, I need to be gone.

It's now or never. I run out, hoping I won't bump into the gigglers, and race down the hall, exiting at the far end of the train. Hesitating on the platform, I opt to get off the side of the car facing the field rather than the circus. I leap from the top step to the graveled ground below, crouch down and hug the metal side of the car, listening for any sound. After a moment's silence, I assume a normal stance, jump over the hitch that connects one car to the other and run right into the gigglers. They stare at me, wide-eyed.

"Where did you come from?" the man asks. I recognize him as half of a married juggling team.

"I dropped a flashlight the other day when I was looking for wildflowers in the field over there." I point to the other side of the train. "Still can't find it," I say, walking away.

"Gee, if we come across it, I'll save it for you, Jeri," the girl says in a breathy, high pitched voice. She is one of the First of May's and not his wife.

"Thanks." I look over my shoulder to wave at them. That's when I catch Constantin standing on the train steps, staring at us. I can feel his curious eyes following me, as I jog alongside the line of railcars back toward the Virgin Car.

Small groups of people are cooking their dinner over campfires or taking in clothes from makeshift lines strung up between bushes. Two jugglers practice throws to one another in the pathway and I wait for them to finish, all the while thinking.

Maybe Constantin only saw me outside with the gigglers. He didn't have an accusatory look on his face, only one of puzzlement. But I may be kidding myself. He must have seen or heard something in the hall, something that brought him out from the compartment to the steps. Maybe it was an unrecognizable blur running down the hall, but it was something.

I move on to my behavior with the gigglers. Dropping a flashlight while I was searching for wildflowers is a pretty lame excuse, even if they bought it.

In the past, I had a level of spirited brazenness that enabled me to face potential danger without letting my fears get in the way. I have to remember how I did that. I'll have to remember a lot of what I did. Two years with the circus has dulled my detective skills. That isn't good. I'm dealing with a murderer.

Inside my berth with the ends of the curtains tucked under the mattress, I switch on the light and remove Catalena's diary from my purse. I think I might have trouble with the lock but it opens easily. That's the last part of easy.

I leaf through the pages in dismay. It's written in a cramped, repressed hand and in Romanian, no less. Stunned, I realize that even though she speaks English well after only a year in this country, she's still spent her formative years in Romania. This gives me a problem I didn't anticipate but should have. My limited Italian isn't going to be much help. I shake the book to see if anything might be hidden inside. A bus ticket falls out from the back, a bus ticket to Salt Lake City.

Bingo. She planned on running away with Eddie.

Finding the ticket spurs me on. I decide to try reading the diary, word by word. Deciphering the most recent events of the diary seems like a good idea, so I flip to the back page. Good luck to me.

After about fifteen minutes of straining to figure out a badly scribbled word here and there, I feel a headache coming on. I close my eyes for what seems like a moment, only waking when Margie shakes my foot, telling me to get ready for the night's show.

Stuffing the book under my mattress, I climb down from the berth. On the way to the dressing rooms, I get an earful about my involvement in investigating Eddie's death from Doris and Margie. Ultimately, they understand I'm going to do this whether they like it or not, which they don't. They're sassy but I'm sassier. We agree to disagree and move on to wondering if Eddie had family back in Salt Lake City and if they know about his death.

I look at my watch. We have fifteen minutes to spare. At half hour, everyone has to be in their dressing rooms but I have some time and every minute counts. I get an idea, unsnap my purse and take out the photo Tony gave me, clenching it in the palm of my hand.

"Ladies," I say, veering off in another direction, "You go ahead. I've got a small errand. I'll meet you at the dressing rooms."

"Wait a minute. Where you going, Jeri?" asks Doris.

"What's up? Why the side step?" says Margie.

"I'm off to find Constantin and show something to him," I answer, walking away with a wave. This is as good a time as any to see how Constantin greets me after the fiasco at the C car. "I won't be long. See you later."

My two friends ignore my farewell and join me, hurriedly walking on either side.

"I'm in," Margie says. "You know, I've been helping Constantin learn English."

"You?" I shoot back. "What's he learning, Boogie Baby? How to talk jive?" Both Doris and I let out a hoot of laughter.

Margie draws herself up. "No jive, just English. You know, I was hot to be an English teacher once, just like my parents."

"Well, I swan," comments Doris, tossing blonde curls in wonderment. "Professor Margie."

"What happened?" I ask, still not quite believing her story.

"I got a load of their salaries," Margie says. "After twenty years as a college professor, Dad makes thirteen-hundred a year, Mom nine-fifty teaching little kids. I make twice that in a season here."

I know her parents are teachers, her mother from Boston and her father a Jewish transplant from Lithuania, both now living in New York City. Considering what they do for a living, they're very accepting of her career choice, to say the least.

"In any event," Margie goes on primly, "when I found out that Constantin was having trouble learning English, I offered to help."

"He just wants to have his way with you, honey child," says Doris, with a dark edge.

Margie turns on her. "No, he doesn't. We meet once a week in the chow tent and he practices talking to me in English. A couple of times his girls have joined us."

"Hmmmm," I say. "He might open up to me more with you around. But when we get there, you have to let me do the talking."

"Aye, aye, captain." Margie salutes.

Doris says, "I don't understand how you can stand to be in the same room with that man, Margie, I really don't."

Margie stops and turns on our friend. "What's your gripe? His wife was shot down in cold blood. He had to come to this country and start over, just like my father. He needs all the friends he can get."

Doris shakes her head, says nothing, and walks ahead, followed by a perplexed Margie and me. I have to admit, I'm thrown by Doris' strong feelings against the man. I admire Constantin's ability in the ring and his love for his children.

He's a bit of a hothead, but I chalk that up to being a temperamental artiste.

We take a shortcut around the Menagerie Tent, which holds various domestic and wild animals in side-by-side pens. As part of the entrance fee, the audience can walk through this mammoth tent before and after the show to see the "beasts" up close. But behind it, in makeshift cages and fences, are many of their babies, enjoying the remains of a breezy, warm afternoon.

Margie pauses for a moment by a pen holding a baby giraffe, Sally. She is being weaned from her mother and is more resistant than most to kicking the habit. Trotting over, she nuzzles Margie's proffered hand and finds the usual parsley leaf. The gangly quadruped loves the green herb and Margie always carries some in her pocket for the calf, now fourteen months old.

Doris' features soften at the sight and she and Margie smile at one another. I know the rift won't last long and nudge us away. Sally's eyes follow Margie until she knows it's useless to stay near the edge of her pen. She ambles back to the shade tree and scratches her long neck on the trunk before reaching up to snag a leaf or two.

The sight gives me a momentary burst of happiness. I love sharing my life with the animals, whether I'm performing with them or not. We all have our personal favorites. Sally is Margie's doll baby. Doris is smitten with a smelly camel named Methuselah that tries to follow her everywhere. Old Kirby is mine. That's a bonus of life in the circus: the odder-than-usual pet.

By the time we get to the knife thrower's tent, the late afternoon's heat returns. Even with the setting of the sun, I'm starting to feel perspiration on my forehead and back.

I knock on the wooden pole in the center of the tent flap. There's no answer but I hear rustling inside. I knock harder and call out his name.

The flap flies open in a spirited, almost angry way, and the small, but muscular, man stands before us. At first wary of the intrusion by three women, he becomes cordial when he sees one of them is Margie. With a smile, he takes her hand in his and kisses the top of it, continental style, and gives her an effusive greeting.

"Ah! It is my good friend, Marjorie. Good day to you or should I say, good evening?" he asks, looking up at her. His English is halting and barely understandable with deep, rolling 'r's.

"'Good evening' will do, Connie. And call me Margie. It's a nickname," she says in a teacher-like tone. "The way I call you Connie instead of Constantin."

He grins broadly and nods in agreement, but I'm not sure he fully understands.

Margie prattles on brightly. "Do you remember my friend, Doris?" Doris nods curtly and backs away. "And this, of course, is Jeri," Margie says, gesturing to me. She pauses and looks at me expectantly. "She has something to show you."

His eyes rest on me, a flicker of confusion in them. Is he wondering why he's seeing me again in such a short span of time? More importantly, did he witness me running down the corridor of his rail car, as well as outside with the gigglers? Whatever it is, he says nothing but offers a questioning smile.

I smile back, stretch out my hand and open it, palm up. The crumpled photo seems to come to life, unfolding itself before us. The movement catches his eye and he glances down at the photo. Puzzlement still sparks his eyes.

"Someone found this," I say. "I believe this is yours, so I wanted to return it."

He hesitates but picks up the small crumpled mass from my hand and presses it open. "From where you get this? Near the sleeping cars?"

"No, it was found near the lion's cage," I answer, watching the expression on his face. "This morning," I add.

"Why you do this? Why you destroy?" He steps forward, almost in a challenge. I can smell garlic and spices on his breath from another culture, foreign even to me, used to my family's ways of cooking from the old country.

"I didn't," I say, standing taller, eye to eye with him. "This is how it was found in Eddie Connors' hand right after he was murdered. Do you know how it might have gotten there?"

Constantin takes a faltering step backwards, clutching the photo.

"Any idea how it got there?" I repeat, when he doesn't answer. His eyes dart around in his head, as if he's seeing something inside his mind the rest of us can't see.

"I do not know," he says. "This is strange. But they are given out at the ticket booth for the publicly..." He hesitates on the word and stops speaking.

Margie jumps in. "Publicity."

"Yes, thank you. Publicity. These are everywhere, the photographs of me and my family." He smiles and gives me a stiff, formal bow. "I thank you for returning it."

"You're welcome."

He turns to Margie, who throws him one of her dazzling smiles.

He visibly relaxes. "Forgive me. I must go now and get ready for tonight's performance," he says, bowing to her and then again to me. Doris, out of his line of vision, is ignored by this gentlemanly gesture.

"Goodbye and thank you," he says, closing the flap behind him.

We turn on our heels almost as one and walk away.

"So what the hell came from confronting the man like that, Jer?" Margie finally asks, kicking at the fresh straw laid down over the muddy path about an hour before.

"I learned the photo makes him nervous."

"Maybe you make him nervous, kiddo," says Margie. "When you're out to drop kick a mule, it can get nervous."

"He's one mean son-of-a-bitch," Doris mutters. "I don't care how he acts around you, Margie. And I don't care that he escaped Nazi persecution. In his case, they knew what they were doing."

"Doris," I say, coming to a stop. "Nothing the Nazis do is justified. How can you even say that?"

Her attitude astonishes me. Doris comes from the south but is one of the most liberal-thinking people I know. She once stood in front of a growing mob in Biloxi, Mississippi, to protect a black youth from being beaten for daring to look her

way. When the rabble demanded she step aside, she threw rocks at them, shouting, defying them in any way she could, while Margie and I searched for a policeman. Even after the cop broke up the mob, Doris never backed down one iota and almost got herself arrested.

Either the shock in my voice or the look on Margie's face forces her to open up. She stops walking, turns and faces us, her stature tall and unyielding.

"All right, I'll tell you and it isn't pretty. I saw him slap the little girl one day --"

"Come on," Margie interrupts with impatience. "Some cultures are different. Parents lose their cool. I'm not saying it's right --"

It's Doris' turn to interrupt. "He slapped her a couple of times, Margie, and hard. It was just short of a beating. Only because she didn't do a trick right."

Margie is silent, as am I.

"He didn't think anybody could see him because it was behind his tent. But I did. I ran right over and told him to stop it. He turned on me. I thought he might hit me, too. I'd like to have seen him try. Little weasel. Then he said 'Oh, I'm so sorry. I didn't mean to do it,'" Doris says, doing a fair imitation of his accent. "But he didn't sound sorry and the little girl was bawling her eyes out."

"When did this happen?" I ask.

Doris becomes evasive. "Some time back. You had an all-day rehearsal with Zolina and Margie was with her trumpet...no, it was the sax player. The one with the goatee." She looks at both of us and inhales a ragged breath.

"That would have made it four or five months ago," Margie sums up quickly, not concentrating on Doris but on something inside her memory. She turns to our friend.

"But why keep a lid on it? Why the mum act?" Margie glances over at me for backup. I nod in agreement.

Doris licks her red lips and looks down. Guilt runs over her features much like storm clouds racing through an open field. Her voice is so quiet I can hardly hear her.

"I went to Tony that very day and told him. He made me promise to keep still about it to everyone, even you two. He knows how some folks feel about Constantin. I expect he wanted to give the man an opportunity to make it right. Anyway, Tony made me promise. He did go and talk to the bastard, though. I never saw him touch the little girl again and believe me, I've been looking for it." She pauses, still looking down at her shoes. Neither Margie nor I say anything.

"I'm as sorry as I can be that I didn't tell you," Doris continues. "But I swore on my mama's grave I wouldn't. And Tony said he would make it right," she repeats, her voice wavering.

At this moment I fully understand what Boss Man means to Doris. This is not her usual passing fling. Tony isn't just a guy buying her jewelry, furs, and expensive meals, with her having the upper hand on the romance. Whatever Tony and Doris have, it's serious to her and not to be dealt with lightly by her friends.

Margie looks over at me and I see the same thoughts reflected in her eyes. "Aw, forget it, kiddo," she says slipping a graceful arm around Doris' shoulder. "I'm just glad you came clean about it now."

"Me, too," I say. "All is forgiven."

I come to the other side of Doris and put my arm around her waist. She wraps her arms around both our shoulders and gives us a good squeeze.

"You two are my darlings, just my sweet darlings," she says in a shaky voice. "I was feeling heavier than a fifty-pound sack of manure about keeping it from you. And just as smelly, too."

We all three laugh and I decide it's easy to forgive her. And to understand. I haven't told them anything about the diary or the ticket and have no intention of doing so. And probably this is just the beginning of what I'm not going to tell them.

Chapter Thirteen
9:25 p.m., Sunday

The evening performance goes better, thanks to Boss Man's speech beforehand. Tony asks performers and staff alike to band together and to cooperate with any investigation that might be taking place. He takes care not to look in my direction. After his talk, there's a small round of applause and I can tell spirits are lifted.

We're well received by a larger than usual attendance. Curiosity about the murdered clown causes ticket sales to go through the roof. Other than the audience being particularly attentive to the clown act, though, it's a normal show.

The last number has finally arrived and we're getting ready for the Grand Finale, chatting away, as usual. I let my hair down for the Spanish costume and reach for my hairbrush.

Missing from where it's usually stashed, I yell out, "Hey! Which one of you girls took my brush?"

The women either ignore me or shake their heads, with a round of "not me, not me." God, I think to myself, another incident like my watch. Where the hell did I leave it? I'm forgetting everything these days.

Doris turns to me. "So Jeri, take my mind off things. With the heat and everything, I'm so depressed I could eat dirt. I need a distraction. What's your word of the day, Sugar?"

The rest of the girls groan loudly before laughing. The first thing I do every morning is to thumb through my Webster's and pick a new word to learn at random. Throughout the day, I rope people into having a conversation with me using that word, particularly if we're trapped together, like in a dressing room. These conversations help to keep the word lodged in my brain but it makes the other girls nuts.

"Let me think back that far, Doris. Oh, yes. Today's word is kleptomania," I say. "An 'irresistible urge to steal in the absence of any economic motive.' A person overcome with that urge is a kleptomaniac."

"Tag, I'm it," Margie says. "When it comes to anything in pants, I'm a klepto."

"Don't you mean nympho?" Doris replies, putting on more fake eyelashes.

"Naw. I have an irresistible urge to steal..." She pauses dramatically, "... men. I'm a sucker for someone else's man."

And we're off. Margie, Doris and I often put on a verbal show for our tent mates and have a lot of fun doing it. I can see the rest of the girls in the room listening and laughing, eager for some frivolity to the day.

Margie applies lipstick while saying, "My horn blower's mouse came in on the sly last night and had the screaming meemees when she got a load of me lip-locked with her Galahad. Belted him right in the smackaroo. They were still mixing it up when I blew."

"I don't see why these ladies get so overwrought," Doris says with a straight face. "When you get through with the gentleman in question, you give him back. I've seen you do it."

"Dozens of times," I added.

"And it's not like they don't get their yum-yums back in better shape than before," Margie says, looking from Doris to me, as if she doesn't understand it.

"Some girls can be touchy, Margie," I answer, lacing up my satin ballet slippers. "They don't like their men manhandled, especially by another woman."

Margie's penchant for men, especially musicians, is a running joke between the three of us. We have a 'hands off' rule about stealing each other's men, although I've always felt that if a man can be stolen like a wallet, there isn't much there to begin with.

"Back home in Charleston," Doris goes on, livening up the conversation, "we'd call you a debutante. Up North, you're a slut." With her southern accent she managed to make two syllables out of the word 'slut.'

"Hey, hey, watch them four-letter words," Margie says. "Don't make me slap a fine on you. And I'm not a slut. I'm just misunderstood." Everyone laughs, Margie being the loudest.

"Maybe Margie needs to head down south, where she'll be appreciated," I say to Doris.

"I expect so, Sugar," drawls Doris, adding a large beauty mark to her cheek. "They need something else to talk about besides the War Between the States."

Margie throws a makeup sponge at Doris, hitting her on the back of the head. It bounces off and lands on the floor. Without saying a word, Doris picks it up and flips it to me.

"Look what's falling from the sky," she says in mock surprise.

"Chicken Little uses makeup sponges?" I say. "I had no idea."

"You should throw that nasty old thing out, Jeri. Trash can's right behind you."

"Sez you!" Margie retorts. "They're up to a nickel apiece, when you can get them. Give."

I laugh and toss it back to Margie, who catches it with one hand, while she applies rouge with the other. The ringmaster's introduction of the finale comes over the loudspeaker, quieting us down.

Doris checks her makeup in the mirror and adds more Vaseline to her lips. Reaching down, she grabs her four-foot high, hot pink feather headdress with both hands and puts it on her head. She straightens it and tightens the elastic band under her chin, dangling silver beads glittering next to her painted, blue eyes. She adjusts her breasts in the hot pink-and-silver spangled bare-midriff top before standing to add the matching full-length, beaded cape to her costume. She sparkles like a marquee in Times Square on New Year's Eve.

Margie stands up in her magenta and green job and looks at me, expectantly.

I rise in my Spanish number and put more bobby pins in my mantilla to keep it in place.

"Let's go get 'em, girls," I say.

Followed by the other women, we leave the dressing area and spread out to our assigned places. I go to the side entrance to find Mabel, the largest of the elephants. Mabel is as large as a male and often just as wily. She has a reputation for being untrustworthy and I am one of the few girls willing to ride her.

Whitey is by her side, holding on to her head harness. It's unusual to see him at this time. Normally, one of the lesser handlers deals with the Grand Finale. It might be because of our earlier conversation, I realize. I've been too busy to get back to him. Coming around the back end of Mabel, I hurry toward the platform and ladder on the left side to climb up to the howdah.

"Hi, Jeri," Whitey says, flashing his winning, gorgeous smile. He's a tough man to resist.

"Hi." I return his smile.

His face becomes somber. "Listen, Jeri, Mabel's been acting up tonight. She was fine for the first show. I don't know what could have happened." He gives me a worried look, then looks to the elephant.

I glance at the pachyderm and see Mabel is shaking her head from side to side, even trembling the way a dog does when you give it a bath. These are clear signs she's nervous.

"Maybe we should cancel her tonight," Whitey goes on. "You can just walk around the ring, instead of riding. I don't trust her without me close by."

I get onto the platform and hike up my skirt. Stepping on the first rung of the ladder, I turn and say, "Then you come with us, Whitey. She listens to you. All the ladies do. This is the only chance I get during the show to sit down and I'm going to take it." I climb up the ladder and into the canopied seat without looking back.

"Okay," he says reluctantly. "Let me grab my show hat."

He lets go of the harness for a moment, as the music for the grand finale starts up. Prancing animals, brightly painted wagons, juggling and dancing performers, all dressed in a kaleidoscope of colorful costumes, start pouring in from the four entrances. The crowd is on its feet, clapping and shouting.

Mabel lunges forward. She passes the bareback riders on their horses waiting in line, then the trick ponies that whinny in surprise to have her beside them. I look back and see a startled Whitey running after us. He fights to get through, past the elephant drawn calliope coming into place behind the horses. Mabel picks up speed and the howdah bounces precariously, more so than I've ever felt. I try not to panic, telling myself that I'm safe enough on her back no matter what she does.

Mabel overtakes the float pulled by the six white Lipizzaner horses with the showgirls on it. As she passes, an astonished Doris and Margie stare at me.

I consider jumping out of the howdah onto the float but Mabel is moving too damned fast. Most people think elephants are slow. This is not so. They can outrun a man and many smaller animals. They can outdistance a Cheetah.

The audience thinks it's part of the show and cheer wildly, not realizing a rampaging elephant can destroy anything in its path, including bleachers holding hundreds of people.

I hear a snap and the howdah begins to slide to one side. Now I panic. Mabel hears it, too, or feels it. She looks back at me balancing on one side of the top of her ribcage. With a high-pitched trumpet, she bolts out through one of the entrances into the black night, incoming performers and animals scurrying to get out of her way.

The howdah smashes against anything and everything, with me cowering inside. I flatten my body into its base, trying not to be hit, while she heads for the visitors' parking lot. In her frenzy, Mabel runs in between a narrow row of vehicles barely wide enough for her, let alone the howdah dropping lower and lower on her side. We sideswipe light poles, thick as tree trunks, and bang into cars and trucks.

Ripped off chunks of howdah fly everywhere. My dress becomes wrapped around my head and arms, protecting me from the debris but often catching on things, almost pulling me out. I have to fight to stay inside. The howdah continues to slip, until soon I'll fall out to be trampled under the elephant's feet.

As suddenly as she started her rampage, Mabel stops. She gives another trumpet but stands shivering. I hear Whitey's voice calling to her, calming her down. He sounds like he's standing in front of her. Later on I learn he saw she was heading for a small clearing on the other side of the parking lot and took a short cut, racing to get there first. He stops her with his very body, counting on the fact that she'll listen to him.

"Easy, girl," he says. "Easy now, girl. It's all right. Shhhhhh."

I let go of what's left of the howdah and fall to the ground, trying to roll away from Mabel's feet. Entangled in ripped fabric, I'm unable to move more than a couple of feet away. I sit in the dirt, pulling at the gown that encumbers me.

"Jeri! Jeri," Whitey says, coming over and kneeling down. He envelopes me in his arms. "Are you all right? Let me see."

He turns back to one of his men who takes over dealing with the trembling elephant. "Keep Mabel quiet but don't hit her." He's referring to the eyehook that the men keep in their back pockets for emergencies. Some try to cow the elephants with them when Whitey isn't looking. He finds the practice to be unnecessary and barbaric.

"That will only upset her more," he says with emphasis. "So don't hit her. Just keep talking to her in a soothing voice. Stroke her trunk." The man obeys.

He turns back to me. "Honey, say something. Are you hurt?"

I don't think I am, but can't talk. I try to rise but fall back down, sobbing and laughing at the same time. I hear Tin Foot shout my name. He's running faster than I've ever seen him, followed by several of the roustabouts. Margie and Doris trail behind holding onto their headdresses, costumes flapping as they run.

"Jeri!" Tin Foot pushes Whitey out of the way and holds onto me.

"He saved me," I whisper into Tin Foot's neck. "Whitey saved me."

Whitey stands up and looks down at Tin Foot. "Tin, someone cut the cinch to the howdah. I saw it. Only the gauze covering was keeping the damned thing on."

The two men exchange looks. Mabel makes several grunting noises, sounds of fear mixed with impatience.

"I've got to get Mabel out of here and take care of her. Jeri, I'll see you later, okay?" Whitey says. All I can do is nod. He bends down, lips brushing my forehead.

"Tin, can you stop by the Bull Ring later on and let me know how Jeri is doing?"

"Sure, Whitey. We'll take care of her. Don't worry."

Whitey crosses over to the elephant and speaks in gentle tones, leading her away. While I watch them leave, it hits me this is no accident.

Margie and Doris are by my side. Tin Foot and my two friends try to pick me up, hindered by yards of shredded fabric surrounding me.

"Stop," Doris says. "We keep standing on this damned dress. Here." She unclips her cape and wraps it around me while Margie goes underneath it and undoes the hooks at the front of my bodice. Together, they pull me out of the tattered ex-Spanish costume, with an anxious Tin Foot and roustabouts standing by, unable to help.

"Oh, God," I murmur, shivering inside the cape. "Wardrobe is going to kill me for what I did to that dress."

"Tell them to take it up with Mabel," Margie says.

"They need to put that horror out to pasture," Doris says. "She's not to be trusted."

I hear one of the roustabouts say, "The audience is coming out now. You'd better get her out of here. They think this is all part of the show. We'll clean up what's left of the howdah."

Tin Foot mutters a "thank you" to the guys and tries to lift me in his arms.

I fight him off, saying, "I can walk, Tin. I'm okay."

"No you're not," Margie replies and turns to Tin Foot. "But she likes to stand on her own two pins. You walk with her and we'll take this rag to wardrobe and clue them in."

Doris adds, "We'll see you back at the car as soon as we change, honey lamb. Tin is going to take you there and I don't want to hear another word about it."

I don't have the energy to fight. I stumble to the train, supported by my friend, and am glad of the help. When we get to the Virgin Car, Tin Foot calls out to Lillian, as we stagger up the stairs. She appears at the door, surprised to see us. We all have a routine and it's usually another ten or fifteen minutes before anyone shows up after the last performance.

"Have mercy," she says when she sees me. "Child, are you all right?"

Tin Foot helps me inside and brings me into Lillian's small room and kitchen area.

"You just set her down there." She gestures to her neatly made bed. "I'll take care of her."

Shooing Tin out, Lillian makes me a cup of her wonder tea. It's delicious, all spicy with cinnamon, nutmeg and a tablespoon of whiskey. I gulp it down and feel like I'm coming back to myself.

Meanwhile, she's been carrying buckets of hot water from the bathroom, filling up the portable tub she keeps in her room for the times when the girls want to take a bath. Lillian undresses me and helps me into the warm water.

"Oh my," she says, when she examines my arms and legs. "We've got some splinters in us. It's nothing for you to worry about, just a few here and there. Let me get my tweezers."

She grooms my body much as I've seen the gorillas and chimps do, removing one or two splinters from my scalp. She has a gentle, motherly touch, humming as she works. While she shampoos my hair, I lean into her, feeling safe for the moment.

"Someone tried to kill me, Lillian."

She stops humming and laughs softly. "Now you hush, Jeri. Why would anybody want to do something like that?"

"Why, indeed?" I whisper and slide under the water into its warmth and silence.

I don't fall asleep that night as much as pass out. There are no dreams, no light slumber, just a black, death-like sleep that comes when the mind and body have had more than enough.

Chapter Fourteen
7:30 am, Monday, July 6th

The curtains to my bunk are whipped open. The metal sound of the hooks scratching against the rod pierces my ear drums. I open my eyes to see both Margie and Doris staring at me, troubled and tearful.

"What?" I lay there, afraid to move, afraid to find out how wounded the day before has left me, but more afraid of the look on their faces. "What is it?"

Doris opens her mouth to speak but all that escapes is a sob. I sit upright and look from one friend to the other.

"It's Catalena," Margie says. I watch a tear glide down her face. "Oh, Jeri," she says, clasping my hands in hers. "I can't believe it. We can't believe it," she adds, looking at Doris. Both are silent, looking at each other.

"Tell me," I demand. "One of you, tell me."

"She hanged herself. Last night. In the First Aid Tent," Doris murmurs. "She's dead."

"Hanged herself," I try to say, the words caught in my throat. "Are you sure?" I manage to get out. They don't answer but look down, heads bowed.

"When? When did this happen?" I jump down from the berth too fast and wobble a bit on my landing. Margie grabs my arm to steady me.

"Sometime during the night," Margie says, her jive talk noticeably absent. "We saw a commotion at the First Aid Tent on our way to get coffee and went to see what was going on. He said the nurse left her side for just a few minutes to go to the bathroom. She thought Catalena was sleeping. He said when she came back, it was too late." Margie stops talking and bites her lower, quivering lip.

"Who's 'he?'" I say. "Who said?"

"Doc Williams found her," my golden-haired friend answers. "But he was in with the sheriff. We didn't talk to him."

During this time, other curtains open one after another and some of the girls watch and listen in silence.

"Tony came out and told us what happened when he found out we were there," Doris adds, wiping tears from her face with a lace-trimmed hanky.

"Why didn't someone wake me?" I ask. "Why didn't I hear any sirens?"

"I don't know," Doris says, backing up from my intensity. "Oh, God, that poor, sweet girl." She buries her face in the hanky, sobbing loudly.

"We did wake you, Jeri," Margie answers me, with a touch of belligerence. "Just now. You knew as soon as we could get back to tell you. As for why there were no sirens, you'll have to ask the sheriff."

"I've got to go," I say, reaching up for my robe hanging on a hook.

"Jeri..." I hear Margie call out, as I fling myself out of the car and run full-out to the First Aid Tent. I arrive out of breath and lightheaded.

Two roustabouts are standing on either side of the tent entrance and stop me from going inside. When I see I can't force my way past them, I begin to yell.

"Doc! Tony! It's Jeri. Let me come inside. Doc! Tony!"

Tony appears at the door, his face ashen and drawn. He nods to the two men and they step aside. Turning, Tony goes back inside without saying a word. I follow. With a fleeting look over to the three hospital beds, I half-expect to see Catalena lying in one of them, as if this is a big misunderstanding. Instead, a sheet-covered body lies on the ground just inside the doorway. Dangling from one of overhead tent poles is the pale blue belt of a robe, a ragged cut at the bottom.

Constantin sits on one of the beds, holding his head in his hands, intermittently wailing or crying out words I can't understand. Ioana is on the floor at his feet, tears streaming down her face.

"Oh, God, Tony," I whisper, looking down at the white sheeted form. "Is that...?

Before he can answer, Sheriff Draeger emerges from a corner of the patient's area carrying a notepad and pencil. He walks around the body, but stops when he sees me. Looking back at the grieving family, he gestures for us to move away to another part of the tent.

"What's she doing here?" he asks Tony, while looking at me.

"I'd asked Miss Deane to help out with some things," Tony answers vaguely, then turns to me. "Maybe you'd better leave, Jeri. I'll talk to you later."

"This little lady seems to be in on everything, Mr. Phillips," the sheriff says in an accusing tone of voice. I'm about to say something, fight for my right to be there when he focuses on Tony. "Well, it looks like you and your circus are in a packet of trouble."

"Maybe not," Tony says. "Maybe this is the end of the trouble."

"What are you thinking, mister?" The sheriff's eyes narrow on Boss Man.

I stand speechless, watching this exchange.

Tony pulls himself up to his full height, putting on what I have come to know as his mock-sincere, showman face. "Maybe the girl was fooling around with the clown, got pregnant and found out he was leaving. One thing led to another. Hell hath no fury like a woman scorned."

"What are you saying?" I ask, horrified.

A look of comprehension crosses Sheriff Draeger's face and he begins to nod his head. "I see what you're getting at. She gets in the family way. This Connors decides to run out on her, leaving her holding the bag. She finds out, creeps up behind him and strangles him with the wire. Then she loses the baby, and in a fit of remorse, hangs herself. I already got that nurse's testimony about finding her swinging."

"I'm not saying that's the way it was," Tony says smoothly. "I'm merely offering that as a possible --"

"How could she strangle Eddie?" I interrupt, louder than I intend. Lowering my voice, I add, "That's absurd."

"Now, now," the sheriff says, looking at me. "We all know you gals aren't the same as other women. You're stronger, a lot like a man. I saw them muscles on you yesterday, Miss Deane. You could lick a lot of men I know. Not me, of course, but — "

"I'm not saying that's the way it was but..." Tony says again, letting his words drop off and looking at the shorter man. His expression is filled with expectation.

"It fits, it fits." The sheriff has a smug look on his face.

"It doesn't fit," I retort.

The sheriff glares at me. "Yes, it does and that's what I'm putting in my report." He looks at Tony. "That might mean you don't have to close your circus, Mr. Phillips. We got our killer, a scorned woman."

"I can't believe either of you --" I start.

Tony's voice overrides mine. "What happens now, sheriff?" he says, putting a hand on the pudgy sheriff's arm and steering him away from me. I follow. Tony shoots me a warning look over his shoulder.

Draeger closes his notebook and puts the pencil in his shirt pocket, chatting in a low voice, as he walks. "First thing, we'll remove the body to the mortuary. Her family can take it from there. Then I'll give my report to the city council. There'll be an inquest but that's a formality."

I ignore Tony and go around to the other side of the sheriff. "You can't mean this--"

"That's enough, Jeri," Tony interrupts. His voice is low and menacing. He turns to Sheriff Draeger with a smile. "The circus will cooperate in any way we can. Let me know if there's anything we can do."

Yeah, I think, *what are you going to do, Tony? Throw another thousand bucks his way?*

"I'll get my men in here to take the body away. I'll leave you to take care of your own people, Mr. Phillips," the sheriff says, giving me a disgusted look.

I watch Tony escort the sheriff to the tent exit. When he turns around, I open my mouth to speak but he grabs me roughly by the arm and pulls me back to the same corner as before.

"Shut up, Jeri. It's over."

I break free of his grasp. "It's over? What's over? Catalena didn't kill that boy."

"You don't know that."

"I *do* know that. Even if she could strangle him with the wire, how the hell could she pull his dead weight into the lion's cage? She hardly weighed a hundred pounds. And why would she drag him there? It doesn't make any sense." I glare at him. "Listen, you hired me to find out who murdered Eddie and that's what I'm going to do."

He glares back. "Well, I'm un-hiring you."

"Tony, it wasn't Catalena. She was running away with Eddie. She had a bus ticket to Salt Lake City. I found it in her diary."

He pulls at his mustache. "Listen to me, Jeri. I don't know if the girl killed Eddie or not, but I've got a circus to think about. And did you see what happened just hours after I hired you to look into it? Someone put a hairbrush under your howdah, then cut the cinch for good measure. You were almost killed."

His words stop me cold. "Someone put a hairbrush under the cinch?"

"Yes, it acted like a burr. No wonder Mabel went on a rampage." I start to speak but he overrides me again. "Jeri, in two months time, we can get Brinks in here, real detectives.

They can find out what happened, if we still want to know. Let the sheriff think what he's going to think. We can stay open. Once the press gets wind of his version of this, there will be no more threats of cancellations."

I stare at Constantin and his daughter wrapped in a world of tragedy.

"Meanwhile, the real killer is out there, Tony. And thanks to you and the stupidity of the sheriff, her poor family gets to believe that Catalena killed another human being, as well as taking her own life. That's not right."

"I don't care about right. I care about protecting you and keeping the Big Top open."

"I don't want your protection." I say through clenched teeth.

"Then it's about keeping the circus open." His voice is low and hard. "It's over, Jeri. I've made my decision. I'll want the keys and the chart back before tonight's show." And with that, he turns on his heels and walks away, exiting the tent.

I lean against one of the tent poles and study the Baboescu family's grief from a distance. Constantin is inconsolable, surrounded by thick walls of desolation, not letting his younger daughter in. I observe the little girl reach out to her father, using a gentle hand or a soft word, and he will have none of it. The scene is all so familiar, it almost kills me.

I suspect Ioana has always tried to comfort her father, gaining some solace herself by the very act. Maybe now he will stop shutting her out. Or maybe one day, something would die inside of her and she'll stop trying.

I'm torn between staying in the shadows and going to comfort Ioana, telling her everything will be all right, which is a downright lie. I stay in the shadows.

Two deputies come in with a gurney and lift the sheeted body onto it. Constantin tries to stop them, yelling incoherently, but is restrained by a third deputy. It's a terrible, terrible sight.

I remain in my corner, trying to give the family as much privacy as possible, yet unwilling to leave. The gurney is carried out, bearing its young burden. I forget to ask about the sirens.

Doc's whereabouts come into my mind. I haven't seen him and know he has to be somewhere nearby. I creep back to his office. He's sitting at his desk finding relief, once again, in a bottle of Johnnie Walker Red. I call out several times before he hears me.

"Jeri, is that you?" he says, his back to me. He twists around, watery blue eyes small and swollen. I go over and put my hand on his shoulder.

"You look like you could use some food, Doc. Let me go get you something."

He doesn't answer. I notice the label has been virtually peeled off this bottle, too; curling, ragged pieces laying about the desk. I take the whiskey from his hand.

"You've had enough, Doc."

He smiles. "Now you sound like a wife." He loses the smile. "I had one once. She's dead." I can tell he's caught up in the past, not a recent one but the past of many years, a past that sweeps him away more and more these days.

"Doc," I say, trying to bring him back.

"Killed waiting at a bus stop. Hit-and-run."

I open my mouth to say something but think better of it. He probably won't hear me, anyway. I sit in the chair on the other side of the desk.

"I should have been there," he says, ruffling his grey-white hair with slender fingers. "I should have driven her where she needed to go. Eight and a half months pregnant, standing on a street corner waiting for a bus, but I was too busy making a name for myself." He looks at me from across the desk. It might as well be from across an ocean.

"Death is everywhere, you know, just waiting. When you're a doctor, you think you're trained to expect it, wait for it, challenge it. But you're not. I'm not."

"I'm sorry, Doc, for all the things that have happened in your life. But right now I need you to tell me about last night. It's important." He doesn't answer, so I press him. "Time's running out, Doc. Tell me. Please."

He looks down and brushes at the curled papers, then worries one of the flaws on his scratched desk. I wait. I can see him fighting something inside of him, maybe those personal demons that hound him so much these days. When he speaks, his voice takes on a monotone.

"I was asleep. I'd left for my compartment around midnight. The nurse was spending the night with Catalena, as a precaution. We don't like to leave a patient alone overnight. You know the portable toilets are outside, quite a ways down, near the gorillas. Around four a.m. Laverne had to go to the lavatory. Catalena was sleeping or that's what the nurse thought. Laverne says she was gone maybe fifteen minutes, twenty at the most. When she came back, she saw Catalena hanging from one of the overhead poles, a chair kicked out from under her. Laverne climbed up and tried to free the knot, get her down. Then she found some shears and cut the belt. All the time she was screaming for help, for what she says seemed like hours, but there was nobody around to hear. I'd gone back to my compartment. I thought the danger was over. It's my fault."

"It's not your fault."

"I should have stayed with my patient."

"You had your nurse stay with the patient. That's the same thing."

He looks me dead in the eye. "It wasn't enough." He turns away. "It's never enough."

"Where's the nurse now?"

"Laverne's lying on a cot back there." He gestures to the supply room. "I gave her a sedative, a heavy dose. She should be out the rest of the day. She has to live with this, you know, for the rest of her life."

"I know about things you have to live with, Doc," I say, my mind flashing back to my last day with Brinks. "Did she find a suicide note?"

Doc shakes his head. "The sheriff looked but couldn't find one, either."

"What that might mean, Doc, is that if Catalena didn't take the time to write one, she was a pretty desperate, driven person. It was probably going to happen no matter what anybody did. Maybe Catalena had been awake for awhile, only pretending to sleep, waiting for the right time."

Doc lay his head down on the desk, pillowed by crossed arms. "I didn't think about a suicide watch, Jeri, and I should have. The death of her lover, the loss of her baby; it was too much for her. She was only sixteen." He swallows hard and is still.

I want to say something of comfort but nothing comes to mind. I feel helpless and inept. The silence becomes stifling.

"I should go, Doc," I say, standing. "I can't do anything here."

He nods without looking up. I come to the other side of the desk and lay a hesitant hand on his shoulder.

"I want you to promise me you'll get something to eat."

"Sure," he says without moving.

I know he won't and I'm not completely sure why I said it. Doc is right. Sometimes, no matter what you do or say, it's never enough.

Chapter Fifteen
8:30 a.m., Monday

Outside in the bright morning, I lean against a small tractor used to carry feed and grain to the animals around the lot. Birds chirp, the sun shines, the world sparkles. It all feels wrong to me.

I pluck at my dark green robe. I should go back to the sleeper and dress, I think, but I can't move, cry or utter a sound. I sink down to the runner of the tractor and close my eyes, putting my head in my hands. The darkness feels good. I'm not sure I ever want to open my eyes again.

I don't know how long I sit there but I hear Tin Foot call my name, not once but several times. It sounds as if he's standing directly above me. I shade my eyes from the sun and look up. The hulking, red-headed man holds two mugs of something hot, tendrils of steam rising, carried off by a soft breeze.

"Hi, Jeri," he says, when he knows he has my attention.

"Hi." My voice cracks on the word and I clear my throat.

"I brought you some hot tea with milk. Just the way you like it." He thrusts the mug in my direction, waving it under my nose.

"Thanks, Tin," I say, taking it. I hold it in my hand, watching the steam rise and disappear.

"Best drink it while it's hot." He squats down beside me. I can smell the coffee in his mug.

I take a sip of tea, but find I can't swallow. It's like my throat is too small. The liquid runs down the sides of my mouth and I wipe at it with the sleeve of my robe.

"I can't..." I begin to say then stop.

"Just hold it then, Jeri. It'll warm your hands. You look cold."

I nod and wrap my hands around the thick, white mug, looking at my friend.

"You know about Catalena?" My voice sounds tight and constricted; the words too insignificant.

"Yes. Everybody knows. It's been going on for a couple of hours. I was glad you missed most of it. Nothing you could do. Nothing any of us could do."

"She was so young, Tin. She had her whole life before her. I can't understand it." My voice breaks.

"I guess the last twenty-four hours were too much for her."

"We'll never know," I whisper. "She didn't leave a suicide note."

"How are you doing today?" Tin Foot asks, changing the subject. "You don't look too bad, considering what you went through last night." His voice is soft, almost without inflection.

I glance at my hands and arms. "No, I guess I don't. I haven't had a chance to think about it."

I take a tenuous sip of tea. This one goes down. It tastes grand. "The sheriff thinks that Catalena killed Eddie and in a fit of remorse, hanged herself."

I gulp at the tea and look over the top of my mug at him. While his face registers bafflement, he doesn't say anything. He drinks more coffee, his expression dark and pensive.

"He's going to write that up in his report," I go on. "That lets the circus off the hook. He says the town won't close us down now."

He grunts. "What did Boss Man say to all of that?"

"He planted the seed in the sheriff's mind, Tin. Tony says he wants me – us -- to stop the investigation."

"I'm not surprised."

"I'm not going to stop."

"I'm not surprised."

We sit in silence drinking from our mugs, thinking our own thoughts. Tin Foot turns to me.

"Well, if we're not stopping then I've got some news for you, Jeri. Actually, a couple of things. Maybe you don't want to hear them."

I look at him and take another swig of tea. "I do. I don't want to think about Catalena right now. Tell me."

"First of all, yesterday at the poker game, the guys were talking about how Eddie owed each of them money they'd never collect. They weren't mad about it but you know how it is. They'll never see that money now."

"I take it he was a better clown than he was a poker player."

"Seems like," Tin agrees. "After I left, I wrote the names and amounts down on this piece of paper." He reaches into a pocket and pulls out a folded sheet. "The most was twenty-five bucks to the Bard. He's the one who dresses up sort of like Shakespeare. He didn't play cards with us. Said he had a headache or something like that. The guys mentioned that the Bard took Eddie under his wing when the kid first showed up. Strange little man."

"That's the clown who wears the ruff around his neck and drives the little car they all pile into?" Tin Foot nods. I take the sheet without looking at it. "Vince is still the largest amount that you know of?"

"By a lot," Tin says. "And here's something the guys were shocked by. Not that Eddie was running away – he owed a lot of people -- but about the girl."

"No one knew about him and Catalena?"

"They saw the two kids talking now and then but figured they were just pals. Eddie came from a pretty strict Mormon family a few months back."

"That doesn't mean anything. Mormons know what goes where. So the guys didn't know about the baby?"

"Not until it got out this morning. I overheard them talking a while ago. They couldn't believe that he...well... knew Catalena in a Biblical way. Although..." He breaks off.

"Although what?"

"Although he might have had a brief fling with Rosie when he first got here."

"Rosie?" I say. "You're kidding."

He shakes his head. "He hung around her only a week or two, at best. But men and women have been known to be friends. Like us," he adds.

"Or it might have been something she did to try to make Whitey jealous and it didn't work. Eddie was a good looking kid." I think for a moment. "You know, that's an odd expression, what you said before. 'In a Biblical way'" I drink more tea. "You ever read the Bible, Tin?"

He gives me a quizzical look. "Sure. Every kid had to go to Bible School on Sunday mornings. Didn't you?"

I shake my head and down the rest of the tea. "My father stopped going to mass after my mother died. I guess I never got into the habit. But I've read a lot of the Bible on my own. It's a well-written book. It has a lot of catchy phrases."

Tin Foot laughs with a toss of his head.

"Vince has a Bible." I ponder. "I noticed it yesterday on top of one of the filing cabinets. Constantin does, too."

"A lot of people do, Jeri. I do. Does that mean something?"

"Not sure yet."

"One last thing, Whitey's got your hairbrush. The one I saw you using yesterday morning. He found it under Mabel's cinch." He pauses. "You look like you knew that."

"I suspected it was mine. How'd you find this out?"

"I overheard Whitey and Tony talking at the training ring."

I grin at him. "Well, if you're not aces in my book. You've been listening in on conversations everywhere. You make one swell investigator."

Tin Foot blushes. "Just doing my job, ma'am."

"Well, it's a non-paying job now. So Whitey has my hairbrush? Or does Tony? I want it back."

"Whitey wouldn't hand it over to him. Said he wanted to talk to you first, but they both knew it was yours by the initials."

I let out a sigh. "I guess Boss Man did fire me partly because he wanted to protect me. But it still means I can't get into the personnel files. I'll have to find another way to find out what I need to know."

"Are you sure you shouldn't stop?"

"Not on your life. Do you know that Tony said he might want to bring in 'real detectives' from Brinks in two months? I've never been so insulted. But it's more than that. I don't want this lain at Catalena's feet. It's not right."

"No," Tin agrees reluctantly, "but…"

"But nothing. I know what it's like when life slams you in the face. It doesn't care that you're young and innocent. If you don't fight back, take on whatever's out there, you're going down …" I stop talking and study the inside of my mug.

"Then I'm with you all the way, Jeri." He sticks out a ruddy, muscular hand. I take it in mine and we shake on it.

"Thanks. Besides, I need something to occupy my mind. I feel like Doris, I'm so depressed I could eat dirt. I don't want to just sit around and wait for the next bad thing to happen, because there's a lot more to come. Call it woman's intuition, if you will, but I can feel it. And then there's the sister."

"Ioana," Tin murmurs. "Poor kid."

"I think she's spent most of her life being called 'poor kid.' She's always on the outside looking in."

"I don't think she has any friends. At least, I've never seen her with any."

"I know. I feel for her."

"Do you, Jeri? I've never seen you say two words to her. Seems to me like you sort of avoid Ioana." Tin casts a swift glance to me then looks down at his mug. "Not that it's any of my business."

I think about it. "I probably do, Tin. She reminds me of me at that age. Awkward... lost... lonely...maybe even unloved. I was a change of life baby, the last of eight, born so late nobody wanted or expected me. My mother died of complications four days after my birth, as my father so often reminded me. When I look back on it, I see a little girl who tried to sing and dance her way out of unhappiness."

"That's too bad," Tin comments.

"When I was twelve years old, my father caught me dancing in the same room as his makeshift alter to St. Joseph. To him, that was sacrilege. Or maybe he was just looking for something. He beat me with a broom and threw me out of the house. I slept on my older sister's living room couch until I got my first job at fourteen. I haven't seen him since that day." I pause. "I think you're right, Tin. I do avoid Ioana. Seeing her with her father reminds me of how my father treated me. I didn't think it was obvious to others."

"Probably only to me, Jeri."

"I wonder what kind of person that makes me? Shallow, I guess." I let out a small chortle that dies in my throat.

"No, just hurting. If this is truth time, Jeri..."

"Oh, it is, Tin." I say, trying to lighten the mood. "This is True Confessions time."

Tin clears his throat. "About a month or two after this happened to my foot, I was at the movies with some friends. A newsreel came on about Jesse Owens running the Track and

Field in Berlin, showing up Hitler's Aryan race. I was proud of him like everybody else, but I had to leave the theatre. It reminded me too much of what I'd lost. But I'd like to think I could watch it now. You get over things." Tin looks at me.

I look back at him.

"I don't know, Tin. Some things you never get over." I throw the soggy tea leaves into the bushes.

Back at the sleeper I change clothes and think. I can't get at Vince's files but I can try to read Catalena's diary again. Privacy being an issue around here, I'll have to find a place to be by myself for a couple of hours.

The curtains to my berth are wide open. The morning sun streams in through the window, wearing the note found at Old Kirby's wagon, forgotten about in all the chaos. Dry and backlit, I see what remains of the blue inked writing, despite the punishing rain and mud.

Blue is volatile dye in almost every form. A fading dress or shirt often takes on a reddish undertone to replace the vanishing blue. So too, this paper has an impression of words no longer blue but with a faint hint of red diluted to pale pink by the water. It's enough for me to make out a word here and there but reveals little. The words "earlier" "meet" and "worry" leaps out at me, and of course, Eddie's name at the end. I peel the note from the window, thin and crisp from the abuse it's taken. Carefully, I fold it and put it into my bag.

The car is empty save for me. Maybe I can stay put for awhile and concentrate on the diary. Best laid plans of mice and men; Margie and Doris show up as I finish dressing. Something's up with both of them, but I can't tell what it is.

"Okay, Toots," Margie says, "Let's hit the Cookhouse for some chow." She smacks me on the rear. "And 'no' is not an answer."

"They've got real eggs today," Doris says. "None of those regurgitated ones."

"Reconstituted, Doris, not regurgitated," says Margie.

"You use your words, Sugar, and I'll use mine."

"After that," adds Margie with forced brightness, "if there's no rehearsal, let's put on our glad rags, go into the berg and catch *Mrs. Miniver*. I hear it's a real tear jerker. It'll get our mind off of things around here."

"What a lovely idea," says Doris, in a rehearsed sort of way. I think they've planned this maneuver before they came into the car. "Somebody told me that Greer Garson has been nominated for an academy award. I just love how she does a British accent."

"It comes naturally to her, Doris. She's English," I say, relenting and joining them in their light banter. I grab my bag from my berth and tie it around my waist. "But I thought you were spending the day with Tony."

"Tony and I are through," Doris says. I look at her in stunned silence. Her face is pinched and red. She swallows several times, fighting back tears.

Margie gives me a warning shake of her head. Whatever it is, she knows about it.

"I don't understand," I stutter. "I thought you and Tony --"

"I followed you to the First Aid tent," Doris says, her voice flat and emotionless. "I overheard what Tony said to you, what he did. I...." She breaks off and moves to the exit. I trail behind.

"Doris," I rush in to say, "He's under a lot of stress. He's in a panic --"

"No," she answers, turning around and facing both of us. There is no more red face or a threat of tears.

"That's no excuse," she goes on. "I don't know who he is. I thought I did, but I don't. And the man who said those horrible things this morning, I don't want to know."

Doris throws her head back and struts forward. I stand frozen for a moment, as does Margie. Then I run to catch up with Doris.

"There's more," Margie says, stopping us with something in her voice. "While we're all going on like the third act of a melodrama, you may as well get the low-down from me than somebody else." She takes a deep breath. "I've been canned."

"What?" Both Doris and I say it in unison.

"You've been fired?" I can't believe it.

"Not from the circus," Margie says with an impatient toss of her head. "From being the SA. I'm to 'step down until certain allegations can be cleared up'. One of our roommates went to management and told them what happened last night. Not everybody thinks we're the living dolls we do." She lets out a mirthless laugh. "There go my ambitions to rise in the ranks, to be the first woman in management. Cut off at the knees."

"Maybe not," I say, hurrying back to Margie. I hug her briefly. "There'll be a review. You can contest it; tell them what happened...." My words drift off.

"You're talking through your hat, Jeri," She replies. "We know what happened."

I don't say anything. Neither does anyone else. Wordless, the three of us move to the exit and hop off the car.

"This is my fault, ladies," I finally say. "If I hadn't --"

They both start talking at the same time. I can't tell who's saying what.

"Absolutely not. You were doing the right thing."

"No, it isn't. It's Tony's fault."

I persist. "I should stop all this. I should --"

"You do and I'll slap you silly." Doris grabs me by the arm and twirls me around to face her, going on with a force I rarely see in her. "I for one am glad to find out I was sleeping with a man no better than a carpet bagger. We don't hold with that kind in the south."

"As for me," Margie adds in a more reasonable tone, "I like to be footloose and fancy free. There's a lot of paperwork doing that job and the pay stinks. An extra three bucks a week. Who needs it?"

"Is this one of those 'everything happens for the best' moments?" I look from one to the other. "Okay, I guess it's settled then. We continue on and see what happens."

"Hon, as long as we got each other," says Doris, "we'll be fine. To hell with them all."

"You betcha," Margie adds. "If you're ever up a tree, call on me," she sings. Margie never had a bad voice and Doris and I join in. It doesn't make things go away but it makes them better.

"Let's go get some breakfast," Doris says. "I'm so hungry I could eat a whale-bone corset."

We link arms and start for the chow tent.

"I'll go into town with you," I say, "but instead of going to the movie, I'll spend the time in the library reading." I don't mention the reading would be of Catalena's diary, hopefully, aided by a Romanian dictionary. "I'll try to get in a visit in with Coke, too. See how he's doing. Oh, my God."

I stop and stand transfixed, staring up at one of the 3-by 5-foot circus posters plastered eye-level everywhere. A montage of images on a red background, it includes true to life depictions of Topsy in her pink tutu, the master of ceremony, Emmett Kelly, a seal balancing a ball on its nose, and a dancing bear wearing a bellboy cap. It also features the face of our most gorgeous showgirl, Doris, wearing her sparkling, finale headdress. Only Doris' eyes, her beautiful blue eyes, have been methodically gouged out, two empty holes in their place. It's so sick and unexpected, I'm speechless.

"What? What?" Margie looks around her for the cause of my halted, statue-like form.

I gesture toward the poster where it dangles from one of the many posts that run the length of the train. Both friends follow my pointing finger. Doris lets out a small scream and clutches at her throat. She, too, freezes in place, staring at the ghoulish mutilation.

"Well, if it ain't one thing, it's another," Margie mutters. "Who would do that?"

She dashes to another hanging poster, about twenty-yards away. "This one's the same thing. I never noticed it when we left this morning. How long have these been like this?"

"Are they all that way?" I race in the opposite direction to another poster. "This one, too," I shout. I move to the next one further down the line. It hasn't been touched. Apparently, only the ones closest to the Virgin Car have been disfigured.

I jog back, my breath coming in short spurts, but keeping Margie's face in my sights. She mouths to me, "Rosie?" I agree but shrug.

Both of us focus on Doris, still staring up, hand at throat. She suddenly drops her hand and turns to us. "I wish I had my daddy's horsewhip."

"I didn't know your father was into horses," Margie jokes, but something catches in her throat.

"He was a turkey farmer and you know it," Doris says with spirit. "But he taught me how to use a mean horsewhip and I wish I had it now." She spins around and heads for the chow line, taking long, purposeful strides. We trail behind, staring at her back, and give each other troubled glances.

"Someone should tell Tony, if he already doesn't know," Margie shouts up to Doris.

"I don't care if he knows or not. And if I see that bitch first, I just might have to scratch *her* eyes out."

I catch up with Doris and try to match her gait, which is not easy with her long legs. Margie attaches herself to the other side of our friend. Her stride comes easier than mine. I start to jog again.

"We don't know for sure it's Rosie, Doris. Not yet," I say, trying to contain this.

"Yes, we do," pipes up Margie. I give her a 'stop stirring up the pot' look. She sticks her tongue out at me but adds, "She'd need a ladder to do it, though. She's shorter than you, Jeri. So maybe it was one of the roustabouts. You piss anybody off lately?"

Doris comes to such an abrupt halt; we're about two feet ahead of her before either Margie or I can slow down. We swivel back to her almost as one. Doris assumes a proper lady-like pose. "I am not the sort of person who 'pisses' people off, I'll have you know, my dear Marjory. I am always a lady."

"Except when you threw that pail at Ernie last week," Marjory answers.

"He was teasing Methuselah. I told him to stop and he wouldn't, so I threw the pail at him to get his attention."

"You got his attention, all right," I say. "Doc said Ernie had a knot on the back of his head the size of a walnut the next day."

"He deserved it." Doris sniffs and struts off. We tag along, Margie and I, and start to giggle. Doris begins giggling, too, and the three of us are out-and-out laughing by the time we near the chow tent.

"So we need to face it. It could be someone else, Doris," I say, as we round the corner.

"Fat chance." Margie rolls her eyes. "I think what Rosie needs is a good lay."

Doris turns a shocked face to her friend.

"What's the big deal?" Margie gives us both an innocent look. "We all *do* it."

"Yes, but we don't *say* it," Doris reprimands. "We may do it behind closed doors, but we don't talk about it."

"I keep forgetting," Margie grumbles. "You're a lady."

"Damn straight," Doris snaps, and all three of us burst out laughing again.

We swing by the bulletin board first to see if a rehearsal is posted or if there are any announcements. Other than the bandmaster, Merle Evans, calling for a rehearsal of the orchestra, there's nothing. That means the day is ours until the seven p.m. call.

I finish eating and promise to meet the girls in an hour. I get another plate of scrambled eggs, toast and hash browns for Doc, cover it with a napkin and head for the First Aid Tent. I steel myself in case the wailing Constantin is still there, but it's eerily empty and quiet inside.

Heading back to Doc's office, I hear the soft murmur of voices. I peek in and see Ioana in Doc's chair, with him sitting on the edge of the desk. She's hunched over, sobbing into a soggy handkerchief. Doc bends over her, saying words I can't make out, but the sound of his voice soothes even me, someone they aren't intended for.

I step inside, extending the plate of hot food. Doc sees me out of the corner of his eye. I pull a Tootsie Roll from my pocket, show it to him, and drop it on the side of the plate. Doc rewards me with a half-smile. He signals for me to be quiet, reaches out and takes the food, gesturing for me to leave.

On my way out, I hear him tell the girl that he has something for her to eat, encouraging her to do so. He's changed, rallied even, since I last saw him.

Doc's one of these men who needs to be needed, more so than most of us. That's what gives him his strength but I suspect it's also his downfall.

Chapter Sixteen
10:30 a.m., Monday

Outside, I pull out my watch, so I can see the time. Whitey should be with the elephants right about now, supervising the grooming of them, making sure they are well and happy. Sometimes I think that if we ever become more serious, I'll have to take a backseat to a bunch of pachyderms.

Sure enough, I find Whitey in the Bull Tent with a long handled brush and several buckets of water, scrubbing down Mabel. This isn't his job to do, it hasn't been for years, but he's the type of guy who pitches in and does the dirty work right alongside his men. If one of the elephants misbehaves or becomes unruly, Whitey takes over, even to the cleaning up after them.

This morning Mabel looks content, throwing straw over her back, first from the left and then the right. Sometimes she aims for Whitey's face with the straw and he tells her to stop it, laughing all the time. It's a game the two play. He's a good man. The way he loves these animals is one of his major attractions to me.

"Hi, Jeri." His face lights up with a smile. God, he's gorgeous, with his blonde hair and bronzed skin, glistening from the sweat of his work.

"How are you feeling?" He looks me up and down but keeps on working. "You seem okay. I hope there's no lasting damage. I've been looking for you when I could get away; we've been pretty busy around here. It's a shame about that knife thrower's daughter. You never know what makes people do something like that."

I don't answer, feeling a large lump in my throat. He looks over, sees how it affects me and changes the subject.

"I ran into Margie a while ago. She told me you were feeling better."

"A little stiff, a few scratches here and there, but otherwise, fine." I force a smile and look at him.

He leans against the side of Mabel's ribcage as if it's a wall and stares at me. I stare back, wondering what's on his mind.

"Jesus, you have such a beautiful face, Jeri. I like to think your face is what Helen of Troy's must have looked like to Paris before he launched those thousand ships."

The tent heats up a few degrees. I try to bring it down a little. "Well, thank you, kind sir. Most people tell me I look a lot like Hedy Lamarr, which is pretty good. But Helen of Troy, that's even better."

"Well, after almost getting you killed, I have to slather it on a bit thicker than most." He forces a laugh.

"None of this is your fault, Whitey."

"I let go of the harness. Plus I should have never let you climb up into the howdah. I knew Mabel was out of sorts."

"I was up there before you knew what happened. I can be like that, you know, determined and stubborn. I like to win. It's the American way."

"You sound like you're selling war bonds, Jeri." He lets out an easier laugh and disappears behind Mabel's massive backside. I can hear him scrubbing her butt. "If you are, I'm buying," he shouts.

"Not today, but I'll keep that in mind."

I come closer to Mabel's face and watch her ears flapping to keep cool. She seems very content. I reach out and touch the top of her trunk near her mouth, determined not to let what happened scare me off her.

I offer her an apple, having made sure to bring another one for Topsy, who stands right next to her. She and Mabel are best friends, happiest when placed side by side. There is a ritual about who is placed where and who gets along with whom. You can't have disharmony among the troupes, especially when each troupe member weighs as much as a boxcar.

Mabel takes the apple with her "finger," the delicate and talented appendage at the end of her trunk and tosses the fruit into her mouth. With a noisy exhale, she touches my face with her finger tip, so gently it tickles. The finger is very flexible and sensitive. I've known them to pick up a dime with it.

I step closer to Mabel and she nuzzles my neck with her trunk, pulling me toward her, almost as if she's apologizing for the night before. I forgive her on the spot and hug her big, grey face. She can be so sweet sometimes.

Topsy looks over to me for her apple and snorts. I pull it from my pocket, show it to her and she gives out a little squeal of delight. Laughing, I free myself from Mable's embrace. Outside of riding Mabel during the spec, all the tricks I do are with Topsy. She's one of the most reliable and easy going of the elephants. I love her dearly. I stand back and admired my two performing pals, feeling the tension inside me ease a little. Animals can do that for you, even ones this big.

Elephants are one of the smartest animals I know. They have a good sense of humor and can be a lot of fun. They love to play games, like softball. They can hold a bat with their trunk and swing at a ball. They understand the concept of a game, especially team against team.

During off-season, we often play softball with them and their antics are hilarious. They'll do anything to win; cheating is not beyond them. Sometimes, they'll hide the ball by placing their foot on it when you're not looking or meander from one base to the next thinking you can't see them.

Whatever they do, they are extremely gentle in the doing of it, which makes their pranks all the funnier.

On the flip side, I've seen an elephant pick a handler up and fling him high across the arena. Another time, an elephant pulled a handler under her, and with her trunk, "kneed" him a few times, before he could be get free. He had to wear a body cast for ten months, but got very little sympathy. He was a rough man, and odds are, he'd asked for it. When this happens, elephants are never reprimanded too harshly, because it's known there's always a good reason for their behavior. The blame and the responsibility ultimately falls to the handler. If an incident happens more than once, a handler will be discharged on the spot. Whitey helps them pack.

I step to my left, coming face to face with my favorite Big Gal, Topsy, and hand the apple over. Sometimes I let her search my pockets with her truck for her treat but I don't feel like it today. I look over to see if Whitey is done, but he's still scouring Mabel.

"I understand you've got my hairbrush," I say, reaching up and patting Topsy's forehead.

"Let me finish Mabel's bath, okay?" he says from somewhere behind her. I hear a bucket of water being thrown, and then more scrubbing. "We need to talk and I don't want any distractions."

"Sure."

I move to the side of Topsy's face and reach out to her eye. She has long lashes, over an inch long, soft and pliant. She loves to have them stroked, as all the elephants do, and I'm always happy to oblige. I look at her body, clean and slightly damp. She's been groomed earlier.

"Come over here, Jeri," Whitey says after a time. "I want to show you something."

I leave Topsy and go to the other side of Mabel, where Whitey waits, gazing up. "You can still see the red spot where the hairbrush was," he says. "I'm sure it irritated the hell out of her. I wanted you to see that, so you would know that Mabel's not dangerous. Any one of them would have acted the same way."

Whitey is defending Mabel's position in the circus. She was mistreated several years ago by someone fired and long gone, but it has left her skittish. A skittish elephant is usually an invitation to danger. I am one of the few willing to ride Mabel. If there's another incident she might be farmed out, left to live out her days without companionship or purpose. I'm sure that's why Whitey showed Tony the hairbrush and I'm getting the lecture.

He throws the last bucket of water on Mabel and turns away, heading for a long wooden table filled with harnesses, chains, ropes and other paraphernalia. My silver hairbrush sits at the end, looking odd man out among the gear. Whitey picks it up and offers it to me.

"I told Tony what I think happened and now I'm going to tell you," he says.

"Okay." I take the brush from his hand.

"I can't prove it but I think Rosie's the one who did this."

Knowing my run-in with her in the dressing room, she's at the top of my list. However, why Whitey should think so, is another matter.

He goes on, "Jeri, Rosie and I were seeing each other about the time you joined the Big Top."

"I know."

"Do you?" he says, straightening up gear on the table. "I'm not sure why that should surprise me, given that everyone seems to know everything around here. Then I'm not being ungentlemanly to say she wanted something more and I plain didn't. When I finally broke it off with her, she came at me with one of these eyehooks."

"What?" I look down at one of the long handled, four-inch hooks sitting on the table.

"Then a couple of days later she set fire to my tack box. She's got a bad temper. Sometimes I don't think she's quite right in the head. She does things without thinking them through. She could have burned the whole tent down, animals and all, if I hadn't smelled the smoke. Anyway, the next day I took her aside and told her that if she did one more thing, I would go to Tony and have her fired. I could have done it, you know. A couple of the boys saw her come at me with the hook. It missed slicing my face by inches."

"Did you ever tell management about the run-in or the fire?"

"No. A man doesn't like to think he can't control an old flame, you know?"

"No pun intended," I say. He doesn't laugh.

"Now I wish I had. I didn't date anyone after that and maybe she thought we'd get back together. She'd give me little notes or presents from time to time. I was sure she'd given up when you and I started seeing each other."

He reflects for a moment. I don't say anything and he continues. "I can't prove it, Jeri, but this business with the cinch has her earmarks all over it. She knows how I feel about my bulls." He hesitated. "And you. By putting the brush under Mabel's cinch, she got two for one. That's why I went to Tony. It's something I should have done when Rosie first started this business. Because of me, you could have been killed. I'm sorry. I'm more than sorry; this is my fault."

"Not really. If it makes you feel any better, I've given her plenty of reasons to put the brush under the cinch." We smile at one another. "Did Tony say what he was going to do?"

"What can he do? There's no proof it was Rosie, no matter how strongly I feel about it. I've been asking around. A performer in costume wandering around the Bull Tent isn't going to attract a lot of attention. Once you get inside, too, there are plenty of places to hide, if you want. That's changed. As of this morning, I've got three guards patrolling twenty-four hours a day. No one's allowed in unless I say so. Last

night, none of my men saw her come in here, but that has to have been when it was done. The howdah goes on Mabel right

after intermission and I checked it myself, so the brush had to have been added and the cinch cut after that."

"I'll ask if any of the girls saw her back in our section. Unfortunately, we don't spend a lot of time in the dressing room. She could have taken it at almost any time."

"I know it was her, Jeri, I know it. And she's not through yet. I can feel it."

"Woman's intuition?" I ask with a smile, remembering I'd said a similar thing earlier to Tin. Whitey doesn't smile back.

"I haven't mentioned the dead rat I found in one of my boots. That was right before the fire. It had its throat cut. I think it was bled out into the boot, too, before it was thrown inside."

While I reel from this bit of information, Whitey goes on, "There's more. I found this outside my compartment door. That's why I was trying to talk to you before the elephant ballet. But when I thought about it and saw you riding away on Topsy, I knew you couldn't do anything like this."

He crosses over to a large trash bin near one of the exits and retrieved his muddy jacket. Unfolding the bundle of clothing, he shakes it out. The jacket has been methodically shredded with a knife or scissors from the bottom up to the neckline. Even the sleeves are sliced. It looks like confetti attached to a string rather than a garment.

"Rosie must have taken it from outside the Virgin Car yesterday morning. She saw me leave it there." I look at him, knowing my eyes reflect the horror I'm feeling. "Whitey, this woman's lethal."

"You'd better believe it."

Running late to meet Margie and Doris, I take a short cut through a small, crooked path that runs in between a row of back-to-back tents for three or four hundred feet. It's more like an obstacle course than a path but I'm hoping it will cut the time of getting to the waiting bus for town.

About half way through, I realize the folly of my ways. Wooden stakes stick up into the track on either side at different angles and heights. Attached to the stakes and overhead, loops of thick hemp are strung from the back of one tent to the other and across the path, almost like a midget's clothesline, making it necessary to squat down to get through. Often the tent backs are so close to each other there's no way I can avoid scraping my arms or shoulders against the ropes or tripping over pegs and stakes.

I sit down on my haunches, taking a breather. I hear footsteps coming up behind me from one of the turns.

"Hello?" I yell out with a laugh, trying to see who it is. "Who else is stupid enough to try to use this short cut?"

The movement stops and there is silence.

I stand up and wait, straining my ears for another sound on the far side of the crook.

"Hello?" I say again. "Anybody there?"

I feel my heart quicken, suddenly afraid. I push forward, picking my way over and under the low strung hemp, trying to avoid the stakes sticking up from the ground in some places like wooden blades of grass. The faster I go, the more I bang myself around. I twist my ankle, not enough to do any lasting damage, but enough to remind me to slow down.

There's a slight rustle behind me and I wheel around, still unable to see anyone.

"All right," I say. "Who's there? Show yourself."

Again silence.

Turning back around, I note it's only another twenty or so feet to go before I'm clear of this maze. Stay calm and do this, I tell myself. I bend over to use a battered stake as a purchase, when I hear a 'whoosh' overhead, followed by the sound of sharp steel slicing into something solid. I look up and several feet in front of me a still quivering knife protrudes from a line of taut hemp.

Shocked, I lose my balance and stumble to the ground. Behind me there is the noise of fleeing footsteps, crashing into pegs and ropes. For one brief moment I consider trying to pursue him or her, but that moment of insanity passes. If somebody's willing to throw a knife at you, they're probably willing to do a lot more, should you catch up with them.

I near the knife jutting out from the dense rope, its sharp blade glittering in the morning sun from the other side. The closer I get, the more familiar it looks to me. When I waggle it out of the hemp, I see for sure it's Tin Foot's whittling knife.

Somebody has a sense of humor. Or I'm the worst judge of character since Julius Caesar called out to his good pal, Brutus.

Chapter Seventeen
11:15 a.m., Monday

The bus ride into town is uneventful, but reminders of the war are everywhere. Bulletin boards alongside the road are plastered with posters in red, white and blue, large print screaming Uncle Sam Wants You. The only thing competing with the sheer volume of them is billboards advertising the Big Top. It seems like either or both are attached to any tree, electrical or telephone pole, and sign post that can't run away.

Trips like this are always a reminder of how much circus people are removed. Rationing is not as severe. With radios and time being scarce, we don't hear what's happening on a daily basis. The only ones we talk to are each other. You could say our world is very circumspect.

But the war is out there, always looming. The image of Lillian pacing in the lot, waiting for a letter that has yet to arrive rushes back at me. This damned war.

I find myself thinking about Eddie. It's hard to believe he was killed only a little more than twenty-four hours ago. I shake my head with sadness and wonder, not for the first time, why? The unknown motive hangs around me like no-see-ums on a hot day. Why would anybody want to kill such a sweet kid? Or was he so sweet? I just learned about his gambling habit, his impregnating Catalena and his friendship or possible affair with Rosie. Who or what else is out there?

You would think that given our isolation, there would be a dearth of suspects. Not true. The circus has nineteen-hundred occupants, more than many of the small towns we pass through. Eddie got around a lot more in our little world than I thought he did. And in the getting, he seems to have rubbed a lot of people the wrong way.

He owed most of the other clowns money – some a lot, some a little - meaning it could be any one of them. Or was this a joint effort on their part, payback mob style? Not likely but possible. I need to talk to a few of the clowns.

Then there's Vince, owed two hundred dollars by the kid. Two hundred bucks is a lot of money, two months' salary for me. People have been known to kill for a lot less. Maybe Vince knew Eddie was taking off, going back to Salt Lake City, and sought revenge. Vince has a dicey past or, at least, that's what the rumor mongers say.

Rosie keeps popping up in this. If she did cut the cinch- -and it's not for certain she did, I have to remind myself--she may have done it either because of my involvement with Whitey or my investigation into Eddie's death. Maybe she was seriously involved with Eddie, even if only in her mind, a mind whose lucidity I am questioning more and more by the minute. If she came at one ex-lover with an eyehook, she might come at another with a wire, especially if he was leaving the circus with another woman.

Then there's Tony. He sure is anxious to pin this on Catalena, but why? Is it to protect the circus or himself? I'd hate for it to be him, because of Doris, but he does have access to everything imaginable within the circus. He could have strangled Eddie, opened the lion's cage and dragged the boy up the stairs of the wagon and left him on the platform. He has the strength. Yes, but does he have the motive?

Ah, back to the no-see-ums. Maybe Eddie owed Tony money. I know Tony plays cards with the guys every now or then. I'll have to check on that.

Enter Constantin, a fairly volatile man. I'm trying not to be swayed by what Doris told us about him slapping around his youngest daughter. Yes, it's wrong, but some of his tricks are life and death. If Ioana is jeopardizing her life, maybe he got carried away in his attempt to discipline her.

His love for his two girls is apparent, especially for Catalena. Maybe he knew Eddie impregnated his sixteen-year old daughter and was taking a powder. Fathers have been known to protect their children, up to and including murder. I let out a sigh; this scenario is weak. Wouldn't it have been better to force Eddie to marry the girl rather than strangling the potential groom?

Then there is Catalena, herself. I guess she could have found out he was leaving her and her baby, come up behind him and strangled him with the wire. On one hand, I found the bus ticket. But on the other hand, maybe Eddie had changed his mind and told her he wasn't taking her with him. Could he have been that much of a rat and I never saw it? Maybe I can learn more when I get the chance to read Catalena's diary.

Maybe, maybe, maybe. That's all I have. What I don't know could fill up Yankee Stadium. If only I could get into the personnel files, I might learn a few things. It's not going to be easy, no longer being the official investigator. I'll have to go about it another way, more on the sly.

I finish running through my paltry little list as we come upon Five Points on the outskirts of town, named for the convergence of five small roads. Martini's Drug Store, run by a pharmacist and his family, houses the only public telephone for miles around, the one Wally used to call the sheriff the previous morning. As usual, we're in the middle of nowhere.

A large circus is set up in an isolated spot on the outskirts of a town or city. The Big Top needs a minimum of fifteen acres for the set up of tents, the pasturing of animals and the parking of ticket holders' cars. It's often a vacant field or fairground. Sometimes it's a farm taken over by the county for non-payment of taxes, the depression having gone but its aftermath still with us.

We pass a schoolyard burbling with children's voices. One voice that reaches out to me is from a small girl with a

jump rope chanting the words 'Strawberry shortcake, sweetening pie, V-I-C-T-O-R-Y' in rhythm with her jumps. Sadness sweeps over me.

We are a nation at war. Every day sacrifices are being made, from egg rationing to dying on a foreign field. There is no certainty we will win the war, as secure as we try to feel, as big as we try to talk. There is no certainty of anything, anymore.

Other thoughts, such as the whittling knife, blade wrapped in a scarf and resting in my bag, surge forward. I'll have to deal with it and Tin when we return to the Big Top. I force everything on the back burner of my mind, lean my head against the window, and try to think of nothing.

Fifteen minutes later, we're inside the town limits, turning onto Main Street. Like everything else, Springfield's hospital and library are both off Main Street, within walking distance of each other. The hospital sits at the opposite end from where the bus enters. The movie theatre is in the center of town surrounded by small mom and pop stores, a Woolworth's, and a seedy looking bar on the corner, already open. A peeling sign advertising draft beer for a nickel swings overhead in the late morning's breeze. There's one in every town.

Across the street, a butcher shop has gone out of business. Forlorn and empty, a faded sign hangs in the window reading, 'Meat for our boys overseas, none for us.' Next to it, a small general store contains red and yellow signs outlining food rationing and what day which coupons will be honored. People are lined up for fresh milk. Limit, one quart per family.

The bus drops off the twenty of us, the movie house being its only stop. The driver tells us he will return in four hours, time enough to allow for the movie and a little shopping. I note a number for the cab company in case I don't get finished before the bus returns.

Townspeople stare at us as we disperse. It isn't just that we're strangers. We act and dress differently. I'd like to think more exotic and colorful, but maybe we look just plain peculiar.

I wave goodbye to Margie and Doris, promising to meet them in front of the theatre after the movie gets out. With a lengthy intermission for a drive on war bonds, it'll probably go until two-thirty.

During the short four blocks to the hospital, I pass a funeral home. The words 'Fitzsimmons Mortuary' is discreetly written in small gold letters over the heavy, dark oak door. A black hearse is parked in front. I wonder if it's waiting for Catalena or Eddie, ready to take them to a graveyard I saw outside the city limits. No, not so soon, I realize.

There's the care of the dead, legal processes, papers to sign. Rituals come much later after the business of death is taken care of. My mind rakes back to that day in the bank and the little boy. I had gone to his funeral, five days after he died, and watched them slip his small coffin into the ground. I may not have shot him, but I caused the shot to be fired. Any right to happiness I may have had in my life was buried that day with the child.

I come to the hospital, a small two-story job, and I hope I've hit visiting hours. I would have said I was Coke's sister to make sure I get in to see him but I don't know his real name. After describing him to the nurses, they point me to the second floor, men's ward. Leroy Patterson is his name. Coke and Aspirin fits him better.

Coke's bandaged head is lying with the rest of him at the end of a row of beds. A man coughs as I pass by and I hold my breath. TB is rampant these days and everyone is aware of it. Maybe someday there will be a cure but right now, there isn't. We all have to be careful.

At first I think Coke is sleeping but the closer I get, I see his eyes are open, staring at nothing. When he notices me, he waves then sits up slowly, grinning from ear to ear. What teeth Coke has left are ragged and blackened. I don't know if it's the constant intake of sugar from the cokes or if he just has lousy teeth. In any event, I can smell his breath almost from the foot of the bed.

"How you doing, Coke?"

His smile becomes shaky. He's shaky all over, maybe from the lack of caffeine in his body. I've read in a medical book that caffeine is as addictive as booze or gambling.

"I'm okay, okay, Miss Jeri. Fancy you coming here to see me." A trembling hand goes to his head and then settles in his lap. "I got this headache, though."

I reach into my bag and bring out a bottle of Coca-cola, still cold from the icebox. His eyes light up and he reaches out for the bottle, practically snatching it from my hand.

He scrutinizes the bottle and turns to me in disappointment. "This ain't one of my bottles. I can tell by the neck. It ain't one of my bottles," he repeats.

"I know, Coke. I got this at the Cookhouse before I left. It's just an ordinary Coca-cola. You want it or not?" He sighs but nods. I hand him a bottle opener and he tries to pry the cap off with shaking, useless hands.

"Here," I say. "Let me do it." I take both from him and flip the lid off, handing him back the bottle. He downs it in fast, long gulps. I take another bottle out and hold it up.

"Want another one?" He nods again, this time more content. I pry the lid off this one and hand it over. I watch him gulp it down like the first one, then look at me as if I would keep pulling out bottles like a magician.

"That's it, Coke. I only brought two."

He's let down, but more relaxed. The shaking has subsided somewhat, too.

I sit in a chair by his bed and get right to it. "Coke, I'd like to ask you a few questions, all right?"

"Sure but I don't know nothing," he says. "Nobody ever asks me anything 'cause I don't know much. I just do what I'm told."

"What do you remember about night before last?"

"Oh, that." He shrugs. "I got hit on the head."

"Do you remember what time that was?"

"Lessee," he answers. "Sometime after five in the morning. Maybe six but I don't think so. It were still pretty dark and I don't have no watch or nothing."

"Good." I'm encouraged. "That's very good. Before you got hit, did you hear anything? See anything? Anything happen that was strange? Did the animals seem nervous, like a stranger might be hanging around?"

With each question, he looks more bewildered and shakes his head slightly.

"Try to think, Coke." I'm pressuring him but I don't care. "Put yourself back there. Was there anything unusual or different?"

He obliges me and thinks for a moment.

"There was them boots I saw."

"What boots?" I nearly jump out of the chair.

"I was leaning down under the tiger cubs' wagon getting me a Coke, one of mine. Don't' tell anybody, Miss Jeri, but that's where I keep one of my stashes. Anyway, I was looking down at the ground when I seen two boots come stand in front of me. Appeared out of nowhere, too. I was starting to look up, you know, to see who it was and whammo! Ow," he says. "My head." He became animated toward the end and sinks down into the bed, closing his eyes.

"Can you describe the boots? What did they look like?"

"Naw. It was under a light pole but I just seen them fast

like. They was thick and newish. Maybe black or dark brown. I don't know." His eyes are still closed. He opens them suddenly. "They didn't have much mud on them, though. Not like the rest of us who work outside in our boots, rain or shine."

I reflect on the boots I saw kicking at the dead clown. And the ones propped up on Vince's desk attached to Tony.

Even the ones owned by Tin. None had much mud on them, other than around the soles. A lack of mud probably does rule out the workmen and roustabouts. I should have thought of that myself. Coke is sharper than I'm giving him credit for. But then I have to remember this is a man who can find bootleg Coke anywhere in the forty-eight states, when he needs to.

"Thanks, Coke. That's a big help."

"You should see mine," he says, warming to the subject. "Them boots look like I roll around in mud for the fun of it. I don't even bother to scrape it off no more." He grins at me again and yawns; giving me a full view of the most rotten teeth I've ever seen.

"I should go, Coke, and let you get your rest."

"Do you know when they're going to let me out of here, Miss Jeri?"

"Tell you what, I'll ask the nurse and if I find out anything, I'll let come back and tell you. Meanwhile, take care of yourself."

"You sure you don't have another Coke on you? Even them straight ones is better than nothing." I give my head a quick shake. "God, I got all the aspirin in here a body could want and no Coke to go with them."

I smile and turn away, passing a nurse on her way to Coke's bedside. I overhear her tell him he'll be there another day or two. Coke asks for a Coca-cola but the nurse laughs and says no. Poor Coke. Maybe I'll try to sneak in some more tomorrow.

Chapter Eighteen
12:10 p.m., Monday

I head straight for the library, one of my old haunts. I've been in just about every public library across the nation since I joined the circus. There isn't a book I don't pick up and read, always looking to learn, and these places hold all I could want.

I recall this library from last year and its most contemporary and racy writer is Mark Twain. They have a decent collection of classical writers going back to the Greeks, philosophers such as Aristotle and Des Carte, and a healthy catalogue of important plays pre-Moliere, all donated from an estate that went bust in the late twenties. If I remember right, they also have several dictionaries in different languages. Maybe it's too much to hope they'll have a Romanian one, but I'll see what I can dig up.

The librarian remembers me from last year and points me in the direction of the dictionaries. The only ones they have that might prove useful are Italian and Latin. Armed with those two and the magnifying glass I brought with me, I open Catalena's diary to the last few pages of the book.

It's tedious work trying to decipher her writing, so small and tight, guessing at the spelling of words, and then looking them up in two dictionaries that aren't even in the same language. I'm making little headway. Her last entry on the day before she died is disturbing, although I can't put my finger on exactly what's going on.

It seems to be filled with sadness, fear and something else. Maybe it's a guilty conscious about running away and leaving her family. There is the mention of Ioana and Eddie, plus one word at the bottom written in large, block letters. Nothing in either dictionary helps me out with its meaning. At twenty minutes after two, it's time to fold up my tent and go to the front desk. I'm disappointed and the librarian sees it on my face.

"Not finding what you want?" She smiles at me. Her middle-aged, scrubbed face looks kind and concerned.

"No, I'm afraid not. I actually need a Romanian dictionary. These others aren't much use."

A startled look crosses her face. "You're looking for a Romanian dictionary?"

"Yes. I have to--"

"If it's about a Romanian word," she interrupts, "Mr. Patrescu is here today. He's from Romania. He's over there," she whispers, "sitting in Reference."

She comes out from behind the desk and walks me over to a sectioned-off part of the library, complete with wingback chairs and a rickety coffee table holding neat stacks of magazines. A well rounded, elderly man rests in one chair, legs crossed at the ankles, hands folded in his lap, white thatched head lolled back, almost asleep.

"His granddaughter has a job at the bakery down the street and he comes in with her two or three times a week," she whispers. "That's when her mother works at the munitions factory in Piedmont." She stares at him tenderly. "I don't think they want to leave him home alone. He's such a sweet man and he reads everything he can get his hands on."

She goes over and touches him on the arm. "Mr. Patrescu. I hope I'm not bothering you."

His head snaps into an upright position and he looks around for a moment taking stock of where he is. "Ah! Lucille," he says, taking her hand and kissing the back of it. "You're not bothering me. I was just resting." His accent is not as heavy as Constantin's and easier to understand.

Lucille points to me. I smile. "Mr. Patrescu, this is Miss…" She turns to me questioningly.

"Deane," I say, "but please call me Jeri."

"Jeri? That is a boy's name, yes?" he asks, blue eyes twinkling.

"Not always. It can be male or female," I say, smiling.

"That is good. We would not want you to have the wrong name." He grins.

I laugh.

Lucille says, "She needs to know a Romanian word and we don't have a dictionary. Do you think you could…" She leaves off speaking and smiles at him.

"Of course, of course," he says, rising awkwardly. "I will be happy to assist such a lovely young lady." He looks at the librarian. "Two such lovely ladies." He bows slightly.

I say, "This is very kind of you, Mr. Patrescu."

"Nonsense. What are we if we cannot help each other? Now what is this word you need me to look at?"

"I should really get back to my desk," Lucille says in a hushed voice. "I'll leave you to this."

"Yes, thank you, Lucille," I say.

I sit down in the wingback chair next to the one he occupies. He half sits, half falls back down into his. I can tell that he's not in the best shape.

"It's in this book." I open the diary to the last entry and offer it to him.

He takes it and looks at both the front and back covers. "I know this kind of book," he says. "It is called a dowry. No, that's not it…" he breaks off thinking.

"It's a diary, sir."

"Diary." He rolls the word around in his mouth. "It is yours?" he asks with a smile.

"No, it's not."

"Of course not. Otherwise, you would not need me to tell you what one of the words mean," he says impishly.

"That's right. It belongs to…" I hesitate. "Belonged to someone no longer with us."

"Oh, I am sorry." His smile fades and he studies the pages. "The writing is not easy and today I forget my glasses."

"No, the writing is not easy," I agree. "Would you like to use this magnifying glass?"

He takes the offered implement and scrutinizes the page. "Which is the word?"

I get up and go around to his side. "The one in big letters."

"Yes, that one is clear but it is difficult to know. Let me think." He closes his eyes for a time. I wonder if he's gone back to sleep. I sit down again and watch him. His eyes flash open and he looks at me. "It is a word that is used only by small group of Romanians, gypsies, in the mountains. Not everywhere is this word but now I remember."

"A dialect, you mean?" I ask.

"Yes. It means to notify… to tell…no stronger than that…to warn. Yes, that is it. To warn." He studies the book again. I can tell he's trying to read the last page in its entirety. I let him. "Such a sad writer. My eyes are not what they used to be and I do not have my glasses but she…" He breaks off. "This is a young girl, no?"

"It was, yes."

"She is troubled. Oh, so troubled. I hope my Magdalena is never so troubled. She is my granddaughter who bakes the bread," he explains.

"I hope not, too, sir."

He hands the book back to me and says, "You wish to help free this girl from some of those troubles, even though she is gone?"

I nod. Not only does he understand what I want to do, but he's put it into the words I hadn't quite found yet.

"Exactly. I want to help free her, even thought she is gone. That's why I am trying to read her diary, yes." I reach in my bag and unfold the note containing the underlined words I scribbled down from Constantine's Bible.

"One more thing, if you don't mind, sir. Some of this I can translate but not all of it. Could you tell me word for word what this says?"

Puzzled, he accepts the paper, studies it and reads aloud in a halting voice, *"'There is a conspiracy of her prophets in the midst thereof, like a roaring lion ravening the prey; they have devoured souls; they have taken the treasure and precious things; they have made her many widows in the midst thereof.'"* He looks at me. "This is a quote from the Bible."

"Yes. Thank you, Mr. Patrescu, for your help." I take the note from his hand and stand. "I should go now. I'm meeting friends."

"I will be here tomorrow, if you need me. I will bring my glasses, so I can read better."

"I don't think it will be necessary but I'll remember that. You've been a big help, sir." Instead of leaving, I stare at the diary in my hand.

"Now you are the one who looks troubled," he observes. "You know something you do not share."

"Possibly." I look at him, smile and offer my hand. "Thank you, Mr. Patrescu."

He rises awkwardly, the leather of the chair creaking and straining under his movements, and grasps my hand. Mr. Patrescu shakes it with a firmer grip than I expect. My eyes find his and I can tell that he is a man who has seen much of life. He, in turn, stares into my eyes, holding onto my hand.

"You are an old soul, Jeri-with-a-boy-or-girl's-name. You are young but you have been by yourself most of your life. It has made you strong, but it has made you lonely. Do not become too comfortable in this loneliness." He smiles at what must be a surprised look on my face.

"My mother, she was a fortune teller in the old country. She had what they call The Sight. Sometimes I think I have it, too. But maybe not." He releases my hand with a shrug and a smile.

"You've been very kind, sir. I hope we meet again."

"I am always here," the old man says and sits back down heavily in his chair. He picks up a magazine and begins to thumb through it.

I turn away, going out the door, down the steps, and toward my waiting friends, wondering just how comfortable I've become in my loneliness. It's a scary thought. I push it out of my mind.

We stop off at a local five and dime store and Margie and Doris stock up on make-up. I buy Tootsie Rolls, two for a penny. We wait for the bus to shuttle us home. I'm silent most of the time, thinking random thoughts, but both girls are so taken with the movie and telling me all about it, they don't notice. Apparently, Greer Garson can cry better than any actress on stage or screen.

On the drive back, I gnaw on a Tootsie Roll, my one big vice, and speculate on how I can get out of returning the master keys to Tony. I probably can't, so I'll have to figure out another way of getting into the compartment Rosie shares with three other girls.

Chapter Nineteen
3:00 p.m., Monday

We arrive back at the lot and Vince is waiting for the bus. He steps up as I got off and signals to me.

"I been waiting for you, Jeri." He's angry and doesn't bother to hide it. "Tony wants to talk to you. His trailer."

"I don't have the keys on me, Vince," I say, thinking that's what Tony wanted. "I left them in my locker. I'll have to go get them first."

"Never mind the keys, Jeri. Tony wants to see you right away. Something's come up."

I wave to Doris and Margie, who are watching this exchange. "I'll bet you this is about the graffitied poster, girls. I'll be at the car in a minute. I--"

"She's got to see a man about a dog, girls," Vince interrupts, grabbing on to my arm. "Let's go." He pulls me along with him.

"What's with the strong arm, Vince? I can walk on my own," I say, breaking free.

He grabs me again, talking the whole time. "I'm told to haul you over to see Tony and that's what I aim to do. Thanks to you, I'm leaving in a few minutes to join Advance. Locked out of my own trailer. Thrown out of my own circus. All because of you. You did this." He holds on so tightly to my upper arm, it hurts.

I twist and look into his face. "Let go of my arm, Vince. Right now. Let go or I'll make you." I know jujitsu and have no qualms about using it when necessary.

He senses I mean what I say, releases me, and looks away. His voice takes on a whining tinge. "I didn't do anything. I didn't kill Eddie. I didn't kill anybody."

"Then you've got nothing to worry about," I say, the anger over my bruised arm showing in my voice. "And this way, should anything else happen everyone will know it isn't you, because you're in the next town." I can see him thinking, his expression changing from anger to confusion to resignation.

"Maybe so." He looks at me. "I didn't kill anybody," he repeats.

"You said that."

"I've done a lot of things in my life I'm not proud of, but murder isn't one of them."

"If that's true, we're going to find out who did and then you'll be back."

"From your mouth to God's ears, sister." He gives me a fleeting smile and becomes grim again. "Yeah, but being with Advance. Putting up posters and handing out flyers and all that. It's humiliating."

"Try to look on it as an important job. Otherwise, how would anybody know about us and come to see the show?" He seems unconvinced. "Never mind, Vince. Tell me about the key to Old Kirby's cage. Do you have it on you?"

"Why would I carry the key to that old lion's cage on me?"

"Then where is it?"

He stares at me. "What do you mean, where it is? It's hanging on a nail on the wall in back of my desk."

I don't say anything and start walking toward his office trailer. He falls in step with me, like an old dog learning to heel. "Isn't it?"

"It wasn't there yesterday," I say. "I noticed the keys when I was having dinner with Tony. The one marked Old Kirby was missing. You're responsible for them. Who else could have it?"

"I don't know. I haven't been inside that trailer since Tony threw me out yesterday," he sputters. "I slept in Coke's bunk. I spend most times in the supply tent. Tony's only going to let me go back in the trailer to pack. Then he's going to watch me like a hawk. That key was there the last time I checked."

"When was that?"

"I check them every night before I go to bed, around ten, ten-thirty. All the keys were there, I swear. Turned out of my own office." Now he grumbles.

"And yet when I was there the afternoon of the murder, the key was missing." I stop walking and turn to Vince. "Who has access to your trailer?"

"Nobody but Tony comes in when I'm not there. Otherwise, it's locked. A lot of people come in and out when they have business, but I'm always there. I would have seen it if somebody lifted that key." He pauses. "Wait a minute."

"What?"

"You know that sick orangutan named Ollie, the one the vet's been isolating in the cage next door to me?"

"Go on."

"Well, it must have been eleven or eleven-thirty the night before last and I hear this squawking come from Ollie. I just flew out in my pajamas to see what was going on and I saw that somebody had put a balloon in his cage. The vet was close on my tail, too, wondering what all the noise was about. Anyway, we grabbed the balloon by the string and pulled it out. Ollie quieted down after a minute or two. When I went back to the trailer, the door was wide open. I couldn't believe I'd left it open like that, I never did it before, but after I looked around and saw nothing was bothered, I figured I must have." He muses for a moment. So do I.

"Funny about that balloon," he says. "I thought it was one of the townies that did it but they're usually cleared out by that time." He looks at me, waiting for a response. I give none.

We continue past Vince's trailer to Tony's Silver Airstream, a shining and beautiful piece of aluminum and steel, twice the size of Vince's beat up and dented one. Vince

grabs the door handle and yanks it open, standing to one side of the steps. His face is dark with anger and insult at not being allowed to go inside.

I go up the steps and into the expensively decorated but functional office. Tony sits behind his mahogany carved desk, tapping on the surface with rapid fingers, either so deep in thought he doesn't see me or purposefully ignoring me. Either way, I don't like it.

I've been in his office many times before, both professionally and socially. The opulence doesn't impress me but I still give the room a once over as if I've never been in it before. Nothing looks out of place or different save for a three-by five- foot partially unwrapped painting, peeking out of its brown paper from a corner of the room.

My eyes land back on Tony. This time there are no filet mignons or radio, only the strong smell of stale cigarette smoke and an even stronger smell of anxiety.

"What do you want, Tony?" I remain in the doorway, ready to leave. I cross my arms over my chest in annoyance. "I think you've said everything you needed to say to me earlier."

He looks up but doesn't answer my question as he reaches for a dead cigarette from the overflowing ashtray.

"What is it, Tony?" I ask. My voice has an unconcealed edge of exasperation to it. "I don't have the keys on me. I'll have to give them to you--"

"The sheriff was here again," he interrupts, further stubbing out the already bent and crushed cigarette butt.

"So?"

"Jeri, we've got a problem, a huge problem." He tugs at that infernal mustache. "Please come in, sit down, and hear me out."

I don't move.

His face tries a half-way smile. "I want to apologize for being so rude to you earlier today. Look, I was trying to make things go back to normal for everyone on the lot."

"You must be kidding," I say. "With one murder and one suicide? You're either living in a fool's paradise or you're an idiot. Maybe both."

He doesn't respond at first, but swivels back and forth in his chair. Then he says,

"You've got every right to be mad at me, even Doris --" He stops moving and looks down. "But let's put that aside for a moment, can we? This is serious."

I lose some of my anger to curiosity and sit down across from him. When I study his face, it doesn't look so good. Strain and lack of sleep are not conducive to looking good.

"What is it?"

"Eddie's mother placed a long distance call to the sheriff today to read him a letter she received this morning from her son."

"That must have been hard for her, receiving a letter from him right after his death."

"I guess." Tony fidgets and goes on. "According to the letter dated three days ago, Eddie was bringing home a girl, a girl named Catalena, and he wanted his family to accept her as one of their own. He was going to marry her; they were going to have a baby and start a new life back in the folds of his family." I watch Tony's eyes well up. He brushes at them. "It was all rather sad, really. Even the sheriff was touched."

"I told you I found that ticket to Salt Lake City in her diary. They were going away together." My voice is quiet. "She had no reason to kill him."

"I know, I know." He holds up his hands as if to ward off a physical blow. "One of the bad things about me, Jeri, is I tend to take the easy way out. I've done it all my life. Just ask my father." He tries to smile winningly at me. It doesn't work.

"You can't do that this time."

"Doesn't seem like it." He sighs, pulls out a pack of Camels from his breast pocket, and lights a cigarette. I glance down at an overflowing ashtray.

"I thought you gave up smoking."

"I did. Doris doesn't like the smell," he says, after he exhaled. He picks a piece of tobacco off his tongue. "The letter convinced Sheriff Draeger and the town council that even though Catalena took her own life, she probably didn't kill Eddie. Somebody else did."

"So back to square one."

"The clock is still ticking. We've got little more than thirty-six hours before they keep their promise to close us down. If you'll go back on the job for double the money --"

I interrupt, standing up. "It's not about the money. I told you that the first time."

"All right. Never mind the money. What do you want?" he persists. "I'm desperate. The Brothers are angry I took you off the job. They feel I've been wasting precious time."

"Well, if it's any consolation to you, I was never really off the job, Tony. I've been clearing up a few things in town. But as for what I want, I want you to stay with it even when things get rough."

"I promise," he says. "And thank you. I can't tell you how much I --"

"Never mind the sweet talk, Tony."

"I promise to do whatever you say, Jeri. The entire Big Top is at your disposal."

"Let's make it more than rhetoric this time." I glance over at the package leaning against the wall in the corner and got up.

"What is this?" I ask, reaching out and touching a corner of the painting.

"Oh, that? That's a portrait I commissioned of Emmett Kelly with the Brothers, a commemoration of his first year with the circus. I thought I'd hang it somewhere in here when I get a chance."

"Have you noticed the wire that was used to bind the packaging?" I turn back to him and watch his reaction.

"The wire? No, I've barely looked at it since it arrived, with all that's been going on. What's wrong with the wire?"

"It's flat and wide," I say, but his face reveals nothing.

He gets up and walks toward me, wearing the same boots I saw on him yesterday. "Oh, that. They must use that so that it doesn't bite through the paper into the wood in handling. That's a pure mahogany frame. I wouldn't want it to get scratched. I paid over a hundred dollars for it."

I turn away from Tony, take hold of the top of the heavy painting, lean it forward and examine the rear. "Some of the wire's been cut away in the back."

"Oh, yes. I was fiddling around with it yesterday morning about the time I heard the ruckus over the murder. I stopped what I was doing and haven't been back to it since."

"When did it arrive?"

"Day before yesterday. Now listen, Jeri. What is all this? Who gives a damn about a portrait painting?"

I stare at him but don't answer. Is it possible he doesn't know what type of wire was used to strangle Eddie? Or is he a much better actor than I give him credit for?

"Never mind, Tony, I'll go get Tin. Do you have keys for that file cabinet or is that the set you gave me? Those are in my berth."

"I gave you Vince's set," he says. "Speaking of Vince, I should tell you that in going through his file, which I keep here, I was reminded that he was in Juvenile Hall for about sixteen months when he was a teenager. That's probably why he's so good to those kids that travel with us. I don't think it has anything to do with anything but I'm telling you."

"He was a Juvie? What for?"

"The file is sealed but I asked Vince about it before we hired him. He said he was in a street gang for a year or two, right after his parents parked him with an uncle. He did some petty crimes, nothing serious. Got hauled in for stealing some records from a record store. Right after that, he broke free from the gang and joined the circus in Detroit."

"And you hired him knowing this?"

Tony shrugs. "Sure. He started out as a roustabout. He'd been here about five years when the general manager had a heart attack and had to retire. Vince was a pretty sharp guy and interested in doing the job. That was ten years ago. Other than not being very good in a crisis, he does an okay job. Pays a lot of attention to detail. Maybe too much. Wait until you see how he keeps his files." He lets out a small laugh.

"So where are your keys?" I ask.

"Right here." He taps his pocket. "I've got my own."

"Good, I'll take those." I put out my hand. "You go about the business of running the circus. Tin and I will look through the files. We've got about two hours before half-hour call. That should do it."

After a moment's hesitation, he reaches into his pocket and hands them over. If he knows I don't want him around when I go through the files, he doesn't say anything.

"I understand you won't let Vince into his own trailer without you being there. You better go watch him pack up and leave all this to me," I say and leave, slamming the door behind me. A tinny sound mixes with an echo and follows me down the stairs. With the latest development, I'd neglected to mention the defamation of Doris on the circus poster. He'll find out soon enough. Not much gets by Boss Man.

Vince is waiting outside, once again like the old, family dog not allowed inside the house. I almost feel sorry for him.

"Jeri, I know how this looks, Eddie owing me all that money, but I want you to know I didn't kill him."

"Uh-huh," I say, noncommittally.

"If you only got thirty-six hours then you're wasting time looking at me," he says, assuming an inflated pose before deflating again when I narrow my eyes at him.

"Sounds like you were listening at the door."

He gulps. "Well, it's kind of hard not to hear things through that piece of tin. I sometimes wonder if people don't hear me in the john."

"Boss Man's waiting for you. You have a bus to catch."

He nods and slinks away.

Chapter Twenty
3:30 p.m., Monday

Tin Foot is in his usual place checking over the rigging. I sit down beside him. I tell him we're officially back on the job and to come help me search through the files in Vince's office. He takes it like he takes everything else, with a shrug and a smile.

"How's your whittling coming, Tin? I don't see it anywhere around you."

He has a quizzical look on his face. "I can't seem to find my knife at the moment. I got to stop leaving it lying around like that." Tin looks behind him on the ground. "I thought I left it right here."

I reach into my bag and pull the scarf covered knife out. I unwrap it and hold it out to him, handle first. "Voilá," I say.

His eyes open in astonishment. "Where'd you get it? I could have sworn I left it right here this morning."

"How are you at throwing this thing?"

"Throwing this? A whittling knife? You can't throw one of these things." Tin takes it from my hand. "They don't have any balance. The handle's too heavy."

"Try," I suggest. "Aim for something on that poster over there." I point to one of the undamaged posters featuring Doris hanging from a light pole about ten feet away.

Tin shrugs and rises. "Okay but don't judge me by this. These knives aren't meant for throwing," he emphasizes again.

"I never judge you, Tin."

He throws the knife and hits the caricature drawing of the ring master in the middle of the gut.

"That's pretty good," I comment.

"I was aiming for the ball on top of the seal's nose at the bottom." He laughs. "That's how good these things are for throwing."

He walks over, pulls the knife out of the poster, and turns back to me. "So what now? Want me to do it again?" he asks in an amiable tone.

"Nope. I just wanted to see how accurate they were."

"God awful," he interjects.

I smile at Tin and stand up. "Enough of that. Let's get back to work. We'll start with Vince, Rosie, Constantin, Eddie, and the list of men Eddie owed money. There's about twelve of them. By the time we're done, I hope to know something about them, in particular, their religious leanings and background. From what Tony tells me, Vince is obsessed about his files on all of us."

"I'd better look through mine and see what he says about me, then." Tin laughs. "You never know."

"It's probably something about your love for cows." We both laugh, then sober.

"While we're at it, we'll pull Whitey," I say. "Things may not be what they seem. I sure wish I could see Tony's file but I doubt Vince would have it. If there is one, it's probably with the Brothers."

The day is turning out to be oppressively hot, over ninety degrees and muggy as hell. With the animals being the number one concern, roustabouts, handlers and staff are scurrying about, carrying buckets of water every which way.

We sit in Vince's sweltering trailer, cooled slightly by a rinky-dink fan that rattles every time it rotates, surrounded by well-read, thick files, holding clippings and an assortment of papers. We decide to divide the stack up, make notes about each person and only talk when we're finished.

"Find anything?" I ask, after about an hour and a half of this.

"You know Bard, the clown I mentioned Eddie owed?" asks Tin Foot, looking up at me.

"Short guy," I answer. "Twenty-five bucks."

"Turns out he had a liking for Eddie," he says and turns away in embarrassment.

"You mean as in a homosexual liking?"

He nods.

"Does it really say that in there?" It's unusual to have something like this put down in writing in the Circus, especially in any type of formal documentation. The rule of thumb is, keep it to yourself; it's nobody's business.

"There's a written complaint from Eddie, plus some notes from Vince in Henry's file, dated four months ago," says Tin Foot. He picks up the Bard's file and begins to read aloud.

"Spear carrier in the Royal Shakespeare Repertory Company before coming to the States back in twenty-seven, blah, blah, blah. Ah! Here it is, 'I've had to speak to Henry on his unnatural attention toward Eddie Connors. I told Henry to keep a professional distance.' But apparently, Henry didn't take it well, according to this follow-up note, dated two weeks later. Vince writes about a screaming match in the dressing room between Henry and Eddie. Didn't come to blows, but it says here that Vince and some other guys had to intervene. Whatever it was about, the clowns seemed to blame Eddie for it, but nobody would talk about it to Vince." Tin thinks for a moment. "I'll bet the guys didn't like Eddie squealing on one of their own, even if he is queer. The Bard's one of our old timers."

"I'm sure that's why Vince tried to make it blow over." I reflect. "I guess Eddie was green in a lot of ways."

"Anything on Rosie?" Tin Foot asks.

"She seems to like the odd assortment of pets."

"What does that mean?"

"Vince had to tell her to get rid of a tarantula a couple of years ago her roommates complained about."

Tin's mouth drops open. "Jeri Deane, are you making this up?"

I chuckle at his response. "I wish I was. There's more, too, but I'll save it for later. Tell me what else you got."

"I found out something interesting on Whitey," Tin Foot offers, with hesitation.

"Oh?" My eyebrows shoot up.

"Did you know he graduated college? Went to some fancy university."

"No, I didn't know that."

It was unusual for someone in the circus to have a higher education, unless you were in a position like Tony's. Most employees are high school dropouts, if they even get that far. Almost no one I know has been to college. Certainly no one in my family ever has. I'm intrigued.

"What college?"

"Northwestern University. Has a Bachelors in Business Administration."

"I'll be right back." I get up, wipe the perspiration from my forehead, and go out to the larger trailer next door. Knocking, I barge right in. Tony is writing in his ledger but puts it aside when he sees me.

"Didn't you graduate from Northwestern, Tony, same as Whitey?"

"Yes, Whitey and I were there at the same time." He closes his ledger book and folds his hands on top of it, but says no more.

"So, you know him from before? And a long time."

"Yes, I know him." There is silence.

I sit down across from him. "When were you going to tell me?"

"Tell you what? My knowing Whitey outside the circus doesn't have anything to do with this."

"But why so quiet about it, Tony?" I ask. "This is something you should have mentioned to me."

He pushes back in his chair and sighs. "Okay, I've known Whitey since high school. We ran around with some of the same kids back in Grand Rapids. Even though he doesn't come from a moneyed family like mine, he managed to get a track scholarship and scrape enough money together to go to Northwestern, where we both were accepted. That's about it."

"Are you friends?"

"Friends enough." He reopens the ledger, feigning immersion in it.

I don't let go. "I never see you together. So what are you not telling me?"

His voice takes on a casual air, a little too casual for my liking. "Nothing, Jeri. He's a nice guy. He's busy with his elephants. I'm busy running a circus. We've had beers together from time to time. He's a nice guy," he repeats. "I hear he's got a thing for you. You could do a lot worse."

"Don't change the subject. What's he doing here? I'm assuming he's 4-F or he'd be in the army. But being that he isn't, a man with a business degree from a prestigious university could get a job just about anywhere. Right?"

Tony puts down the ledger and looks at me with annoyance.

"As to why he's here, you'll have to ask him that. As to why he's not serving, he's got flat feet."

"You need two good ones, I know that," I say, thinking of Tin Foot. I study Tony's face for a second. "So what's your story, Tony? Why aren't you in the army?"

"Heart murmur." He smiles at me. "Sometimes it's the small things that get you."

"And that's why I'm always looking at the small things." I stare at him and he returns the gaze, unblinking.

Chapter Twenty-one
6:45 p.m., Monday

Odds are Henry, aka the Bard, is probably inside the large Clown Tent right about now. With all the makeup, costumes, shoes and hats the clowns have to deal with, prep time usually takes them longer than other performers. After a matinee a lot of the men don't remove their makeup, not only to save time for the evening performance but also to stretch their greasepaint dollar. It's good on the pocketbook but hard on the face. A lot of these clowns have skin that looks like the surface of the moon after years of this practice.

When I approach the entrance, I hear angry words inside between two or three men, one of them sounding like it could be Henry, British accent and all. Instead of doing my usual announcement of "knock, knock," I pause and wait. You never know what useful tidbit you might overhear.

Just then the flap is pushed open and a thin, tall clown comes out and bumps into me. His wig and makeup aren't on yet, but his green and black checkered pants hang by red suspenders over a bright yellow shirt. After a look of surprise, he recognizes me and I, him. Jimmy, the String, is his name and he's a nice guy whose only vice seems to be playing the ponies and eating cotton candy.

"Well, hello there, Jeri." He has a nice smile, the String, and I like him. String is one of the few clowns I know who socializes with other performers outside his group. "I'm off to collect money for Eddie's funeral. Something to help out the family. Interested?"

"Sure, String." I reach into my slacks pocket and pull out two singles. "Here you go."

"Cripes," he says, taking the cash from my outstretched hand. "I wish everybody'd give that much. The most I can get from these guys is fifty cents apiece." He turns and shouts back to the tent. "And some cheap bastard's won't give one thin dime."

"Oh, shut up, you skinny, Nancy boy," comes a bass profundo reply. I smile up at the lanky clown who winks down at me in amusement.

"I came to see the Bard, String. Was that him?"

"The very tightwad." He opens the flap and sticks his head inside. "Henry, you've got company. Zip up your flies, gentlemen, lady coming through." String winks again and takes off.

I go inside, closing the flap behind me. There are about fifteen men in various stages of dress. Outlandish hats, shoes and costumes, in garish patterns of stripes, flowers, plaid and so forth, are strewn about over chairs, tables and the tops of wardrobe racks. If the Wardrobe supervisor sees this display, she'll have a fit. She likes things hung nice and neat.

I spot the small clown named Henry in a corner, meticulously applying makeup at his vanity mirror. Beside him sits a large tin of lard-based makeup remover. I can't get any for love nor money, and haven't even seen any in over a year. I make a mental note to ask him where he got it, if we wind up being on the friendly side.

"Hi, Henry." He looks me up and down, with black eyebrows painted on in a half circle over his eyes. "Mind if I talk to you for a minute?"

"You are the famous Jerull Deane, are you not? The wench whose Balendron bag of tricks is bandied about by the press?" For a little man, his voice is low, almost unnaturally so, and his British accent resonates off the canvas walls.

"I think Zolina has been getting most of the press, but I've gotten a line here or there. Nice of you to notice."

He lets out a snort. "What choice do I have? Your picture is everywhere and in every town. The face that launched a thousand snaps." Another man's reference to Helen of Troy, but not quite so nice.

"There's a clever play on words," I say, smiling. "Shakespeare, isn't it?"

"Christopher Marlowe," he replies in an acid tone. "Now what do you want? I am otherwise engaged. So if it's idle chit-chat, be gone. There's a good lass," he says, turning back to his mirror and dabbing paint from various jars on his chin and forehead. Bright yellow, red and black colors begin to appear from practiced hands in a pattern, de-emphasizing a round and chinless face, short on appeal but long on peevishness.

"Gee, most people who meet me for the first time aren't quite so hostile. They have to know me for a while."

He doesn't laugh. "I repeat, what do you want?"

I look around the room. Five men have gathered around a card table at the other end of the tent, playing Seven Card Stud. Others are concentrating on their makeup or have left. One nearby clown, in full makeup and costume, looks engrossed in a magazine. I walk over and sit down on a trunk by Henry's side, leaning in to him. Surprised by my forwardness, Henry turns and faces me, spreading more goop on his cheeks in a circular fashion.

"I thought we could talk a little about Eddie Connors," I say, keeping my voice low.

His hand freezes mid-circle. He looks away and back into the mirror. "'As flies to wanton boys are we to the gods, they kill us for their sport.' *That* was Shakespeare. King Lear. I have nothing to say about that deceitful boy, Edward Connors. Go away."

I stay right where I am. "I'll bet you've got plenty to say. I understand you were one of his first friends in the circus, Henry. I'll bet his death hit you hard."

Henry slams his hand down on his vanity table and members of the card game pause from across the tent and glance our way. Henry and I glare at one another without

moving. Shrugging, the players go back to their game. The clown reading the magazine turns a page, but I can sense him straining to hear our words.

"Surely you jest." Henry almost snarls, leaning into me and searching my face. I continue to stare at him. "No, I can see you jesteth not. Get thee to a nunnery, Jerull Deane, and good riddance to you." He picks up a brush and begins to do the finer work on his makeup.

I lean over and whisper in his ear, "Henry, don't think because you're being obnoxious to me that I'm going to go away. It doesn't work like that. Basically, you can talk to me or I'll point some big guns in your direction who might come after you, especially if I tell them to. They might not be as understanding or sweet natured as me."

"What 'big guns?'" he asks, giving me his full attention. "What are you talking about?"

"Everybody wants to know who killed Eddie: the local sheriff, the owners of the circus, maybe even the Mormon Tabernacle Choir. And you, my friend, have got motive in spades. There's that charming little letter from Eddie in your file, for starters. So if I were you, I'd talk to me. And if you give me the right answers, your part in this might be over with sooner rather than later."

Henry throws down his brush in disgust and studies me. "Very well. 'I will wear my heart upon my sleeve for daws to peck at.' What do you want to know? I've got nothing to hide."

"What was the big fight about? The one noted in your file?"

"Edward Connors was an ungrateful, spoiled brat," he says between clenched teeth but enunciating carefully. He turns to me, his whole body radiating self-righteousness fury.

"I was the first friend he had here. Not one of the first but the first! I taught him everything. How to walk, talk, act, even gave him his face. You know, these faces don't come free! You have to create one or buy one. Everyone's is

different, unique. It's your trademark. None of the clowns have the same face. You must have noticed that."

I haven't, but decide not to mention it. Henry, just warming up, prattles on.

"See this star over here?" He points to a spot above his left cheek, where a large, red star lives. "That cost me one hundred dollars. One hundred! A gentleman in the Sparks Circus was using it and I had to pay him to stop, so it could be exclusively mine."

"Very nice but let's get back to Eddie. The argument."

"Very well," he says, applying glue to the perimeter of the hairline around his face. "I had advanced him money to buy supplies for his clown outfit, in the amount of twenty dollars. He'd already owed me twenty-five from a time when I was foolish enough to play cards with him and take his IOU. Anyway, I demanded the money's return in toto and, bold as brass, he said he couldn't pay me back; he needed all his money for his future. Well, one word led to another and if some of the boys hadn't been here, it might have led to fisticuffs."

"As I understand it, it did lead to fisticuffs. Vince and some of the boys had to pull you off of him. At least that's what it says in the file."

"Grievous exaggeration, madam, grievous."

The Bard's hand is shaking so much, he spreads glue too far down on his forehead. He snatches another cloth and wipes at the sticky stuff. A hot pink wig dangling from the side of his mirror is next. He slaps it on top of his head, lines it up with the streak of glue, and seals the hold by pressing down with one of the many clean rags lying in a bucket by his side. I watch him in silence.

"I showed the lad every single trick of the trade," Henry mutters. "Things it took me years to learn, I handed to him on a silver platter. And what was my reward? 'How sharper than a serpent's tooth is it to have a thankless child.'"

He flings the cloth down on the table, knocking over several tubes of greasepaint. Behind them rests a small brass ring of keys. Henry fights for control and picks up the tubes, carefully lining them back up against the mirror with trembling fingers.

"I'll bet that made you plenty mad, Henry. I know it would me," I say, egging him on. I like him better with less control. He's libel to say more.

The Bard drops his grander speech pattern and lapses into a cockney accent.

"The little bastard spread lies about me to management, vicious, 'orrible lies. He wrote them a letter saying awful things about me."

"Like what? What lies?"

"Don't play the innocent with me," he growls, turning his attention back to me. "You know. You read the letter, ducky, or you wouldn't be 'ere."

The nearby reader drops the magazine on the floor, gets up and leaves without a backward glance. While Henry watches him exit the tent. I lean in and palm the keys.

"But what's your side of it?" I ask, after putting them in my pocket.

"Listen," he turns back to me and answers softly. "I can't help who I am, but I never force it down anyone's throat. You know what they call most of us behind closed doors?"

"No, I don't."

"Of course, you do. Even in the circus, we're different."

"Explain it to me."

"We're the third sex. We're the elephant in the room, love, the one everyone knows is there but nobody talks about. But once fingers point, it comes out in the open and I could lose my job. That little creep tried to cost me my job! Then what would I have done?" His royal self returns full volume, along with the accent. "I gave that boy my heart and he ripped it up and threw it on the ground like so much garbage. That's all I was to him, garbage."

"Bard, keep it down, will you?" demands a rotund clown with a large yellow wig. "We're trying to play cards."

"Sorry about that, gentlemen." Henry concentrates on gluing on a red nose. I watch him, thinking even we girls don't wear that much crap for a show.

"So where were you early yesterday morning, Henry, say between five and seven?" I smile at him.

A look of horror crosses his face. Taking me unaware, he jumps up, knocking his chair over and lunges at me, one powerful hand at my throat.

"Get thee gone, strumpet," he hisses, spraying saliva in my face. "And take with you your crack of doom. I don't care if you are management's little tart." He tries to lift me off the ground by my neck.

I feel my spine stretch and my throat squeeze shut. Henry's small but very strong. I give a moment's struggle, but bring up my knee and aim for his groin. I get, as the Bard might say, 'a palpable hit.'

He releases me and drops to the floor with a small cry. The card players glance over at us again, but can see little. I force a smile and wave at them, as I bend down, locking eyes with Henry.

"You ever do that again, you miserable son of a bitch, and I will make you very sorry." I reach down with one hand and haul him up. With the other, I pick up his overturned chair and push him into it.

Whatever aggressive manliness he was feeling moments before is gone. He whimpers into his hands. "Here I am, being nice and answering your questions and you go and accuse me of killing that boy."

"I never said that, Henry, but I don't see why you can't tell me where you were."

"It was the girl," he says, leaning against his makeup table. "She turned him against me. Everything was fine until she came along. Even that other tart didn't have that effect on him."

"What other tart?"

"That trapeze one; the bitch that thinks she's too good for everybody. He dumped her for the little knife girl. Came to him, whining, crying, making him feel sorry for her." A look of loathing crosses his face. "You women are all alike. You should all go and hang yourselves."

I lean down into his face. "That's a pretty hateful thing to say, all things considered, Henry. I can see where you might be the kind of person who wouldn't think twice about slipping a piece of wire around someone's neck." My hand goes to my throat.

The Bard is silent, his thoughts somewhere else. I wait while he stares into the mirror.

"I loved that boy," he tells his reflection. "I was good to that boy. I gave that boy everything. And then he went and did this to me. 'Ingratitude, more strong than traitors' arms.'" And with that the Bard starts to cry, huge tears running down his cheeks.

"Damn," he says, snapping up one of the rags and blotting his cheeks. "I'm ruining my makeup." He looks over at my reflection in his mirror. "Why can't you leave me alone? I was finished with Edward over four months ago. Why should I enact revenge now?"

"Because 'revenge is a dish best served cold,'" I answer, getting up. "It isn't Shakespeare but it'll do." Henry stares at me, his mouth hanging open.

I leave in search of the magazine-reading clown, who was listening to Henry and me so intently before. He's one of the older clowns, hailing from Brooklyn, and I think he goes by the name of Dinghas. I find him around the corner of an adjacent tent smoking a cigarette and pacing back and forth. He halts when he sees me.

"Hi. You're Dinghas, aren't you?" He doesn't reply but merely nods. "Mind if I ask you a few questions?"

I think he might bolt but he doesn't. He grinds his cigarette into the earth, looks at me, breathing hard, and says, "He told you, didn't he?"

I try not to act surprised. "Yes, he did, but I thought I should get your side of it." I smile knowingly, like the good little actress I can be.

"I knew he would," Dinghas says. "I knew it. He can't keep his mouth shut. Always going off in that phony accent of his, spilling his guts."

"Some people are like that. So what's the real story?"

"Real story? Hah! The guy was crazy about Eddie or, as he would say, 'Edward.'" He does a fair imitation of Henry's voice. "Followed him everywhere. Did everything for him. Mooned over him."

"That must have hurt," I put in.

"Sure it did. You think we don't have feelings? Here it's been the Bard and me for five years, and then this pipsqueak comes along and Henry..." He stops speaking and pulls a pack of Lucky Strikes out from inside one of his puffy black and white polka dot sleeves. He taps one out and offers me another, a good sign. I'm his new pal. I take the cigarette and murmur my thanks. He lights his, deep in thought and seems to forget about lighting mine. I'm just as glad. I don't smoke.

"Of course, you have feelings," I say, revving the conversation back up. "But I really need to hear your side of the story. Otherwise --" I stop speaking and shrug, indicating I wouldn't be responsible for the outcome. I won't anyway, but I lay it on thick.

He throws his hands in the air, moved by great emotion. "God, that idiot! I tell him to stop, but no. He has to take the note to her father."

I fight to keep surprise from registering on my face. Dinghas turns on me, shaking his finger in my face.

"Listen, I didn't have nothing to do with it. It was Henry who done it. All Henry. I says to him, I says, 'stay out of it, mind your own business' but would he listen? No." He calms down after his outburst, fidgets with his cigarette, and puts it in his mouth.

"When was that? When did he take the note to Constantin?"

Dinghas sucks in cigarette smoke like it was air fresh off the ocean. "He was always following the kid, even when we got back together. I don't know why. That night he sees Eddie acting strange so he watches him even closer. Henry follows the kid to the Pay Wagon, so I follows him."

"What time was that?" I ask.

"Around midnight. They keep the Pay Wagon well lit every night straight through to the morning, whether it's got money in it or not." He looks at me. "Do you know why they do that?"

"It's called reinforcing a pattern. This way no one knows when it has cash and when it doesn't."

He digests this new bit of information. "Maybe that's why the kids chose it for a drop off point; it's always lit up."

"Maybe. Go on about the note."

"Yeah. Anyways, I see Eddie tucking something behind the folded down awning, like it was some secret hiding place. Henry sees it, too, 'cause when Eddie leaves, Henry runs right over and gets it. I come out from where I'm hiding and I says to Henry, I says, 'What do you think you're doing, Hank?' I always call him Hank when he's being bad. I says to him, 'Leave the kid alone. Put that back and leave the kid alone.' He just laughs. Then he reads the note and starts cursing up a blue streak. He says, 'That miserable so and so thinks he can do a bunk and take off like that, well, I'll show him' and so on and so forth. I keep telling him to put the note back, but he says he's bringing it to the girl's father. Jesus, he can be such a bitch."

"Are you sure that's what he did?"

"Dunno for sure." He shrugs, takes another long draw, and absentmindedly exhales in my face. I try not to cough. "Said he was. But I dunno. He changes his mind a lot."

"Did you read the note?"

Dinghas stubs out his cigarette and searches for a new one in the pack. I hand him the one he gave me. He light up before he speaks.

"Yeah. I snatches it from him and I sees some of it before he grabs it back. Didn't say much, just a new time Eddie was meeting the girl." I watch him close his eyes and read the note once more in his mind.

"Oh, yeah, and something about the kid wrote his mother and told her they was getting married. That really ticked Henry off." He takes another long drag off his cigarette. "I felt sorry for the kid. He didn't belong here." Dinghas gestures to the surroundings. "Jesus, he was a Mormon, for Christ's sake." He turns to me. "You know what them is?"

I nod.

"Anyways, Henry takes off with the note. I goes back to the train. Never hear him come in. I guess I fell asleep. He was there when I woke up, though, looking like the cat that swallowed the canary."

"What time was that?"

"Around eight-thirty."

"What else?"

"Then we hear they found the kid dead."

"Anything else?"

The clown slowly shakes his head, puffing on his cigarette. He's through talking, just like a music box that's run down, but I wait anyway. After a moment I say,

"Thanks, Dinghas."

I turn to leave, but he takes hold of my arm. "You won't tell Henry what I said, will you? I mean, him and I are back together now. I don't want him mad. He can be such a bitch."

"Not unless I have to."

He doesn't like my answer, but it will have to do. Dinghas gives me a half smile, pulls another cigarette out of the pack, lights it from the one he has going, and in a cloud of smoke, resumes pacing.

I turn my back on him, draw out Henry's keys and check them over. None look like the key Harold showed me earlier but that doesn't mean the right one isn't somewhere else in Henry's possession.

I put my hand to my throat, still hot from the Bard's grip. Did Henry take the note to Constantin or did he take matters into his own hands? He has a temper, our Bard. I can see why Dinghas doesn't want to make him mad.

I make sure no one is around and toss Henry's keys near the entrance to the clown's tent. If he gets them back, fine. If he doesn't, fine. Frankly, my dear, I don't give a damn.

Chapter Twenty-two
8:45 p.m., Monday

With Constantin's act being cancelled for the night, management asks the clowns and the featured acts to extend their times, 'stretch it out' for the audience so the show won't run short. To the delight of the audience, Emmet Kelly adds back a couple of retired segments from his act. I put my web costume on fast and dash out to watch, a rare treat for me. My favorite part is when Mr. Kelly 'sweeps' the spot light into the dustpan, the finale of his show, and I'm glad to be able to catch the last few minutes of it.

When he's done, the three featured trapeze artists follow. The girls troupe out, Rosie in the middle. I concentrate on her, all done up in gold sequins, and watch her climb up a rope and onto the trapeze. The lights fade in the house and several pin spots come up on the three, making for a sparkling, dramatic effect. Sometimes when I'm performing, I resent how much heat the lights generate in an already hot tent, with me working so hard. I tend to forget how much they add to the excitement, help the audience focus on what we want them to see.

All three girls pose on their trapezes, while their sitters on the ground pull at the ropes, swinging them to and fro. In unison to the music, the girls throw themselves over backward and catch on to the bar with their ankles, as I've done many times in practice. The audience applauds politely.

On the other side of the ring, three male catchers climb up web ropes, mount their own trapezes and swing out, with their backs to the girls. When the men go over the back of their trapezes, they lock their legs around the ropes of the bar, readying for their partners. The music swells as the catchers extend their arms toward the girls.

All six flyers make sure they're in perfect sync. In unison, the girls let go of their trapezes and fly into space toward the men. The men grab them by the wrists, take one swing back and forth then release the girls back toward their own trapeze. Each girl turns around in midair, grabs her bar, throws herself up and over it, landing on her abdomen in the angel pose. They repeat the beginning of the trick, but this time the girls do a backbend inside the catcher's arms and, using the man's shoulders, pushes off toward their own swinging trapeze. An appreciative applause fills the house.

The spotlights die on the two end girls, but remains on Rosie. The audience watches her expectantly, hundreds of head moving back and forth in accord with her swings. She does her release and pulls into a tight somersault, coming out in perfect time to reach for the hands of her catcher. The two swing for two or three moments, posing to an adoring and enthusiastic crowd.

When the catcher returns Rosie to her trapeze, she stands up on the bar, pushing herself higher and higher into the air, like a kid does in a playground. What she has to do is make her arc higher than her catcher's in order to give her more time to do the final trick.

There is a drum roll and Rosie does a swan dive off the bar and into the air, out and down. She whips herself into a somersault and again with perfect timing, straightens out, falling into her catcher's hands. The crowd goes wild. Not only does she thrill her audience, but proves her expertise and wins them over completely.

I've done the first somersault into a catcher's arms, but I've missed more times than not on the second, free-fall trick. I see too much at the beginning of the swan dive and at the end, when I go into the somersault, I can't see anything at all. I have to rely on my instincts and timing. It scares me. There can be no fear, something I haven't conquered yet.

Not true for Rosie. She's a real daredevil. I have to give her that. After her performance, she drops to the safety net, poses on the wooden ring and, to the audience's deafening applause, exits into the aisle where I'm standing. She sees me out of the corner of her eye and, flushed with her triumph, begins to laugh and runs out. I'm certain she put my hairbrush under Mabel's cinch.

I push Rosie out of my mind and concentrate on my routine. The orchestra plays transition music while twenty-five web sitters run out to their spot on the perimeter of the three rings. They release the webs from their various latching, each about thirty feet away from the other. Meanwhile, the ringmaster is announcing to the audience they are about to see twenty-five, yes, count them, twenty-five of the most talented and beautiful girls in the world displaying death-defying skills forty feet in the air. If I ever paid attention to him, I might get a swelled head. On cue, I run out into place with the other girls and strike a pose.

We're wearing voluminous, red and hot pink beaded capes over matching, sparse costumes. The glitter alone when the lights hit all the beading is enough to dazzle half of the state. Along with the other girls, I drop my cape, climb up the web and start the routine. The lights on the ground lower to black and above, spotlights focus on each of us. After various acrobatic tricks sure to thrill, this routine always ends with a breathtaking spin.

Each girl holds onto a hidden loop with her strongest hand, keeping the other arm by her side. The sitter begins to twirl the rope faster and faster until the force lifts each girl into the air, parallel with the ground. For a good thirty seconds we are life size, sparkling spinning tops, a finale made even more sensational by the orchestra's dramatic music. From my point of view, thirty seconds is a long time to hold on when centrifugal force is trying to send me into outer space.

The sitters slow down to a stop in time with the music and we pose for the crowd, forty feet in the air. The showgirls, meanwhile, are strutting around the ring in their four-foot headdresses, complete with ostrich plumes and beads. Applause, applause, applause.

Afterward, I climb down and follow the other girls to our dressing room, out of breath and sweating. It's a hot, muggy night and between the crowd and the lights, it has to be around one hundred degrees near the roof of the Big Top.

I strip and throw a lightweight robe over my g-string, glad to be out of the sticky costume. Sitting at my makeup table, I'm retouching my makeup when Margie lets out a short, high-pitched scream.

She screeches a word that sounds a lot like "snake" over and over and jumps up. She knocks over her makeup table and chair and, still shrieking, runs to the entrance of our dressing room. I beat her there, grab her by the arms, and hold on tight.

"Snake?" I repeat. She continues to scream, struggling to be free of me. "Is that what you said? What snake?" I shake her. "Margie, stop screaming and talk to me."

Doris races to us, reaching out for Margie. The other girls stay frozen where they are, half afraid, half concerned, uncertain of what to do.

"I saw a snake, a Coral snake." She gasps and points. "In my drawer. It's a Coral snake. I touched it." She shudders and begins to cry.

"Did it bite you?" I say, hastily examining her fingers. I don't see any puncture marks.

"No, no, I don't think so. I touched something moving and looked down. Oh, my God," she sobs.

The Coral snake is one of the most deadly snakes in the world, a first cousin to the Cobra. This is one of the things they teach you when you arrive in south Florida, among other safety measures. Not to be confused with the harmless Scarlet King snake, which looks similar, the Coral has a different arrangement of colored stripes. If what Margie saw was a Coral, then we have to find it and kill it right away.

Doris takes over and embraces the shaking Margie, while I search for the snake near her area. The rest of the girls finally move, backing away from me. By now, people are gathered outside the dressing room entrance, demanding to know what's going on inside.

"Everybody stay clear," I yell. "There's a possible poisonous snake in here." My roommates throw on robes and leave. I grab one of the ubiquitous long poles by the entrance, one with a sharp end, and poke at things lying on the ground next to the overturned makeup table. I see the snake, smallish and slow moving, come out from under a magazine.

"Red and yellow, kill a fellow; red and black, friendly Jack," I chant. This is a Coral snake, all right. I prepare to strike.

Just then, Tony barrels into the dressing room. "Jesus Christ! Is there really a snake in here?"

I nod without speaking and jab at the snake's head a couple of times with the sharp end of the pole. One jab finds its mark. The impaled snake writhes in a death throe, pierced through. I lift the pole up, snake twisting in the air.

Tony backs away. "Jesus, it's a Coral," he says. "Where the hell did that come from? We're too far north."

"Get me a bucket with a lid."

Tony hollers for one of the roustabouts to bring an empty bucket with lid and I unload the snake into it. Tony snaps on the lid and shaking, we both let out trapped air from our lungs in unison.

He turns to me. "You're sure no one was bitten?"

"I'm sure. Margie's all right, just hysterical. If anyone had been bitten, they'd be dead by now. You know that." I pull him to one side and lower my voice.

"Tony, I'm not going to do the rest of the show. You and I are going to pay a visit to one of the sleeper cars while everyone's busy with the grand finale. Don't tell anyone. I'll dress for it but I'll let Whitey know I'm out at the last minute." Ever since the cinch business, Whitey hasn't left Mabel's side, especially when she's in harness. I know he'll be there.

"Sure, but what do you---?"

"I'm hoping to find something before it gets thrown away."

"Does this have anything to do with the clown's death?"

"Maybe. You know, the sheriff was right about one thing. Anybody could have killed Eddie, man or woman. Under the right circumstances, a woman can exhibit amazing strength. I read about a mother lifting up a truck by herself in order to pull her five-year old son out from underneath. Something about adrenalin in the bloodstream."

Tony lights a cigarette and pivots to leave. He looks back at me and says, "I don't know what you're talking about, but you're scaring the hell out of me."

Chapter Twenty-three
9:20 p.m., Monday

Since my senorita costume was destroyed, I'm using my old costume from the year before, the Arabian Nights harem outfit. It's less cumbersome and when I leave off the noisy bells, unobtrusive and easy to move around in.

Though still shaky, Margie and the girls dress for the grand finale and head out along with me. I make a detour on my way to Mabel and rendezvous with Tony behind a tent.

"I'll tell Whitey to walk Mabel around the ring without me in the howdah," I say. "You meet me at Rosie's sleeping car, number fifteen, in about five minutes. Everyone else should be performing but I need you as a witness, in case I find what I'm looking for."

He nods and leaves. I find Whitey, briefly tell him I won't be in the finale, but he is to walk Mabel around the ring, anyway. Before he can ask any questions, I dart off to the train cars. I ignore his startled, concerned expression.

Tony is waiting for me, pacing and nervously smoking another cigarette.

"Okay, we've got a few minutes," I say, climbing the stairs and going into the main hallway of the sleeper car. I take the master keys out of my pocket and insert one into the lock of one of the compartments that holds four berths, expecting the door to be locked. It isn't. I turn the knob and push the door open a crack.

"Who is it?" cries out a voice in the dark. "Who's there?"

A light in one of the lower berths goes on. Struggling to sit up is Florence, a featured performer, and one of the four people sharing this compartment. Her nose is red and her eyes are bleary, making her small, elfish face look almost laughable. She coughs into a hanky and pull the covers up to her neck when she sees Tony standing behind me.

"Jeri? Mr. Phillips? What do you want?"

"Shhhh. Sorry, we didn't know you weren't performing tonight. Touch of the flu?" I say with sympathy, turning on the overhead lights. She nods. "You go back to sleep. Mr. Phillips and I need to get something from Rosie's berth. This is it, right?" I point to an upper berth, curtains closed and tucked under the mattress. The remaining two berths have the curtains pulled open for ventilation.

"Yes, but she's not going to like it, you going up there, Jeri," Florence wails, then sneezes. "None of us have ever been up there." I can hear the fear in her voice.

"It's all right," Tony says, in his best managerial voice, "We need to get..." he hesitates and looks at me questioningly.

"Yes," I smile. "Just ignore us, Florence." I put my foot on the lower bunk and lift up.

"She won't like it," the sick girl repeats. "And she'll blame me for not keeping you out."

"I'll make it all right, Florence," Tony assures her. "It will be fine."

Higher in the air I get a whiff of an unpleasant ammonia odor, strong and repellent. I pull open the curtains and the odor becomes almost overpowering, near the ceiling in the hot night. I reach for her overhead light and switch it on. Soiled linen and crumpled clothes litter the unmade bed. A small, foot-long rectangular glass tank, topped with a wire mesh cover, sits at the end of the bed. The tank is empty.

But there's something else. Right above the tank and pinned to the inside of the curtain, is one of the thousands of three and a half inch round buttons people buy for a nickel from the promotional button booth at the front gate.

They pin them to their lapels or hats using the safety pin backing. The buttons have photos of the clowns, animals, or specialty acts, with the words "I love the Big Top," encircling the perimeter. This particular button is of Eddie in his clown face, youth and freshness shining through, even slathered with all that makeup. I must have been staring at it, because Tony calls out my name with impatience.

"What are you doing up there?"

"Sorry," I say, jerking back to the here and now. I ease the tank over to the edge and hand it down to Tony. "Here."

"Jesus.... what the?" Tony holds it at a distance.

I don't say anything, but jump down and take the tank back from him. A whiff of a foul odor is coming from inside, enough to make my eyes water. The tank has not been cleaned in a long time, if ever. Urine and droppings are everywhere. And something else. I look at Tony and Florence.

"Now, you are both witnesses. I went up there empty-handed and came down with this tank, correct?" Tony nods. Florence stares at me, tears brimming in her already fevered hazel eyes.

"Please don't drag me into this," she begs.

"Okay, sweetie," I say. "You don't have to be a part of this. Why don't you get up and go out for a little fresh air? Just say you were outside the whole time and you don't know anything. No one has to know any different."

"No, they don't," Tony agrees.

Florence throws back the covers, gets up and puts on a flannel robe. Coughing, she goes outside without saying a word.

I turn to Tony. "Look at what's inside this tank." He leans in, gets a whiff and backs away.

"Pretty sad conditions," I say, "even for a deadly snake to have to live in. But look here in the corner, Tony." He obeys and then looks back at me, his mouth open in shock.

"That's right. It's the shed skin of a Coral snake. This is proof the snake came from this tank belonging to Rosie. Judging by the filth inside and the way the snake moved, I would say the reptile was half dead when it was put into Margie's drawer. That's probably what saved her or anyone else from being bitten."

I watch Tony's face harden as I speak. He grabs the tank from me. "After I fire her, I'm going to have her arrested. I thought Whitey was exaggerating about her but now I see..."

"Why would you think that?" I ask, surprised at the comment.

"Never mind. Let's go. I want to find her before she comes back here and terrorizes anyone else." He opens the door with his free hand.

"Tony, I wouldn't do anything until you get the sheriff. There's no telling..." Without listening to my final words, he slams the door to Rosie's compartment on his way out.

I stand for a moment, looking at the slammed door, hoping Tony will practice a little self-control when he comes across Rosie. I'm not counting on it, though. Underneath all that elegance and refinement can be a hothead, determined to have his own way.

I decide to leave Tony to his outrage and examine Rosie's bunk further before I leave. The button with Eddie's photo really throws me. Maybe they were close, even lovers. I didn't know it then but I'm about to know it now. I hop up to her bunk and systematically tear the small area apart with determination. I'm looking for love letters, receipts for gifts, photos, something that might show me the state of their relationship.

What I find is a Mormon Book of Prayers lying under a blue silk scarf. It's a small white book, a book a parent might give a young child to start them out on the path to religion. As I open this prayer book, I notice it looks almost unused. On the first page and written in the large, unsure block letters of a child are the words 'Edward Randolph Connors, born February 3, 1923.'

Cripes, the kid wasn't even twenty years old. My eyes burn. Whether the tears are from the sadness of knowing his true age, or from the lingering foul odor, I can't say. But I am now even more resolute. I will find his murderer. And if it's Rosie, God help her.

I pocket the book and take off for the dressing room to change clothes. The grand finale has just ended when I return and the girls come trouping in.

"Where were you, Missy?" Doris demands.

"What do you mean? I was there. Right in my usual place," I say, my eyes flashing her a signal. Doris looks surprised, but nods and turns away.

Margie seems still too stunned to pay attention to either of us. Even though she was told the snake had been killed and was gone, she refuses to go near her table or area. She changes clothes next to the exit.

"I need a drink," she growls, smoothing back her golden hair. "Something long and lethal. But not venomous." She lets out a snort of laughter.

"I've got a jug of my daddy's moonshine back at the sleeper," one girl pipes up. "You can have some. It's pretty good, if it's cold enough."

"I know where we can get some ice," another one says. "And some lemons. Do lemons go with moonshine?"

"I never met anything that didn't go with moonshine, hon," replies Doris. Everyone giggles.

"I've got enough for everyone," the first girl says with pride. "Why don't we have an impromptu party in our car? Fifteen minutes?"

"Sold," says Margie, slapping her thigh with her hand. "And then I'm going to hit the sack and never get up."

"I know what you mean," says Doris, brushing platinum blonde curls. "I never thought I'd say this, but Sherman's March through Georgia is looking pretty tame to me right now."

"Amen, sister." My friend turns to me, the old Margie resurrecting herself. "Dollars to doughnuts that mousy wife put that snake in my drawer to get even. You know, she's from Florida. She probably brought the little monster with her for just such an occasion. What some women won't do for a man!"

The girls laugh and I laugh with them. The atmosphere lightens considerably. Friendly banter and idle chit-chat fill the room until we're dressed and ready to leave.

Doris looks over to me. "You coming?"

I shake my head. "Sorry, I've got something to do. But you and Margie go and have a good time."

Doris come over to me and whispers. "This got anything to do with Tony and that glass container I saw him with? Not that I'm talking to him."

"Something like that." I smile. "Go on! Have a good time. I'll join you later."

"Well, you be careful, honey lamb," she says. "Won't do for you to get bit."

"I'm off to find out the truth about something in the past, Doris."

"My mama used to say the truth can bite you harder than any snake."

"Your mama was a smart woman," I say, and leave the tent in search of Whitey.

He's in the Bull Tent washing down Emma's back foot with some concoction that looks and smells funny. Emma is one of the older elephants, very docile and sweet. When he sees me, he drops his brush in the bucket, comes over and hugs me.

"Are you all right?" He releases me, eyes searching my face. "When you ran off like that, after telling me you weren't doing the spec, I panicked, especially when I heard about Rosie. What's this all about?"

"You know about that already?"

"Sure. Tony came to me, asking if I'd seen her. I hear she took off right after some trouble with a snake. All the men I can spare are out looking for her." He turned back to Emma and picked up her foot. I came closer and listened to him say, "I suspect they'll never find her. There are a lot of places to hide in a circus and she's a crafty girl."

I look around me. Handlers nearby are bedding down their assigned elephants for the night. What I want to talk to Whitey about can't be overheard.

"Whitey, finish up here and let's go someplace private."

His eyes search mine again. "All right."

He checks Emma over, gives her some fresh hay, makes sure her right leg is secured to the stake and comes back to me.

"What's that you were doing to Emma's leg?"

"She's got a fungus infection under one of her toenails," he says. "I wash it in a mixture of Tea Tree Oil and water twice a day. It's getting better."

"Good." I stroll away and out of the tent.

Whitey follows, coming by my side. He puts an arm around me, but I shrug it off.

"Let's take a walk," I say.

"Not a romantic one, I gather. What do you want to talk about, Jeri? You look so serious."

I don't answer. We walk about five minutes out into a clear field on the other side of the parking lot where the light comes from the moon and stars, instead of electricity, and the air is cool and sweet smelling. A mixture of earth and sky fill my lungs, so different from the circus behind us.

Whitey breaks the silence. "What's on your mind, Jeri?"

I turn to him. "What's between you and Tony?"

He shoots me a wary look, made more sinister by the half light. "What do you mean?"

"Listen, there's a murder to solve and this, whatever it is, is getting in the way. I'm going to find out eventually, Whitey, so why don't you do us both a favor and just tell me?"

I can see he's fighting to make a decision. I leave him to it and wait, turning my face up to a moon that hangs in the black vastness, surrounded by hundreds of blue-white stars. I search for the Big Dipper, aware of Whitey's breathing in some part of my mind, but trying to imagine myself on one of the Dipper's stars, any place but here. But here I am, so I can out-wait Whitey if I have to, to find out what I need to know.

"It doesn't have anything to do with what's going on here, Jeri. I swear it," he finally says.

I leave the Big Dipper and return to the sound of Whitey's voice. "Tell me, anyway. I promise it won't go any further than this field."

"Okay," he says, after a beat. "You're going to be the first person to know about this, outside of Tony and me. We took an oath to never talk about it, not even to each other." He exhales and takes a deep breath before speaking again.

"Tony and I go way back. He was the rich kid in school and I was the poor one, but we had a few things in common. We were both good students, wanted to make something of ourselves, get out of Grand Rapids, population boring and going nowhere, even got accepted to the same college. We became friends...of a sort."

Whitey squats down and pulls at weeds in the ground. "Tony was used to things going his way back then, Jeri. He'd led a pretty privileged life, even though it was the height of the depression. He had an indulgent father and a trust fund, those kinds of things. I didn't have any future to speak of, other than the likelihood of working in a factory and dropping dead from exhaustion, like my father." He looks up at me. I stare down at him.

"Hell, I'm not making excuses, Jeri. I'm just telling you how it was." He continues to rip at the weeds around him. A small frog makes a leap for freedom. Whitey doesn't notice.

"One night we were driving in his new roadster together, the one his father had given him for his birthday. Tony had been drinking and was driving too fast. We'd both been having a good time. It was a dark night, no moon, not even stars, blackness all around us in that little car. We were on our way home. It must have been three or four in the morning. There was this hobo, bum, walking down the middle of an unlit road in the middle of the night, dressed in black. It's almost like this man was looking to get..." His voice peters out.

When he speaks again, his tone is husky. "Anyway, Tony hit him, killed him instantly. It wasn't anybody's fault, really. Neither of us knew he was there until.... but Tony had had his license suspended for drunk driving and shouldn't have even been behind the wheel." Whitey pauses and looks down at his hands.

"God, it was terrible. Even now, my palms get sweaty from talking about it." He wipes them on his shirt.

"So he paid you to say you were driving the car," I say. "That's how you went to college."

"I'm not proud of it. I did it half out of friendship but half for the tuition money. I didn't realize that I would carry that man's death with me for the rest of my life, wherever I went, whatever I did. Even though I wasn't the one who hit him, I profited by his death."

"What was the verdict?"

"I was convicted of accidental manslaughter, extenuating circumstances, suspended sentence. But it was noted on my record because I'd just turned eighteen. It didn't affect me getting into college. I'd already been accepted. But

afterwards, I wanted to be a veterinarian, work with animals. That's all I wanted. Most of the vet schools closed during the depression and the ones that were left had the luxury of scrutinizing a person's character more carefully. Once they got a load of my felony record, there wasn't one that would touch me."

"So Tony gave you a job here, working with the elephants? Or did you blackmail him into it?"

He gives me a quick glance, then returns to his grass. "I guess I deserved that, but no. A year or two after we graduated, he found out I was drifting, working here and there in small zoos, so he offered me a job. They needed an elephant handler and I needed a purpose." Whitey lets out a small, knowing laugh.

"I've worked my way up and now I'm the head bull man. But I did it on my own, I swear to you. Tony's not a bad guy, Jeri. I'd like to think I'm not, either. It's just that we can't look at each other and not remember. So we keep our distance when we can, if that makes sense."

"Tony told me he always took the easy way out," I say. "But I don't see that in you."

"Thanks. I guess we both took what we thought was the easier way. It wasn't, though. You think a lot of things when you're eighteen that don't turn out to be true."

I rest my hand on his shoulder. "I'm sorry, Whitey."

"What happens now?" he asks. He stands up, facing me, ready for whatever blow I might deliver.

I have none to deal him. "Nothing. I just needed to know. As far as I'm concerned, you never said anything; we never had this conversation. You have my word on that."

He shakes his head. "But we did have this conversation, Jeri. And this is going to stand between us. I've fallen in love with you, Jeri. I may as well confess that while I'm confessing everything else." He lets out a hollow laugh. "Who did I think I was kidding, a girl like you could care for

me? But I am sorry I'm not the man you thought I was. I'll leave you alone from now on."

I reach out, but he backs up. "I didn't ask you to do that."

"You don't have to."

He turns and starts to walk away. I watch his back for a split-second, a guilt burning inside, always the guilt. He deserves to know. And if I let him leave like this, anything we might have would go away with him. I don't want that.

"Maybe I'm not the girl you think I am, Whitey," I say, louder than I mean to. I drop the volume of my voice and go on. "I wonder if you'd still care for me if you knew my truth. What I've done."

He turns back to me. I can't see his face, really, but his stance is one of hesitation and puzzlement."What could you have done, Jeri? You're such a good, little Italian girl," he jokes. I don't smile.

"You have no idea, Whitey," I pause ,then start talking into the dark night, in a monotone voice I almost don't recognize as my own. "A little over two years ago I was doing undercover work for the Brinks Detective Agency in a bank in Brooklyn, one of ten branches. They'd had a series of robberies, four in less than two months. A security guard had been killed, plus two customer injuries. The bank president began to suspect that in each case, it was an inside job, so he came to Brinks. Six of us posed as tellers in the banks that hadn't been struck yet. I'd only been there for two weeks when one day I noticed the head teller, a pompous, self-important man, was acting nervous, almost apprehensive. I knew something was up, so I managed to stick close to him most of the day.

"Right around closing time, three men came in, tough looking characters, and I saw my mark go to the cage that held the security alarm and stand in front of it, blocking any access.

I had just positioned myself behind him when the three men overpowered the security guard, drew their guns and told everyone to drop to the floor. I should have done that. I should have dropped to the floor, just like everybody else in the bank did but no, I was cocky, full of myself, going to save the world."

I shut up and stare out into the endless dark night.

Whitey reaches out and takes my hand, whisper soft. "What happened?" he says, prodding me on.

"I threw myself in between the head teller and the cage, trying to get to the alarm for the police. I didn't know the man had a pistol hidden there. I didn't know that." I let out a sob. "I saw him panic and reach for the gun. I tried to get there first. We struggled. The gun went off and a little boy, a little four-year old boy, lying on the floor on the other side of the counter next to his mother, got shot in the head. He was killed instantly. The teller was so shocked, he dropped the gun and froze. The three men got away but were captured the next day. I'll never forget that mother's screams. They haunt me every day."

"Oh, Jeri." Whitey strokes my shoulder. "I'm so sorry."

"If I hadn't gone for the alarm or tried to get to the gun first…" I break off.

"What did the police say? And Brinks, what did they say?"

I pull free from his touch and wipe at my wet face. "Oh, the gun was in his hand when it fired, I was just doing my job, it was an unfortunate occurrence, stuff like that. All words. I was offered a month's leave with pay, which I didn't take. I never went back." I finally look at Whitey, who steps closer.

"Don't you see? The gun wouldn't have gone off if I hadn't fought the man for it. If I had just lain down on the floor like everybody else then that little boy would still be alive."

"Maybe. Bank robbers are known to be pretty ruthless," he replies. "You said they had already killed a security guard."

"Whitey, I made the wrong choice, and because of my choice, a child is dead. That's a fact."

We are both silent.

"I'm sorry you carry such a burden," he finally utters. "I know how tough that can be."

"You're never free." My words are carried away on the wind.

"No, you're not." His words stay put.

We are silent after that. I can feel the night breeze on my damp cheeks.

"I still love you, Jeri. No matter what you've done. Or think you've done. It doesn't change a thing."

I half-sob, half-exhale and say, "I'm glad."

Whitey reaches out. I go into his arms and for one small moment, feel peace. I lift up my head and look into his face, partially lit by the moon, partially hidden by the night. His lips find mine and it's a kiss I've never experienced before, filled with passion, yet as comfortable and timeless as the stars themselves.

I break free and cup his cheek with my hand. "Whitey, I have to go."

"Not yet, not yet," he whispers, trying to pull me back into his arms.

"Yes, now. Time's running out and I've got to get back to those files. Just me. You'll only be a distraction. Please understand, my darling. This is something I have to do."

"I understand more than you know."

"To be continued?"

I sense his agreement as he takes my hand from his cheek, and gently kisses my upturned palm. Wordless, Whitey turns away, staring up into the immensity of space.

I walk toward the Big Top, leaving him to the stars.

Chapter Twenty-four
11:00 p.m., Monday

Everywhere I hear people searching for Rosie. I can't stop my eyes from flitting into murky corners and gloomy areas, looking for any movement, as I pass on my way to Vince's office. I'm nervous. Until Rosie is found, that's how I'll be.

I return to Vince's office to immerse myself in the files once more. Picking up Rosie's again, I mull it over. The seeming normalcy of it, outside of her penchant for dangerous, small animals, is eye-catching: She'd been a Brownie in grade school and a cheerleader in high school, living with her mother, father, sisters, brother, and grandparents together in one large house in Evanston, PA.

Vince scribbled the words 'close-knit family' followed by a question mark on a newspaper clipping from an Evanston local rag. There was also an empty envelope addressed to her, with the Napa State Asylum for the Insane as the return address. On the back flap, Vince wrote the word 'uncle.'

This brings some questions to my mind, mostly about Vince. Where did he get the envelope? Why has he saved it? How did he find out about the uncle? I'm thinking blackmail, but there might be more to it. Whatever the answer is, Vince is in the next town with Advance. It'll have to wait.

I give in to my curiosity, go to the file drawer and pull out the files of Margie, Doris, Doc, and Tin Foot plus my own. I start with mine.

It contains several newspaper reviews mentioning me, with my name underlined. There are six or seven recent photos, plus notes. "Smart cookie," "talented newcomer" and "something in her past" are neatly written on the back of certain clippings. He's also noted I rarely get mail and seem to be estranged from my family. One small scribble, reading like an afterthought, is that I seem to keep men at a distance, as if I don't trust them, with the exception of Doc, Tin Foot and until recently, Whitey. I fight to keep his observations purely on a professional level, trying to look at how they can best be used for the job. It's hard. Say what I will about Vince, he has an uncanny knack for painting a realistic picture of a person with a few well-chosen words.

Tin Foot is "honest and trustworthy like a Boy Scout" and "likes to whittle." One small time newspaper article mentions how his family almost lost their dairy farm to back taxes a few years back. Not that it's any of my business, but I didn't know Tin sends part of his paycheck home every week. Apparently, Vince does.

He writes that Doc is "tender hearted" and "skilled with his hands, even does calligraphy." Vince's notes confirm something for me. Several years back, Doc was asked to leave Mount Sinai Hospital due to a drinking problem. I'm surprised to learn Doc won a Distinguished Medal of Honor in nineteen-eighteen for rescuing twenty-three kids from a burning orphanage in the south of France. But when I reflect on it, it seems perfectly in character.

He doesn't have much to say about Doris, other than she's romantically linked with Tony. He remarks she reminds him of one and a half Betty Grables, and has compiled nearly every photo taken of her since she was a teenager.

The words "hussy" and "snooty" are in Margie's file and a big 'x' is scrawled across the only 8 x 10 headshot photo of her. I remember he made a play for her once and she turned him down flat. She turns down a lot more men than she takes on, despite her reputation. She likes her reputation; it's colorful and for her, freeing.

I put my friends' files aside and tackle the others in the drawer, not completely sure what I'm looking for, but there's a lot here. All in all, Vince would have made a perfect desk jockey for Brinks. His files are neat and orderly, almost to the point of obsessive. He's overlooked nothing. Newspaper clippings, brochures, and other types of documents cram each folder, probably taking months to assemble. Every member of the circus, whether performer or staff, are here, complete with small details and his observations. Putting aside his personal insights, I learn tidbits here and there.

It's like Vince is my own private investigator, if I can trust his reliability. There is that. If nothing else, his point of view is eye opening. I can only imagine how Vince feels, knowing someone else is pouring over his private assessments of us circus folk. It's almost as if these files are Vince's private diary.

That thought brings me back to Catalena's diary, resting in the small bag at my waist. I push the book out of my mind for later, thinking this time to start at the beginning of it. I continue reading files trying to overlook nothing. Hours go by.

Somewhere between one-thirty and two in the morning I finish and remove Catalena's diary from my bag. I'm so tired I can hardly see straight. I'm not looking forward to trying to decipher the journal again. I get up and stretch cramped muscles. Deciding to make myself a cup of tea, I carry the small red diary with me into the microscopic kitchen.

While waiting for the water in the kettle to heat, I sit down at Vince's dilapidated kitchen table and open to the first page of the calendar-style, yearly diary. The date January 1, nineteen forty-two is stamped in the upper right hand corner.

The writer is given two blank entry pages per day and Catalena's writing fills them all. Initially, I believe I've gotten used to her handwriting or absorbed more Romanian than I think. I seem to be able to make out words and phrases easier. But I realize my fatigue is making me slow on the uptake.

The beginning shows a normal, young girl on the brink of womanhood. Catalena was more open and free in her life at that time and it's reflected in her penmanship. From what I am able to tell, the next fifty or so pages contain random thoughts and impressions of her new life in the states. Little snippets come through to me about missing her mother, feelings about the Big Top and its people. It's all part of a teenager who's made a big change in her life. Then for two weeks at the beginning of March the pages are blank. When the writing continues, it's cramped and almost unintelligible throughout the remainder of the book.

Before and after the blank pages she's a faithful writer. What happened in those two weeks?

I concentrate on the first section of stilted writing in the last of March and the beginning of April. That part seems to be hardly more than a spasm of words, cross outs and scratches. I read and reread, write down different spellings of certain words, say them out loud, change the order of words, hoping to make sense of them.

When it comes to me, the book falls from my hand. I stand up with a jerk, knocking over the small, Formica table. I don't hear the whistle of the kettle, dry from blasting its head off for over ten minutes or pay attention to the acrid smell of melting metal assaulting my nostrils. Crossing to the stove, I turn off the burner, and set the kettle in the sink, all the while trying to absorb what I've learned, as unfathomable and ugly as it is. I snatch the book from the floor and run out into the night, heading for Tony's car.

One of those sudden summer storms is upon us. Dark clouds obliterate most of the moon's light and only a few stars are able to break through the murk. Lightning flashes in the distance and wind howls. Gusts burst around tent posts and wagons, creating violent, eerie sounds in the dark night. I hear a short, muted cry and muffled voices from somewhere nearby. But they blend in with the groans and creaks of the canvas and rigging and the plaintive cries of anxious animals.

I stop short, trying to figure out which direction the disturbance came from. Whipped up brochures, programs and scraps of paper not yet taken away by the clean-up crew wrap around my legs like the tentacles of an octopus. I begin to wonder if all I heard was the storm and animals, no human cry or voices.

I hesitate. Should I follow the train or head back to the mystifying noises? Close by I hear the sound of two roustabouts yelling to one another, lowering the awnings on the animals' wagons. Only their moving flashlights indicate where they are. Was that what I heard?

I turn and race toward the end of the railroad cars, tripping over stones and uneven patches of earth, almost feeling my way down the train. When I get to Tony's private car, I pound on the door, trying to be heard above the blustery weather.

After a few seconds, the door flies open and Tony stands there, dishevelled and half-asleep in his pajamas, holding a robe in his hands. The door rips from his hand, like it has a life of its own, and pounds against the side of the train keeping rhythm with the wind.

"Oh, God, what's happened now?" Tony falters, his face ashen and hair blowing wildly.

"Get inside," I say, pushing him back into his suite. "I can't talk to you out here." We struggle to pull the door closed against the wind.

"Jesus," he says, windblown and frightened. "What is it?"

"Get me your gun," I say. "We need to find Constantin. We need to stop him. He killed Eddie and he's a dangerous man."

"What?"

"Now! Get it now!" I scream in his face. Tony stumbles toward the bedroom and comes back a second later with the small pistol he offered me a couple of days ago.

"Is it still loaded?" I ask.

"Yes, but what…"

"Come with me." I seize the gun from his hand and turn to the door. Before I go, I point to a large, red flashlight lying on a table by the door. "And bring that light."

He grabs it and we go out into the crying wind. I jog up the length of the cars, followed by Tony. I stop suddenly and Tony bangs into me.

"I'm not sure…" I mutter, breaking off mid-sentence. Even with the wailing wind, Tony knows I said something.

"What?" he shouts at me.

"Where to go," I shout back. "Where to go first? We'll try the compartment; that's my best guess." I begin to run.

"What are we looking for?" Tony hollers, trying to keep up.

I stop short at compartment C and start counting the windows. "It should be here." I shine the light on the glass pane, but all I see is black; the curtains are closed.

I take the steps two at a time, with Tony close behind, run to compartment fifteen, and bang on the door. No answer. With trembling hands, I put in the pass key. Empty. I try the adjacent door to Ioana's room. The door opens easily but that compartment is empty, too.

I turn to Tony. "Let's go."

"Where?"

"His tent."

"At this hour?"

"I've got a feeling," I say. "That might be what I heard. That might be…" I rush out of the car and toward the performers' tents, Tony right behind.

I'm drawn to a lone light coming from inside one of the tents. I can tell by the flickering it's a kerosene lamp hooked onto the center pole. We've been strongly advised not to use kerosene lanterns because of fire. The new battery lamps, while not as long lasting, are far safer. Closer, I see it is Constantin's tent.

"What's he doing using a kerosene lamp?" Tony asks, in voice filled with indignant outrage. "The tent flap's not even tied down. Lord knows what could happen."

Lord knows, indeed.

The wind whips through the loose flap, causing the lantern to swing ominously back and forth on its hook. On the other side of the canvas, the shadow of a standing man moves in and out of focus with the shifting light.

Half-blown inside by the force of the wind, we see the shadow belongs to Doc. He's stock still, looking at a fluttering piece of paper in his hands, hands covered with blood.

"Doc?" I call out and come closer. He turns to me, a dazed expression on his face.

"I found him. He's dead." He looks down at his hands again, opening them palms up. The paper adhered to the drying blood. He doesn't seem to notice. "I tried to help."

Beyond Doc I see Constantin lying on his back in front of a battered, black trunk, one of his show knives with his insignia sticking out of his abdomen, crimson blood running wet on his white shirt. His arms are stretched out as if he was sunbathing. But there is his face, features contorted in anger or pain, maybe both, and eyes wide open.

"Jesus Christ," Tony cries out so loudly, the sound of his voice hurts my ears. I turn around to Boss Man, gaping at Doc's extended, bloody hands.

"He killed Eddie," Doc says with no expression to his voice. He offers me the bloodstained note, oblivious to Tony and his wails.

"I know." I say, watching him, but not moving.

"He says it right here," Doc goes on, shaking the note in my face. Then he drops his arms to his sides and stares straight ahead. I go to him, repeating his name several times, trying to get his attention. When I touch Doc on the arm, he stares at me with heavy-lidded eyes. I can't read anything in them.

"Put the note back, Doc, where you found it. Right now. Put it back. It's evidence. The police are going to want to know where it was."

"I found it over here," he says, pointing a crooked finger. "On the edge of the trunk." He walks over more like a zombie than a man and sets it down. The note, heavy with blood, lays flat on the deep, inside brass rim of the trunk, untouched by the howling wind.

"You're sure he's dead?" Tony asks. "The blood looks so… fresh."

"Only just," Doc answers, coming to life a little. "Probably not more than fifteen or twenty minutes, I would say. I tried to save him," he repeats, looking at his blood soaked hands, as if seeing them for the first time. I notice his trouser pockets are also rimmed with blood. Maybe he tried to put his hands inside to warm them.

Tony collapses into a nearby chair. "This is a nightmare, but I never wake up. I never wake up."

"What are you doing here, Doc?" I say, ignoring Tony. His answer is slow and mechanical.

"I heard yelling, things being knocked about. Then I heard a man's scream, coming from here. That must have been when he stabbed himself. I came to see what was happening."

While he is talking, I take the swaying kerosene lantern off the hook. "We need to send for the police."

Doc's eyes are riveted on his bloody hands. Either he can't or won't respond. I turn to Tony. His face is so blanched of color, I fear he might faint.

"Get up, Boss Man," I jab him on the shoulder. "Get up and take Doc back with you to your suite, then send someone for the sheriff. I'll stay here." Tony stands at my order, swallows hard, but instead of moving, stares down at the dead man.

I turn back to Doc. "Tony will get you some water to wash your hands, sit you down, take care of you. You need to rest. Go on." He doesn't move.

"Tony," I scream, "you need to take care of Doc. Come on, both of you. Somebody, move!" Roughly, I push the men to the entrance, willing them both into action. "I'll keep the flashlight. You take the lantern." I thrust the lantern into Tony's hand.

"What are you going to do?" Tony asks, finally focusing on me. "You can't stay here by yourself."

"Yes, I can. Someone should be here in case Ioana comes looking for her father," I say. I lean in and whisper in Tony's ear, "See if you can send someone out to search for her. I'm worried about where she is, but I'm also worried about Doc. I think he's in shock."

Shaking himself into life, he nods, and put an arm around Doc. "I'll be back as soon as I can," he says.

"I'll be fine. Take care of Doc and go get the sheriff," I repeat.

I watch them leave, the wind swirling around them like a small tornado. Lightning flashes closer now and thunder rolls overhead. I tie the flap down to keep the wind from blowing things around inside the tent any more than it already has.

I aim the torch at the man with the outstretched arms. He hasn't moved. I search the corners of the tent with the light, turning everyday objects into eerie shadows. Satisfied no one is hiding, particularly a traumatized, terrorized Ioana, I relax a little, find an electric lantern, and switch it on. The batteries are low and it gives only half the promised light. But it is better than nothing.

I begin to investigate the tops of several trunks and tables, not only to see what I can find but to keep my nerves from getting the better of me. A narrow wooden box contains several knives rolled up in burlap. Behind the box is a coil of flat wire, the same as I saw wrapped around Eddie's neck.

On his makeup table, a set of keys on a small chain hold a white rabbit's foot. One familiar looking key of blackened silver, short, thick, and blunt edged, causes me to pick them up and slip them into my pocket.

I end my hunt at the edge of the trunk that holds the note, written on the bottom half of a sheet of note-size paper. Bloodstained fingerprints obscured a letter or two but the printing is clear enough, with Constantin's familiar signature finishing off the missive. I lean over and read the contents out loud, my voice eaten up by the shrieking wind outside the tent. I read it again and again.

I strangled the clown to keep him from running away with Catalena. Now she is dead because of me. It is only fitting I go the way of my daughter, by my own hand. May God forgive me. Constantin

I steel myself and turn my attention to the dead man. The knife is buried to the hilt within his chest, just under the sternum and slanted upward. It looks like the only stab wound but there's so much blood, it's hard to tell. I do another search directly around him but come up with no other weapon. Everything is in disarray, presumably from a man who thrashed about in his death throes.

My mind is always on Ioana. Where is she? I'll have to find out later. Right now, I have to stay where I am.

Exhausted, I sit down on a crate several feet away from the body. The storm breaks and I hear rain beating down on the roof of the tent. I shiver and draw up my legs, hugging them with my arms. The electric lamp fades and dies but, fortunately, the flashlight doesn't. I wait, Tony's revolver in my pocket, flashlight in hand, beam focused on the dead man. It seems like hours but it's probably less than thirty minutes.

A blaze of light shoots through the canvas from the headlights of an approaching car. I jump up, turn in that direction and stand, unwilling – maybe unable -- to move. I hear the sound of a car door opening and closing.

Tony calls out my name, while untying the flap and throwing it back. He's left the car's lights on and is backlit, looking like a macabre figure standing in the doorway, dressed in a tan raincoat and hat, both dripping with water.

"The sheriff is on his way," he says, breaking the silence. "I decided to drive to Five Points, myself. The fewer people that know about this right now, the better. I haven't even told the Brothers yet. I'm leaving my headlights on, so Draeger will know where we are. I'll wait with you." He comes toward me but walks past, staring down at the dead body.

I follow Tony, spouting questions. "Where's Doc? How is he? Where is he? Has anyone found the girl?"

He turns back to me. "Doc's okay, but he must have spent ten minutes washing his hands. I gave him a drink and he went back to the First Aid Tent. Ioana's there, sleeping, and he wanted to be there if she woke up."

"She's there? But how...?"

"Doc told me that she came running to the tent around two am, terrified, crying, looking for help. Her father went crazy, she said. Doc calmed her down, gave her something to make her sleep, then went off in search of Constantin. That's what brought him here."

He opens his mouth to say more, but is stopped by the sound of an approaching vehicle. We both watch the oncoming headlights blending in with Tony's own.

The car stops outside the tent, close enough so that we hear two car doors slam shut and loud voices competing with the wind and rain. I withdraw the revolver from my pocket and tap Tony's hand with it, not looking at him.

"You'd better take this back while it's on my mind."

He says nothing, but wraps his fingers around it.

The flap jerks open and the sheriff enters brusquely, dressed in a long grey coat over his uniform, water droplets on his face and hat. Behind him the deputy who stood watch over Tin and I the other day is muttering indistinguishable hell, fire and damnation quotes from the Bible. I only catch a word here or there.

Sheriff Draeger turns on him. "Shut up."

The sheriff is angry. I can almost smell his anger. He looks at Tony. "I am so sick of you people and what's going on around here. What's she doing here?" He glares at me. "Why are you always around, missy? You seem to be everywhere."

He doesn't wait for an answer when he sees Constantin's body. He yells back to his deputy. "Holy Jehoshaphat. That's him all right, the knife throwing man, the one whose daughter killed herself."

Draeger moves forward, past Tony and me. He kneels beside the body while the deputy stays in the doorway, terror stricken. I can see his lips moving but no sound comes forth. I think he's still mumbling quotes from the Bible.

"Where's this suicide note you mentioned?" says the sheriff, rising. Tony looks around for it and points to the edge of the trunk. I feel lightheaded and sit back down on the crate, putting my head between my knees.

"What are all these bloodstains on it? Did he write it after he stabbed himself? Jesus, you people are strange." The sheriff's voice is filled with disgust.

"Doc's the one that found him, sheriff," replies Tony. "He said he tried to help and got blood all over his hands. After he knew the man was dead, Doc picked up the note to read it. Jeri's the one that made him put it back where he found it."

"Where is the doctor now?"

"He went back to the First Aid Tent to take care of the little girl."

I listen to all of this as if it's part of a dream. The sheriff walks toward me, the rustling of his raincoat drawing my attention. I open my eyes to his anger. He shakes the note under my nose.

"This the note you saw in the doctor's hands?"

I nod, too tired to talk.

He reads it through once or twice, then spins around to Tony. "Well, I guess we found our man. I won't be coming here in a few hours to close the circus, like I thought." The sheriff lets out a small laugh. "Too bad."

Sheriff Draeger's eyes turn back to me. "I'll have to talk to this doctor. Then I'm going to talk to you, little lady, I hope for the last time. Meanwhile, you two get out of here. You're in my way."

I rise and go to the doorway, saying nothing. The deputy moves aside, as if I have the plague. I almost laugh. Close on my heels is Tony, who takes off his raincoat and throws it over my shoulders.

"Let's go back to my place," he says, taking control. It seems the more bedraggled I'm feeling, the more he's come to life. "Just give me a minute to turn off my headlights."

He returns, saying, "You can get some sleep without people bothering you asking what's going on. I'm going to give you a drink, too, same as Doc."

"You're getting wet," I say, with a shiver.

"It feels good."

We walk for a few moments in silence. I'm unable to think, running on fumes, as they say. But one thought does break through the wall of fatigue.

"What about Rosie, Tony?"

"I've got everybody out looking for her. She won't be any trouble to us much longer. Let me take care of it, Jeri. It will be all right."

I don't answer, busy shielding my face from the wind and rain, and so weary I can hardly walk. I stumble when a gust of wind all but blows me over.

"Jeri, I've got you," Tony says, putting his arm around me. "Come on."

We trek the length of the train to his suite in silence. He opens the door, ushers me inside and into the bedroom, taking the raincoat from me and hanging it on a nearby hook. He pulls off his wet jacket, throws it in a corner, crosses to the closet and grabs a dry one, shrugging it on. He is a man in a hurry.

"Here," he says, taking two navy blue towels from his bathroom, throwing one to me, and wiping the rain off his face and hands with the other. I towel-dry my hair, saying nothing, but my mind starts to work again, going over and over what happened.

"There are some fresh pajamas in the top drawer, Jeri. You crawl into my bed. You've even got clean sheets; I slept on the couch in the living room last night. Don't worry. No one will disturb you. I'm going to spend the rest of the night talking to the North Brothers about the end of the season. But I think this mess is finally over. Maybe I can even talk Doris into coming back to me."

His voice has almost a cheerful tone, as he picks up a decanter filled with amber liquid, pours a liberal amount into a crystal glass, and hands it to me.

"The way I see it, Constantin killed Eddie and then took his own life. Poor Catalena got caught in the middle. I think it's over," he repeats. "My job will be to convince the sheriff and the town council of that before they burn this place to the ground. I'll wake you if the sheriff wants to talk to you. Drink up. This will help you sleep."

I don't say anything but accept the drink. He watches me sip the scotch, then dons his raincoat and hat once more. He throws me a half smile as he closes the door to his suite behind him. I'm left to collapse into his large, sumptuous bed, more space than I've experienced in two years.

Chapter Twenty-five
11:00 am, Tuesday, July 7th

I wake up not knowing where I am, what time it is or even what day. Groggy and disoriented, I struggle to an upright position. When I remember the night before, I lie back down, close my eyes and will myself not to think.

Outside I hear children playing. I stretch out a hand to pull back the dark blue curtain on the small, oval window and look out. The sun is shining and I can tell by the shadows or lack of them, it's late. I call out Tony's name, wondering if he's in the sitting room. Silence.

I throw back the covers and get up too quickly. Lightheaded, I have to sit back down for a moment. I'm stiff, puffy and carrying so much achiness, I feel hung over. The past few days are catching up with me. I need to do a barre, plus some exercises, even though all I want to do is sleep for a week. I force myself up, put on my now dry clothes, toss Tony's pajamas in the hamper, and make the bed before I leave, good little Italian girl that I am.

Outside, the sun is dazzling and the air is clean and crisp from the storm. Around me some of the specialty acts are going about the business of the day, half-dressed in colorful costumes, practicing routines or talking among themselves in small groups. Roustabouts tote supplies and feed, handlers deal with animals, workmen carry tools, the sound of hammers reinforcing or building something crash like cymbals in the air. Small children burst through each of these scenes at play, going every which way. It is a normal day in the circus, putting aside three deaths.

I linger on the lower step of Tony's car, trying to orient myself. I hear a "Hey, Jer!" and turn in that direction. Tin Foot is waving and hurrying my way. He grabs me in a bear hug and squeezes so hard it knocked the breath out of me. He releases me just as quickly and stands back taking my presence in.

"How are you? I should be mad as heck at you. Why didn't you come and get me last night? I thought we were partners in crime. You know, that kind of stuff." His tone is light but his features express his anxiousness and maybe a little hurt at being left out of the dénouement.

'Tin, it was the middle of the night and it all happened so fast. Once I read the diary --"

"What diary?" he interrupts.

"Catalena's diary and...never mind all that now." I wave the subject away with impatience, wanting to move on. His face registers surprise at my dismissive attitude. I do some backpedaling and link arms with him, patting him on his bulky shoulder at the same time.

"I'm sorry, Tin. There are so many things I need to bring you up to date on. Why don't I tell you over breakfast?"

"Breakfast?" He laughs. "You mean lunch. It's eleven-thirty."

"Tin! Is it really?" I pull him in the direction of the tents. "Well, then the chow tent should be open. Come on. I'm starving!"

Tin doesn't budge. "Wrong way, Jeri. Lillian made up some sandwiches for us back at car fourteen. We can talk there privately and what you have to say better be good. I've been waiting a long time for you to get up."

While we walk up the thirty-five cars to the girls' sleeper, I reflect on how like Tin not to say the words Ballet Broads or Virgin Car. He is a true gentleman. I smile at him and he grins back, holding up a rough wooden figure of a ballerina.

"I got a lot of whittling done while I waited."

"What's been happening while I was in slumber land? What's going on?"

"Balendron called a brush-up rehearsal for the Elephants' Ballet at ten."

"But I'm in --" I say, stopping short.

"Naw. You're off the hook," Tin Foot interjects. "Tony said it was okay if you weren't there. Balendron said it was okay, too; said you know your stuff. Topsy's going through her paces without you, with a little help from Whitey. Tony told me to keep an eye out for you and if you weren't up by noon, to wake you. We've got that special matinee, remember?"

"I remember, all right. It couldn't be coming at a worse time."

We're doing an extra show in support of our troops. The performers donate their time and the Big Top gives all the proceeds to the USO. Anyone in a service uniform is invited in, free of charge.

"How are you feeling?" asks Tin. "I've seen you look better."

"Thanks a lot."

"You're welcome."

"To be honest, Tin, I need to work out some stiffness and take a long, hot shower, something to get my mind going again. I feel like I'm in a fog."

"Maybe I can help. Got lots of things to report," Tin Foot says, with a grin.

"Like what?"

"Tony is with the Springfield City Council right now, trying to talk them into letting the show stay open. They probably think it's more dangerous around here than being in one of Eisenhower's bunkers. Anyway, Tony said he'd see you after the afternoon show to let you know what's going on."

"I see. Any news on Rosie? Have they found her?" I ask.

"No, they're still looking and Tony's got a guard on her compartment. She hasn't been back there to get her clothes or nothing. Maybe she's long gone, half way to Canada by now."

"I don't think so. I think she's still here, Tin."

"You mean, hiding somewhere in her costume?" he says. "Well, that gives me the willies. Thanks a lot."

"You're welcome."

"I still can't believe Constantin killed Eddie and then took his own life." Tin loses his smile. He takes my arm.

"Hurry up," he says, pulling me forward. "Lillian's waiting for us."

"I thought the sheriff was going to talk to me," I say, shaking my head, but picking up my pace. "Where is he?"

"He left first thing this morning along with the coroner. He agreed to interview you tomorrow or the next day down at the station. Tony said it was just a formality."

We continue walking and Tin muses for a moment. "I wonder why Tony didn't wait until the sheriff was here to arrest Rosie. Wasn't very smart."

"Because 'Y' is a crooked letter that can't be straightened out," I answer.

Tin looks at me, puzzled.

"Never mind," I say, linking arms with him again. "That's just one of my smart aleck answers. It's too late now to do any speculating one way or the other. We'll just have to see how it turns out."

"'Speculating.' That one of your daily words? What does it mean?"

"To speculate. It means to reach a conclusion without sufficient facts or reason."

"Sounds a little like faith," he answers amiably.

"That's more of a strong belief in a supernatural power or powers that control destiny."

Tin laughs."You're a walking dictionary, Jeri."

I return his laughter. "And a show off."

He glances my way. "Never that, Jeri, never that. I know you learn things for yourself alone. Sometimes you share them with others."

I give Tin a grateful look, aware and not for the first time, of how well my friend knows me.

"Tin, have you heard how's Ioana doing? Is she okay?"

"Well enough. She stayed in the First Aid Tent last night with Doc and the nurse. Sheriff wanted to take her with him, hand her over to Welfare, but Doc talked him out of it for now. Mentioned an aunt in Chicago the kid really loves, so they're contacting the woman, asking her to come here. I guess Ioana will be going back with her. It's all pretty sad."

We walk the rest of the way in silence.

Lillian brings out a tray laden with hot tea and sandwiches and carries it to one of the picnic tables nearby. Chatting and scolding us while she serves, she wears a smile on her face, but her eyes are red-rimmed.

"You're going to sit out here," she says to Tin. "'Cause you know there's no men allowed inside. But I made you some extra sandwiches." She winks at my friend. "Won't do for you to waste away. And they're your favorite. I got hold of some Virginia ham. Hot coffee for you and tea for my girl, who's going to learn to mind her own business and take care of herself for awhile. No more running around like Mr. Sherlock Holmes."

"But I'm her Watson, Lillian. What about me?" Tin says, grinning in my direction.

"I want you both to stop this meddling. Right now, you hear?"

I want to reach out and hug her, thinking about her son once again. I missed mail call yesterday and today, so when

Lillian goes into the railway car for mustard, I ask Tin about her and any letters.

Tin Foot shakes his head. "It's been almost two weeks. Doris said she caught Lillian crying last night, when she didn't think anyone was looking."

I find myself saying a silent prayer for Duane. Then I add my three brothers. I pray for all our boys over there. This damned war.

I eat half a sandwich and Tin has three, while I tell him everything that happened last night. Except what I found in the diary. If I let go of that one, her secret will be out in the open. I can't do that to her.

Afterward, Tin returns to his compartment. I hope he's satisfied with my answers. I do a strenuous ballet barre for forty-five minutes and finish with some work on the monkey bars set up in the practice area, completely mine due to the rehearsal.

I avoid the trapeze. I'm not sure why but I can't even look at it. It reminds me of Rosie. A wave of anxiety shoots through me. Where is she? I drop down to the ground, ready for a shower.

On my way back from the practice area, I spot two young Negro soldiers standing together. The short and compact one is looking around, his face full of befuddlement and confusion. He's holding the arm of a taller boy, graceful and well groomed, despite the bandages covering his eyes and forehead. I recognize him from his photos right away, even with half his face swathed in bandages.

"Duane!" I yelp and break into a run to him. "Oh, my God! It's you, isn't it?"

To the two soldiers' astonishment, I throw my arms around Duane in my excitement.

"Miss? Miss, are you all right? What are you doing?" the shorter soldier stutters, looking around him. A white girl hugging a black boy. Not done, even up North.

"Do I know you, miss?" Duane asks, cocking his head, as if his ears will give him more information.

"You are Duane Washington, right?"

"Yes, I am. I'm looking for my mother --"

"I know! Lillian! Come with me," I interrupt. "I'm on my way back there now."

I grab his arm and start tugging him toward the Virgin Car. The other soldier follows. We're stared at by some of the performers, but most just go about their business.

My happiness bubbles over and my mouth never shuts. I babble about how much Lillian has missed him, how proud we all are of him, on and on, pulling him to the car. He smiles all the time, sometimes breaking out into easy laughter; a nice kid. When we get close to the Virgin Car, I shout out Lillian's name repeatedly.

She steps out on the upper step, looking around."Who is that yelling? What's on fire around here?" Her focus hones in on the three of us. Then she lets out a scream they could probably hear in New Jersey and runs down the stairs toward us.

"Duane! Duane, my boy! My son!" She throws herself in his outstretched arms, nearly knocking him over. He lets out a laugh to the heavens.

"Mama! Your voice never sounded so good to me."

They hug so tightly, I don't know how they manage to breathe. The other soldier and I look on, sharing in the mother-son happiness.

Lillian breaks away and notices his bandaged eyes for the first time. "What happened? Oh, God. My boy is blind?" She puts her hands over her mouth, as if the words have escaped before she can recapture them.

The smile leaves Duane's face. "Just for awhile, mama. The doctors say I'll get my vision back again in a couple of months." He forces his smile again. "Maybe not all of it, but most of it."

Her lower lip quivers, but her voice is strong. "Well. They should know, boy, and we'll leave the rest up to the Lord. Come sit down, Duane," she says, pulling him toward the table and chairs. She notices the other soldier. He removes his hat and gives her a nervous nod.

"And who are you, young man?" she demands.

"Good afternoon, ma'am," he says. "I'm his friend, Lamar."

"Oh, mama, I'm sorry," Duane says, groping around for his friend's hand and pulling him near. "This is Lamar Baker. He brought me here. There wasn't any other way I could get here."

"I'm on furlough and I live just fifty miles south of here, ma'am," Lamar has a shy smile.

Lillian takes his hand in hers. "Thank you, Lamar, for bringing my son back to me."

"It was nothing, ma'am. He's my friend."

"Sit down, both of you," Lillian orders. Lamar helps Lillian maneuver Duane into a wooden chair. Lillian gives him a grateful look. "Are you boys hungry?"

"Oh, yes, ma'am," Lamar says.

"We could eat a horse," Duane adds.

"We ain't had nothing since yesterday." Lamar looks guiltily at me. "Couldn't find no colored restaurants 'round here."

"I've got some sandwiches. Let me go --" Lillian begins.

"I'll get them, Lillian," I interrupt, leaping onto the platform. "You sit right there and visit." Inside, I grab six of the sandwiches Lillian made for the girls after rehearsal. I hand them down and watch Lillian offer the plate to Lamar and put a ham sandwich in Duane's hand. The two boys, not much older than eighteen, take huge bites of the food, while Lillian hugs and kisses her son.

"Mama!" Duane laughs. "I can't eat with you grabbing on me like this."

"Too bad, too bad," she says. "That's what you get, child, for being gone so long."

I leave the small scene feeling happier and more light-hearted than I can remember.

Chapter Twenty-six
4:15 p.m., Tuesday

I wait in the darkened aisle and watch hundreds of American flags and USO banners transform the Big Top into a sea of undulating red, white and blue. No soldier is turned away, so the house is beyond full capacity, spectators spilling out into the entrances and exits, getting in the way. They're rowdier than usual, too: clapping continually, stamping their feet, voices ringing out with need and anticipation. I feel tension sparking the air, almost a bloodlust.

Roustabouts and security do more crowd control than usual. I don't think any of us are happy performing for this group, patriotic as we feel. We could lose control of them at any moment. Even the animals appear to be on mob alert.

Along with the rest of the girls, I'm dressed in my red and hot pink costume, awaiting my cue for the web, glad the end of the show is near. There's so much noise and revelry going on, it's difficult to understand the words of the ringmaster, just an overriding blast of a mangled, micro-phoned voice.

The lights are focused on the high wire act in the center ring, about to begin their last, chilling trick. No matter how many times I see it, my heart beats faster within me. They are truly defying death at every performance.

Dressed in a sequin-covered green and white leotard, the lead man begins to cross the thin wire riding a bicycle, balancing himself with a long, slim pole. Standing behind him on the back of the bike is another man, similarly dressed. Posing prettily on the handlebars sits a woman in a green and white tutu, legs cross, toes pointed, a glittering tiara upon her head. Welded to the bottom of the bike's frame is a metal pole, which hangs down five feet. Attached to the bottom of the pole is a swing.

Everyone, audience and fellow performer, waits in anticipation, enthralled. For the first time during the show, there is a short span of silence as the bicyclist nears the center of the wire. The acrobat mounts the bicyclist's shoulders, pushes up into a handstand and balances himself, body pointing to the ceiling. The woman slides down the pole to the swing, sits down, and gently swings to and fro, waving to the crowd. The bicyclist balances all three and the bike on the wire. Then he cycles to the other side. Forty feet below, there is no safety net, not now, not ever. One slip and all three could be dead.

The crowd cheers wildly. I think I hear a voice call out my name, but it's lost in someone's whoop. The assemblage is on its feet, yelling and cheering, stamping on the wooden platforms. The finale music swells to a deafening crescendo. The high wire act is over and it's time for me to go to my spot. My name is shouted out again and this time I pause and look around me. They have already lowered the twenty-five ropes into the perimeter aisle surrounding the three rings when Tin Foot comes up behind and spins me around.

"Jeri, you're late! The girls are ready to start the climb. What's the matter with you? Get in the air!"

I follow Tin Foot, run into place, and throw off my cape. I'm the girl at the far outside of the ring, off the exit aisle. The lights dim on the ground, as usual, with the spotlight hitting the ringmaster in his red coat with gold buttons and black pants, top hat and whip. He introduces us again as the death defying beauties, his voice magnified to an ear-splitting level. Spotlights pop up on us as we climb the ropes in unison.

Preparing for our first trick, I look down and spot Whitey on the ground below. He's fighting to get nearer, waving and shouting to me from the middle of the crowd and all its chaos. Soldiers and civilians press in on him, jockeying for a better view, but he continues to force himself closer, looking up at me the entire time. I can only see him from the neck up.

The music for our routine commences. I put my left foot in the loop in time with the music, push out with my right leg on the taut rope into an arabesque and smile down at the raucous crowd.

Whitey shoves a sailor aside, exposing his upper body to me for the first time. He gestures to his chest. There, outlined in blood, a long, ragged slash runs from one side of his shirt to the other. I falter and almost lose my balance. Then he turns and fights his way from the tent, like a man possessed.

As horrified as I am, I have to put it out of my mind. One wrong move and it's possible to tumble to the ground. Because a web artiste holds onto a rope or loop and is supposed to never let go, there is no net underneath. When you're forty-feet in the air, there's no room for error; you need to be in top form. A girl fell six or seven years ago to her death. She was high on some narcotic, but still. It's a gruesome way to die.

The audience is appreciative, and after several catcalls, they settle down. There's even a cool breeze blowing in from the entrances, circulating the air. After a few languid tricks to violin music, a drum roll sounds and the lights go to complete black below, lighting only us. This is the time for the audience to give us their undivided attention for our final trick. I've been trying not to think about Whitey, but he flits back into my thoughts no matter what.

Tin Foot spins the rope, faster and faster. I hang onto the loop with one hand, feeling myself become horizontal and sense the audience focusing on the twenty-five twirling tops. This is the most dangerous time of the routine and after doing it for two years, I know the ways of it down to a micro-second. I whirl and whirl and then it's time for it to slow.

I feel a hesitation in the twirl, a moment when the momentum is not continued. For an instant, I drop down but the slack picks up again only to intensify. The spin becomes faster and faster. I can hear the final fanfare signaling the end of the routine and applause from the audience but my spinning does not slow down. I hang on but begin to get dizzy. This is motion the human body can only take for so long before it begins to respond adversely.

I seize at the loop with my other hand, almost unable to breathe. The force of the spin is so severe I'm losing my grip using both hands. The music for the jugglers begins in the center ring and around me the lights go to black. Still I spin.

Almost when I think I'll be hurtled out to space, there's yelling below and the rope jerks. The spinning stops abruptly and my body crashes against the web rope. I cling to it, dizzy and disoriented, unable to comprehend what's going on. It takes me a second or two to focus and look down.

Below is a ruckus taking place between two of the brown-suited roustabouts. Tin Foot is nowhere to be seen. It's hard to tell with the lights so low but one of the roustabouts seems to be hitting the other. Then one leaps onto the web and pulls himself up, kicking at the man below. His foot makes one connection with the other roustabout's face and that one falls to the sawdust, clutching his nose.

Fear grips me. Even in the dark I sense it's no roustabout climbing the rope, but Rosie. Then I hear her call my name interspersed with obscenities. Though I can't see the expression on her face, I know it's murderous.

I hesitate, unsure of what to do. In one brief flicker I see Whitey run to the bottom of the rope, Tony right behind him. Tony is pointing something up at the climbing figure but I don't have time to think about it.

Rosie is upon me, yanking and scratching at my legs and feet. She seems determined to pull me down, even if it means she has to go with me. Woozy as I am, I have to do something. I kick at her but she's strong, stronger than I am at that moment. She seizes both my ankles, tugging at them with all her might.

My screams have a hollow sound, drowned out by the music and the laughter from the audience. I can't sustain her weight added to mine for much longer; I'm already tired. I get a lucky kick in at her jaw and she drops down a foot or two.

I know I can't go down. I have to go up. I begin the climb to the top of the rope, heading for the canvas sky, sixty feet in the air. Rosie is close behind. I never look back, but I listen to her wild, hysterical laughter. About ten feet higher the rope is no longer covered with soft fabric. Stiff hemp tears at my fingers and the palms of my hands, even with my calluses. I keep climbing.

At the very top of the Big Top is a series of ropes supported by thick beams. These beams come into the center of the canvas like spokes in an oval-shaped wheel. They support all the rigging below.

Set up by the workmen when the tent is raised, a man on a crane checks the beams and ropes periodically. Other than that, no one ever goes up that high. If I can get to one of the ropes near the center, maybe I can cross over on a connecting one to another web and climb down. I have to try to reach it before Rosie gets to me; it's my only chance.

I grip one of the network of hemp ropes, trying to put the pain of my hands out of my mind. I walk hand over hand, feet dangling into nothingness, and move forward, never looking down.

About five feet before I come to the rope leading to safety, I hit a massive wooden beam, too large for me to wrap my arms around. It didn't look that big from far away but up close, it's huge. I'm at a dead end. I'll have to go back. Below, the nearby center ring is alive with the juggling comedy act and the music swells dramatically to their antics.

I turn around on the rope only to see Rosie less than ten feet away. She sees my predicament and laughs. She stops her hand over hand motion and begins to swing back and forth. I know what she's doing. When she builds up enough momentum, Rosie will come at me with legs spread apart and hit me like a projectile. Then she'll wrap her legs around me, adding her full weight to mine. There is no way I can possibly hold on if she does that. Rosie is willing to die just to insure that I do, too.

When I see her take her final swing backward and release herself forward, I pull my body up with shaking arms toward the ceiling, arching my back and flatten out against the rope, hoping it's enough. I close my eyes and feel a rush of air pass by, then a screech from Rosie, a sound of frustration more than fear.

I'm not sure what's happening. Someone directly below me starts yelling. There's a high-pitched scream and a hush comes over a section of the crowd beneath me. I wrap my legs around the barbarous hemp, turn my head and try to look down, but I can't see anything.

The juggling act and the music jolts to a stop, the lights go to black, and there is silence. A moment later the audience lights come up in the center and far left rings. People talk excitedly to each other. The ring that I'm hanging over is still dark.

Minutes go by. The hot, stifling air trapped right beneath the canvas ceiling is almost unbreathable. I don't know how much longer I can hold on. Just as a wave of panic overtakes my fatigue, I hear Tin Foot's voice shouting to me from across the Big Top's covering. He must be twenty feet away but his voice echoes near the fabric sky.

"Jeri! Jeri, are you all right?"

"Tin! Where have you been?" I feel a resurgence of energy brought on by hope.

"Rosie knocked me out when the lights went to black. Don't let go."

"I was afraid no one knew what was going on," I say, letting more fear show in my voice than I intended.

"We knew. I just couldn't get to you before now. Jeri, they're trying to get a portable net under you, but maybe you can make it back over to here. We'll go down your web together. Want to try that?"

I don't answer, but lower my legs and hold on with both hands. My arms quiver from exhaustion but I ignore the fatigue and the pain in my hands and inch toward his voice, walking hand over hand.

When I get there, Tin's waiting for me. He has a smile on his face, even though blood is dripping from his right temple. He lowers himself down the jaggy hemp and I follow. Soon I wrap my legs around the soft, outer covering of the web rope and know I'm home free, just another forty feet to go.

Chapter Twenty-seven
4:45 p.m., Tuesday

When we finally reach the ground, there is sporadic applause from some in the darkened ring. Most are still not too sure what's happening. I hear mumbling, with people half-paying attention to us and half-looking at what's going on within the other two rings.

I stumble and fall into Whitey's waiting arms. He envelopes me.

"Jeri, thank God," he says. "I knew she was somewhere close by. I tried to stop her."

I cling to him for a moment and feel Tin embrace us both. I'm shaking so much I can hardly stand. I hear Tony's voice from somewhere behind me.

"Jesus, I would have shot her but I couldn't get a clean shot. I couldn't get a clean shot."

"Never mind all that, Tony," says Whitey. "You take care of the aftermath. We'll take care of Jeri."

As he goes, I feel Tony touch me on the shoulder. "I'm sorry, Jeri. This is my fault. But you're going to be all right." I feel him brush by.

"Did she cut you, Whitey?" I lean in and whisper into his neck.

"She got me with an eyehook when I found her under the bales of hay. She ran off before I could stop her. I came to warn you, but when that didn't work, I went to get help."

The lights come up full in the center ring, lighting our way a little. I look around for Rosie but don't see her anywhere. The Ring Master makes an announcement from the center ring regarding 'an incident.'

A hush falls over the entire audience and then there is a sea of murmuring. He asks the audience for their indulgence and to remain seated and stay calm. Everyone obeys, sitting quietly and waiting. After a short time, the music starts up again in a half-hearted fashion, and the trained seal act picks up where it left off with perfect timing. In the far ring, comedic jugglers try to return to normalcy, but drop pins here and there. Sometimes the animals have the edge on professionalism.

The third ring, my ring, remains surrounded by subdued, but dark, bedlam. I can hear people running around, whispering in urgent voices. Tin Foot and Whitey guide me to the edge of a riser, place me down, and sit on either side of me protectively. The three of us huddle together, each hurt by a woman who is supposed to be one of us. I can't help but glance over at the center ring from time to time to the spangles, laughter and high-jinx, while I sit engulfed in darkness.

Vince runs over to us. I can't see his face too well but his voice is shaking. I wonder how he returned so fast from Advance but don't ask.

"Thank God you're all right," he says. "We were trying to get a hand-held net under you but nobody's ever dropped from that height. Thank God, you're all right," he repeats.

"Where's Rosie?" I ask. "Is she..." My voice trails off.

"They're about to carry her out. She's still breathing. That's all I know." He turns to Whitey. "Whitey, the elephants are feeling all the chaos and a few have even broken their chains. All we need is a stampede. You've got to do something." He sounds desperate.

"Of course, of course," he answers in a calming voice to Vince, who seems more stressed than the three of us.

"Forgive me, Jeri, I should go," Whitey says, leaning into me. "I wouldn't go unless I had to, believe me, but you're in good hands." He kisses me on the forehead, then rises. "Take care of her, Tin."

"Will do," Tin replies.

I grab Whitey's hand and squeeze it. "You take care of that cut on your chest."

He squeezes mine back, nods and smiles. I watch his retreating back and wish he could have stayed.

I notice a stretcher with someone under a white sheet being lifted by two men a few feet away. It's Rosie. Her hand dangles from under the cover, streaked with blood looking almost black in the dim light. I stare down at my own hands and legs, black blood streaking them, as well. A bout of shivering overtakes me and my teeth actually chatter.

Tin gets up and walks away just as the gurney with Rosie passes; maybe by coincidence or maybe he can't look. I focus on her hand, all that I can see of her, while flashes of a German movie, surrealistic and very disturbing, come to my mind. A beautiful woman had been turned into a freak, half woman, half chicken, by the carnival people she'd worked with and wronged. Am I in a carnival of freaks? I turn around and vomit into the darkness behind me.

Two women dressed in ballerina outfits sit tensely astride white horses in the shadows. The horses are nervous and whinny, pacing in place. Even the animals are used to a certain routine and this is anything but. Tony strides over to them, confident and filled with authority. The old Tony is back.

"You're going to be announced in a minute," he says to the two ballerinas. "Be ready to go. Do two sets of the usual routine but scrap the somersaults. The horses are too skittish." The women nod, grim mouthed.

Tin returns with my spangled cape and wraps it around me. I notice specks of blood on the fabric where he has held it. I search his face and hands, straining my eyes in the dimness. He wipes a handkerchief at the cut on his head with a hand torn and raw from climbing the hemp rope. But not as torn or raw as mine. His legs, covered by the costume, were protected, except for a scratch here or there. I don't want to look at my naked legs and hands. The adrenaline rush is fading; I wince and suck in air between clenched teeth, suddenly overcome with the pain and burning.

Tin says, "Doc's waiting for us, Jeri. Let's go. Can you walk?"

I nod and stand up, leaning against my friend. We trail Rosie's gurney to the First Aid Tent.

Doc is busy trying to deal with Rosie and get an ambulance for her, so I don't see much of him. The nurse cleans Tin Foot and me up, applying ointment and bandages to our legs and hands. She pumps me full of a pain-killer, which comes at me so fast I don't have a chance to refuse it. I hear her say it will only last a few hours, but I don't like drugs; I'd rather have the pain. In the on-coming haze, I'm told I won't be able to perform for two to three weeks, maybe four. Fortunately, she says, I can still use the tips of my fingers, so I have some mobility.

Back at the Virgin Car, I'm clucked over by Doris and Margie, who tell me Doc will visit later. Tony comes by, saying again and again he'll take care of my salary and for me not to worry. My salary is the last thing on my mind, if I've still got a mind. I'm just a drug-induced rag-doll.

The next few hours are long and dream-filled. Every half hour or so I wake up and open my eyes to see the worried blue ones of Doris or the anxious green ones of Margie staring back at me. Then they fuss with my covers, or offer me water. Go away, I think.

While I'm out, small pieces of the past come into my mind, disjointed mental images of everyone I know, detailed and lifelike. But mostly I dream about Rosie and Doc and how life twists and turns on us and we wind up doing things we never imagine we'll do.

The last dream is about the day in the bank and the little boy who is dead because of me. I cry in my sleep, as usual.

Chapter Twenty-eight
8:30 p.m., Tuesday

I wake up hearing the sharp sound of a dog barking under my window. I pull at my watch pinned to the curtains and see I'd been down for nearly four hours. I throw the covers back, remember my hands and legs, stiff and painful, and struggle to sit up. The effort is too much. I lie back down.

"Hey! Hey! Anybody here?" I call out to a supposedly empty sleeping car.

I hear Lillian running from her room in the front. I roll over on my side and look down at a face filled with worry and relief. She grins at me.

"Hay is for horses, not for young ladies," she says. "Now you lie back down. I'm here to take care of you and that's just what I'm going to do. I've made you a nice pot of tea. You stay still and I'll go get it." She turns on her heels and starts back for the kitchen in her rooms.

"I don't want to lie down, Lillian. I've got to go see somebody," I shout to her receding form, forcing myself up into a sitting position.

She wheels around and points her finger at me. "Jerull Dean, don't you make me come up there. Now you stay put until I come back with that tea."

"Yes, ma'am," I answer, and stay perfectly still until I see the last of her. Then I move one side of my butt forward and then the other, inching to the edge of the bed. When I get to the end, I swing my legs over the side. That small amount of effort causes the insides of my legs to burn underneath the bandages. My skin pulls like it's stretched too thin over my thighs. My hands don't feel much better. I rest for a moment, legs spread apart so they won't touch each other and take a couple of deep breaths, saying 'ow, ow, ow' every few seconds.

Lillian returns with a small tray laden with a pot of tea, a tea cup filled with the brew, milk and sugar on the side, and a plate full of cookies, all on the china she saves for Best Occasions.

She slides it next to me on the bed. "Now you just sit there, young lady, and drink that tea and eat those cookies."

"Yes, ma'am."

"I made them special for you. Blackstrap molasses. And the tea's Darjeeling. I know those are your favorites, so don't try to pretend they're not."

"No, ma'am."

"And don't you be ma'am-ing me like that or I'll take a switch to you. I know what you're planning to do. The minute my back is turned, you're going to sidle down from there and go off somewhere to do that meddling you do so well, that landed you here."

"Yes, ma'am," I smile at her. "I am."

She fights a returning smile and goes on, "Well, leastways, eat something before you go, child."

I pick up a cookie with my fingertips and take a big bite. Delicious. She's right. I do love her blackstrap molasses cookies.

"And use your napkin."

"Yes ma'am." I pick up the cloth napkin with the fingers of my other hand and brush my lips with it. It has been carefully washed, starched and ironed.

"Because God didn't raise you to be a savage," Lillian adds.

"No ma'am," I say, putting down what's left of the cookie and picking up the tea cup by the rim, not being able to pick it up by the handle. I swallow a big gulp and feel worlds better. Lillian's tea always seems to work magic on me. I look down at her staring up at me, with a twinkle in her soft brown eyes.

"Where's Duane?" I ask.

"He's sitting outside, waiting for me. Mr. Tony said he'd have someone drive us to that colored rooming house down the road. I know that place, heard all about it when we pulled into town last year. No son of mine is staying in that kind of squalor without his own bed linens, towels, a pillow, everything."

"A real dump, huh? Why can't he just stay here? The circus is a big place; there's always room for one more." I finish the tea and look down at her.

She's silent for a moment then reaches up to straighten the sugar, milk and cookie platter on the tray. "Mr. Tony says he's trying to make arrangements for him to stay here and bunk with someone, maybe take Coke's bunk until he comes back. Mr. Tony says Coke won't be back for three or four days."

"Well then, that solves the problem."

Lillian looks doubtful. "I know Mr. Tony is doing his best, but I don't think the other men in the car will let him stay with them, Duane being colored and all."

"Lillian! You can't believe…I can't believe…you mean some of our men actually…" My voice peters out, as the realization hits me.

"Maybe the war will change things. Duane, he fights side by side with the white boys now. That's got to count for something. Someday it will be different." She gives me a wistful look and changes the subject. I let her.

"Mr. Whitey was here a little while ago, looking for you. You were still sleeping, so I told him to come back later. He spent a few minutes getting to know Duane, while he was here. Such a nice man. He had Duane laughing in no time."

"Did he? That's good." Maybe it's the drugs, but I'm burning with anger over the insult to Lillian and her family, one of our own. The anger gives way to an almost overwhelming sadness. I stare down at the woman who is as close to a mother as I will ever know, wishing I could lighten her burden. Lillian fills the small cup with tea again and hands it to me. I drink it down, looking at her over the rim.

"Lillian, I have to get down and do something no one else can do for me, if you get my meaning. You'd better stand clear."

Lillian removes the tray from the bed and steps to the side. Still sitting on the edge of the bunk I roll over on my belly, legs suspended, and feel for the lower bunk with my naked feet. Once secure, I bend my knees and hop down into a plié. I try keeping my balance when I land, so I don't have to grab at anything with my hands. I just manage it, but I walk to the bathroom like a tinhorn that's been on a horse too long. Lillian is close behind. While I'm in the stall relieving myself, she stands in the doorway. I shout out to her.

"What have you heard about Rosie? Any news?"

"None and you put that wicked girl out of your mind. After you get done, I want you to crawl right back up in bed and --"

"I can't. I have to go see Doc, Lillian," I interrupt.

I hear her set the tray on the edge of the sink and walk to the stall door. When I come out, she hands me a soapy, warm cloth to wash my fingers, a cool wet one to rinse them off and a third dry towel, all the while talking a mile a minute.

"Why you have to go see Doc Williams? You feeling worse? What's wrong? You got a fever? You need some pills? I can go get them for you, child."

I finish drying my fingers, put my arms around her while guarding my hands, and give her a quick hug, loving every ounce of her.

"No, no. This is another thing you can't do for me. I have to go, Lillian. I'll be fine. I promise to walk slowly and be careful."

I hear familiar music coming from the Big Top.

"Listen to that. They're almost to the Elephant Ballet. Intermission will be here in another fifteen, twenty minutes. I've got to go."

I release her and glance down at my nightgown.

"Will you help me get into some clothes? I think I've got a full skirt somewhere."

She looks at me with a frown. "I will, but I don't like it."

"Then I want you to go be with Duane, Okay? And don't go anywhere with him yet. Let's see what we can work out."

Chapter Twenty-nine
9:00 p.m., Tuesday

I hobble across the back lot listening to the orchestra and the sounds of the throng inside the Big Top, another kind of music to me. The night offers little breeze, but the temperature has dropped ten or twelve degrees. I shiver in the thin sweater Lillian threw over my shoulders.

A full moon, brighter than I've seen in months, drenches everything around me in an unearthly, white light. The ghostly flutter of flags on poles over the Big Top, glowing but devoid of color, add to the eeriness.

Dark silhouettes of people stand around the Big Top in waiting mode. Some hold cigarettes, red-orange tips firing up only to go pallid again after the inhale. Exhaled wisps of silvery smoke look like they're being pulled up by the moonlight to become part of the translucent night.

In another ten minutes, the intermission will be upon us, the outside lights will come up full, and the concession stands will be dealing with lines of people clamoring for soft drinks, cotton candy and souvenirs. It's a chance for the circus to fill the coffers and for the performers to take a breather, a good thing all around.

I enter the First Aid Tent and find it empty. Back at Doc's office, I see his shadow through the canvas. He's sitting at his desk, leaning over, maybe writing something. I rap on the pole beside the flap and call out. When he hears me, he rises, comes over and throws back the flap.

"Jeri!" he says in surprise. "I was going to come over to see you in a few minutes." He scrutinizes me from head to foot. "Are you all right? What are you doing here? You don't look so bad, all things considered."

"I don't feel so bad, all things considered, Doc, so here I am."

"Astonishing!" he says, with a shake of his head. "Something like that would have laid me up for a month, at least. Let's go into the examining room. I'll check you over in there."

He steps past me toward a slightly larger sectioned off area, where I was brought earlier in the day. He opens the flap, stands aside, and gestures with slight impatience for me to go in.

"Come on, come on. Let's see what we've got. It's not that I don't trust Laverne. She's a fine nurse, but I like to see these things for myself."

I walk toward the room, with legs spread slightly apart, trying not to let them rub against one another. Inside I stand with my back to him, listening to him chatter on.

"Let me see how those wounds are coming along. In a top notch athlete, and that's what you are, Jeri, the rate at which wounds heal never ceases to amaze me."

He turns me around, puts his hands on my shoulders, and pushes me into a chair. "Sit down."

I obey, saying nothing. He draws a small stool on wheels from the corner, sits down and rolls over to me.

I watch him unwrap my legs with great care. I'm anxious, myself, to see how much permanent damage has been done. Relief spreads through me. My inner thighs, red and swollen, have only one or two deep gashes, the rest are scrapes and cuts, easily healed, leaving little or no scars.

Doc glances up into my face with a warm, professional smile, then bends over to check out my ankles, which are puffy, red, and scratched. He holds each one with a firm but delicate hand, as if they're made of porcelain, and examines them carefully.

I try to focus on the top of his head rather than the thoughts swirling around in my mind. Though his hair is still full on the sides and back, a pink scalp peeks through the thin brown hair laced with silver. I am struck by the fact that Doc is in the fall of his life, maybe early winter, and it makes my eyes mist over.

"Do you know the latest on Rosie?" I ask. "Lillian didn't and I haven't seen anyone else."

He removes my slop shoes and picks up both feet in his hands. I'm not sure he's heard me and am about to ask the question again when his voice stops me.

"The swelling should go down in a day or two, just keep your feet elevated whenever you can. What I've heard is her back is broken in three places," he adds, without looking up. "The word is Rosie will be paralyzed from the neck down for the rest of her life. That much they're pretty sure of."

I let out a gasp. He stops examining my feet and his eyes meet mine.

"She's lucky to be alive, Jeri, falling from that height. You'll forgive me if I'm not too sympathetic about it after what she tried to do to you. Somebody said she grabbed at one of the tightropes on her way down. It slowed her fall somewhat but she'll probably spend the rest of her life in an iron lung. She's lucky at that."

Trapped inside your body, unable to move, to feel, to be free, what kind of luck is that?

"I'm sure she'd rather be gone, Doc. I know that would be true for me."

"You'd be surprised the conditions people are willing to live under, glad to be alive. That's not true for all, but for most."

"Where there's life, there's hope? That sort of thing?"

"Something like that," he answers. He looks up at my face and allows a smile. "For the next few days, come by twice a day, once in the morning and once in the evening, to have the bandages changed and fresh ointment applied. It will give us a chance to talk about philosophy, my favorite subject."

I hesitate then say, "I don't think we share the same philosophy on some things, Doc."

He laughs, wheels around on the stool, opens a well-ordered drawer and removes a tube of ointment. He closes the drawer, turns back, and unscrews the cap, all the while considering me.

"What's bothering you, Jeri? I know you've been through a lot, but there's an expression on your face I've never seen before."

I shake my head and look down, not knowing how to start.

"Come on, Jeri," he prods. I feel his warm voice washing over me, like a sun shower. "Tell me what's on your mind. You look like you're carrying a heavy burden."

I lick dry lips and study the hands that don't even look like they belong to me. My voice comes out in no more than a whisper.

"I was such a smarty pants. I was going to use my brain to reason things out. I thought, maybe I can't make it right but I can find out what happened. Absolve the innocent, ferret out the guilty. Something like that."

He starts applying ointment to my feet. "Everybody around here calls you 'The Thinker' for good reason. You've got a better brain than most."

"Maybe so, but I've made several mistakes, Doc. The really big one was starting at the back of Catalena's diary instead of at the beginning."

"That sounds like a rational approach to me, especially if you want to know about recent events," he says, moving on to examine my legs. His voice is as soothing as the salve.

"Maybe I could have saved her if I started reading from the front. Maybe..." I break off.

Doc thinks for a moment. "Probably not," he says quietly.

"Once I started at the beginning, I found out it wasn't Eddie who made her pregnant. Eddie was just her friend and trying to help her. He paid for it with his life."

"I thought Constantin killed Eddie to keep Catalena from running away with him," Doc says.

"Yes."

He goes on, "And then the sick bastard took his own life when the horror of what he'd done and his daughter's suicide was too much for him."

"No."

Doc shakes his head and pushes back on the stool. Squeaky wheels cry out from the sudden movement, echoing throughout the tent. Doc grimaces.

"I've got to oil this stool." He reaches for a fresh tube of ointment and a roll of bandages. "So you don't think he killed himself?" Doc asks.

"No. That might be the case with a lot of men, but not Constantin."

Doc's hand freezes in midair. Then he smiles, staring back at me. "Why not? Everything says that he did, including his suicide note."

"There was the angle of the knife as it entered his body, for one thing. When a person commits suicide, the strike goes into the abdomen from down to up, like this. Better leverage." I demonstrate with hands that feel foreign and useless to me, gesturing with a thrusting motion into my gut.

"But Constantin's wound was much higher than a self-inflicted strike," I say. "And it went from up to down. Like this."

I put my hands together again and hold them over my head. I strike downwards toward Doc's chest, stopping an inch or two away. Sharp pain courses through the soft parts of my hands, but I ignore it.

"It would be that way, Doc, if someone else did it."

His eyes widen and he looks down at my hands still hovering over his chest.

"That's not much to go on, Jeri."

"Then there's the note. It was in English. Maybe it won't occur to the sheriff, like the angle of the knife. In my opinion, most people would probably write a suicide note in their native tongue, the way Catalena did her diary. But mainly, there's the structure and words. Phrases like 'It is only fitting I go the way of my daughter, by my own hand.' That's something only a person comfortable with English and probably well-educated, would write. Even though the note appears to be in his handwriting, Constantin had only been in this country a year. His English was negligible. And lastly, as you say, underneath it all he was a sick bastard. He would never take his own life."

"You're sure?"

"I'm sure. Last night, when we found you covered in blood, you told us you heard Constantin scream and went to his tent to try to help. But later on, you told Tony Ioana had come running to you, that she told you her father had gone crazy. You said you went off searching for him only after you gave her a sedative to calm her down. That you found him already dead."

Doc picks up a pair of scissors and starts cutting strips of gauze for bandages. "Is that what I said? I can't remember, so much happened."

"I think what you told Tony is some of the truth but not all of it. Ioana did come to you in the middle of the night looking for help. And there was a scream, the one I heard when I was on my way to get Tony. But it came after you went looking for – and found -- Constantin."

"Go on." He lays strips of gauze on the edge of the desk in careful rows.

"Possibly the note was written while you were waiting for the sedative to take effect on Ioana here in the First Aid Tent. You're a good calligrapher. Vince mentioned it in your file. And Constantin's posters carry his signature and they are everywhere."

"You're saying you don't think it was suicide?"

"It was murder. You killed him, Doc. You."

Doc stares at me, unblinking. Then he sits back in the chair, bringing his hands together, as if in prayer. His reply is unemotional.

"You're being silly, Jeri. You're always pointing out the need for a motive. A motive is all, you say. Why should I kill that man? What reason could I have?"

"Because he'd been raping his eldest daughter for months and was about to start in on the younger one."

Doc's face drains of color and he wavers.

I lean forward. "I think Catalena told you when she was first brought here about her father and what he was doing to her. That's one of the reasons why you took her death so hard, why you felt you had to avenge her."

Doc has a faraway look in his eyes again, much as he does when he talks about the First World War or his wife. A myriad of emotions cross his face, some almost too painful to watch, but I will myself not to avert my eyes. He gulps and snuffles, wiping at his nose and face with a hand. Finally, he extends his other hand palm out to me, as if asking for more time to get himself under control.

I watch him push on the little stool over to the other side of the room and reach under a sheet-covered table for a half-full bottle of whiskey hidden there. I wait while he unscrews the top and pulls a long drink, my heart racing every moment. He looks down at the bottle in his hand and finally speaks.

"After Catalena miscarried, I tried to comfort her. She was so...so..." Doc searches for a word. "...desolate. I told her she could have another baby someday. She said she was 'glad it was gone; it was an unclean child.' I asked her, what does that mean, 'unclean?' She wouldn't answer, just turned her head away. Then it occurred to me what it would take to

make a baby unclean. There is a higher percentage of spontaneous abortions in cases of incest, Jeri. Did you know that?" He looks at me. I shake my head and he goes on,

"I asked her outright, 'Has your father been forcing himself on you? Is he…was he… the father of this baby?' She wouldn't answer. I told her I could go to him, make him stop, report him to the authorities, if I had to. She cried and cried. I never saw a more miserable, unhappy girl. But she never admitted it outright."

"So you weren't sure?"

Doc is silent and I don't know if he's heard me. I open my mouth to repeat the question but am cut off by his barely audible words.

"I wasn't one hundred percent sure even after she'd hanged herself. The truth is I couldn't quite believe it, so I left it alone." He covers his face. "I should have done more when I had the chance, should have seen what he'd done to her, helped her."

"You didn't know. I didn't know last night, myself, until I read it in her diary. Not many of us think that kind of thing."

"The man was a monster," Doc says, his voice filled with more anger than despair. He gets up and paces around the small, makeshift room. "I should have acted right away. Now that the older girl was dead, he started in on Ioana. She's only twelve, a child. She wasn't even sure what he was doing but she told me he kept trying to touch her. She told me that for about a month before Catalena died, her sister had started locking the door between the compartments. Night after night, she would hear her father call out, begging for Catalena to unbolt the door but Ioana never knew what was going on." Doc's voice falters. "When Ioana came to me and told me all of that, so small, so frightened, I knew what needed to be done. It wasn't revenge, Jeri. It was protection."

"But you could have told the sheriff --"

"That moron?" Doc explodes. "Maybe he would have believed the child and maybe not. Maybe he would have done something and maybe not. It's so sordid and we're too puritanical a country. We don't want to believe this sort of thing happens."

"But there's the diary. It's proof. We can show it to the sheriff. It will--"

"And the little girl," he goes on, as if I haven't spoken. "Don't you think she'd been through enough? Should we cart her family secrets before the world at large like a sideshow, so she has to endure even more shame and horror? Isn't it enough that she's lost a mother and a sister?"

"But now she's lost her father, too."

Doc makes a sharp, hissing sound. "Not much of a father, Jeri, believe me. From what she told me, he was always cruel or indifferent, except after Catalena died. Suddenly he was paying attention to her when they were alone together, stroking her cheek, or her thigh, pressing her to him. She said he came into her room one night and kissed her on the mouth. It was sickening. Ioana was confused and scared. She came running to me for help. She needed my help. I did what I had to do."

He stops talking, his final words resonating again and again until I think I'll scream from the sound of them. Doc looks over at me, deflated again, his voice sad and far away.

"Poor Jeri. I'm so sorry. I'd hoped you'd never find out but I should have known. You're such a smart girl. It's hard to keep anything from you," he says with something akin to pride in his tone.

I try to speak, but my mouth is too dry.

"Would it make any difference to you if I told you that I only have a few months to live?" He points to the whiskey bottle. "It's the demon rum or, in my case, the demon whiskey. I saw a specialist in New York last winter. Liver. He told me if I changed my ways, I might have a year. Less if I don't." He leans over and takes another swallow. "You can

see I didn't." Doc reaches in a pocket and pulls out a round vial.

"This is for the pain. It affects your motor nerves, makes you act just like you're drunk, but when I take it, no one can tell the difference." His laugh is hollow. "I would say I have perhaps six weeks before I need to be hospitalized. It will be quick after that."

I'm breathing so fast, I think I start to hyperventilate. At any rate, I feel dizzy.

"I'm sorry, Doc," I manage to get out.

He waves me off. "Maybe you can see why I did what I did. I have nothing to lose." He rolls over on the small three-wheeled stool again.

I feel a heaviness in my chest, the unrelenting weight of sorrow. I know it well.

"So you're going to die."

Doc picks up one of my hands in his, as if it is gossamer instead of flesh and blood, and leans in to me. His voice lightens, becoming almost conversational, as he swathes my hand in ointment.

"Jeri, it doesn't matter, because I am content. I finally did something that was enough. That disgusting human being can never hurt another child. I made a difference. If I had the chance to do it again, I would. There's good news in all of this, too. Ioana's aunt arrives soon to take her back with her. Constantin wouldn't let the woman near her before, even though the child has always loved her dearly. She'll have a good life with her mother's sister, or at least a chance at one." He sets my hand palm-up in my lap and studies my face.

"But as for you, my sweet Jeri, I seem to have put you in a bit of a pickle. What are you going to do?" It's as if he's talking about something as mundane as not paying a parking ticket.

"I don't know," I answer. I raise my arms in supplication, then drop them by my side. "I don't know what to do. I need to think."

"I understand," he says, nodding his head. "Meanwhile, let's finish taking care of those hands, shall we?" Doc smiles, using his professional voice. "You can think while I wrap them." He becomes very chatty, while I sit only half-listening.

"We have to make sure none of these abrasions get infected. You know, they have this new medicine called penicillin used to fight infection. They've started manufacturing it in large quantities for our boys at war. I'd hoped to get my hands on some of it for use around here." He laughs softly. "I'll try to get some before I leave."

I watch him bend over the palms of my hands, move my fingers and thumbs before he wraps my right hand. His touch is gentle, with never an unnecessary movement.

"You say you look on me as the daughter you've always wanted. Well, you've been the father I've always dreamed of having." My voice sounds young and detached.

"I know." He doesn't look up. "I didn't intend to put you in the position of wondering whether you should turn me in or let the good Lord take care of me. It's a tough choice for someone like you to make; you have such a strong, moral fiber. It was easier for me. My moral fiber disintegrated a long time ago." His eyes meet mine. "I'd like it if you understood just a little. I hoped to keep you out of it. But sometimes you can be too smart for your own good." He smiles and kisses me on the forehead. I pull back. He wears a look of surprise.

"Tell me what happened last night," I demand.

"Let it go, Jeri."

"Tell me. I need to know."

He finishes wrapping my hand before he speaks. As he starts on the other one, he says, "You're right about most of it. He'd come to Ioana's room last night, a drunken animal, carrying the Bible and chanting about who begat whom, covered her mouth with his hand and then, quite simply, tried

to rape her. She broke free, screamed and there was a pounding on the wall by the next compartment. She managed to get out the door while Constantin was distracted by them. She ran to the first place she thought of, their tent, and hid. He showed up and tore the place apart looking for her, while she cowered behind boxes. When he found her, she pushed some boxes over on him and fled, then came here looking for me. She knows I'm usually here, working on files. I've been getting them in order for my demise." He allows himself a faint smile, then continues.

"While she was telling me all of this, not fully comprehending what she was saying, I knew what I had to do. I gave her a sedative, waited for it to take effect, then took my service revolver from the bottom drawer." He looks at me with shame. "I keep it nearby because sometimes I toy with putting the gun to my head and --"

I wince.

"Sorry. That's neither here nor there. My plan was to shoot him outright and be done with it. There were no thoughts of making it look like suicide until later. The first place I looked for him was where Ioana left him, their tent. I went inside and there he was dead drunk, sound asleep on the floor. He woke up and lunged at me before I could get the revolver out of my pocket. We struggled. He was a strong bugger and I'm not in the best of shape. He threw me to the ground. Then he seized one of his knives lying on the counter and came at me, all the while ranting in broken English that I couldn't have her, she was his, he had killed before and would do it again. He tripped, fell down by the trunk and dropped the knife. That's when he screamed, out of anger or being thwarted; I don't know. Anyway, I picked the knife up right as he threw himself at me again. Before I knew what happened, the knife plunged into his chest, I'm sure, piercing his heart. He was dead before he hit the floor."

"So it was self-defence," I say quickly.

Doc reaches over, sips his whiskey and sets down the bottle. "You're clutching at straws, my dear. I went there to kill him, did so, and don't give a tinker's damn about it. He didn't deserve to live."

I try to absorb Doc's point of view. Do I share it or a part of it somewhere deep inside me? Spoken aloud, it seems callous, more judgmental than one person has a right to be.

"It came to me afterward." Doc says, "If I made it look like suicide, it might be better. No one had to know the shameful things he'd done. It might be better for Ioana. I could watch out for her until she got settled in her new life. I looked around for something to write on but there wasn't anything. Then I remembered I had my notebook in my pocket, as usual, for one of my many obsessive thoughts. Several of his posters were around, so I imitated his handwriting as best I could. I'm pretty good at it, as you say. It didn't occur to me that he probably would have written it in Romanian. Not that it made any difference. I don't know any Romanian. I didn't think about the blood on the note or my pants, either. I guess I'm a better doctor than a killer." He lets out a small, ironic laugh.

"Where is the notebook now? Do you still have it?"

"I threw it in one of the trash bins last night. The cover was spackled with his blood."

"They do a trash pick-up and burn every day," I say, thinking out loud. "It was probably incinerated sometime this morning."

"I guess so." He rises, looking at my hands and legs appraisingly. "We're finished for now."

I stand up and face him. "I can't condone what you've done, Doc. You killed a man and tried to cover it up."

"I know." He pauses. "I excuse none of it. You must do what your heart dictates, my dear Jeri. I accept that. Whatever you decide, I'll abide by."

Done with the conversation, he begins to clean up the examining table and throw away the soiled bandages. Doc seems oblivious to my presence. I make my way to the exit, listening to him straighten up the small room.

Tony hired me to find the killer of Eddie the Clown. I did that. My part in this nightmare is over.

Or is it? Doc became Constantin's judge, jury and executioner. If I say nothing, he'll go scot free, the killer of another human being. But if I turn Doc in, am I being his judge, jury and executioner?

Even though Doc seems content, even blasé, about me determining his fate, I hesitate in the doorway, reluctant to leave, reluctant to leave it like this. But that's just what I do; I leave it like this.

Chapter Thirty
8:00 a.m., Wednesday, July 8th

I toss and turn much of the night, but fall into a heavy sleep around four. When I finally open my eyes, both Doris and Margie are staring at me. Both so tall, they don't need to stand on the lower bunk to look into my upper.

"Hey there, Toots," Margie says, batting her green eyes and turning her head from side to side, tossing her golden hair every which way.

"Are you, as the Northerners say, up and at them, Sugar?" asks Doris, waving at me with graceful hands tipped in red lacquered fingernails.

"Hay is for horses, Margie. That's what Lillian says," I reply, forcing a smile and swinging my legs over the side of the bunk. "And I'm up, Doris, but I don't know how at 'em I am."

Doris laughs. "I'll help you down." She can't decide what part of my body is undamaged enough for her to touch and makes a grab at my waist.

"Wait, wait," I say, getting thrown off balance. If I fall on her, it won't do either of us any good.

"I can do this myself. I've done it before." I roll over, feel for the lower bunk with my foot and hop down. It's a lot easier to do than yesterday. I glance around. Except for the three of us, the car is empty.

"Where is everyone?"

"Rehearsals, hon, all except the showgirls. We're due at nine-thirty call," says Doris.

Margie jumps in. "They have to show the new girl what Hot Stuff does around here. That's you, Toots. They've cut a lot, too, until you get back in the swing of things. Jesus, you do a lot in this show. Who knew?"

"Well, me for one," I chirp.

"We should have been suspicious," adds Doris, looking at Margie. "With all those costumes she totes around."

Margie becomes serious. "Listen. Speaking of being suspicious, I want to apologize to both of you for defending Constantin the way I did. I never thought--"

"Oh, hush up," Doris says, fluttering her hand in Margie's face. "None of us did. Besides, Sugar, if every man in the South strangled the boy who got his daughter pregnant, there would be no weddings at all, shotgun or otherwise."

She and Margie whoop with laughter. I join in, but feel guilty for keeping the truth from them. The baby wasn't Eddie's but Constantin's. I'm not sure if anybody besides Doc and me will ever know that, so I laugh loud and long, in defense of it all.

"Oh, God, you are such a hoot, Doris," Margie says, wiping the corners of her perfectly made up eyes. "No wonder we keep you around."

We sober up and look at each other.

"It's all so sad, though, isn't it?" Margie's voice is soft and honest. It packs all levels of truth in its simplicity. I can only nod. Doris looks away, eyes glistening.

"Let's not dwell on the past, ladies," says Doris, after a moment. "As my mama says, nothing can be done about it and it can only drag you down."

"Besides, we need to fill Jeri in on what's happening right now. I'll start," says Margie, clearing her throat in a pompous way. "Now that Rosie has proven herself a total nut job, I got my job back. You're looking at your new/old Section Captain. No applause, girls. Your turn," she says, turning to Doris with a bow.

"All right," Doris drawls, fluffing her shoulder length, platinum hair, which is being worn down today. "Tony is in town signing a contract with the town council. They're going to keep the show here for another week. And he's being backed by the sheriff."

"You're kidding," I manage to say.

"Cross my heart and hope to die, stick a needle in my eye."

"That sounds gruesome," I say. "What did I miss?"

Margie takes over. "Seems this burg hasn't been so razzle-dazzled since they put indoor plumbing in at City Hall."

"What Margie is trying to say and I will put it into plain Southern English," Doris drawls, "is people are flocking from miles around to see the circus and spending a lot of money in their town, too. Tony told me the merchants have never had it so good."

"You and Tony seem to be having a lot of conversations for a man you're not talking to," I tease.

She grins and winks at me. "Well, he's not off the hook yet, not by a mile, but he's trying to make amends. He wants to buy me a present. I'm thinking of a Blackglama mink coat or maybe sable."

"Just what you need in Florida," I remark.

"You and your skins, Doris. Give me rocks, anytime," said Margie, flashing a diamond ring somebody or other gave her. She looks at her wristwatch. "Gals, I'm on the move. Got to hitch a ride before rehearsal to Five Points. I need an Ameche."

"What's an Ameche?" I ask.

Margie looks at me with a combination of amusement and annoyance. "You never head the telephone is called an Ameche? Sometimes I think you girls live under a rock."

"Oh, right," I say. "Because Don Ameche played Alexander Graham Bell in that movie."

"Bingo! Give the girl a cigar."

"Make it a Tootsie Roll and it's a deal. So why the phone call?"

Margie loses her glowing smile. "I got a letter from my father yesterday. My seventeen-year old cuz wants to join the army. That's all we need, another Jew boy in Germany. He's an idiot but he looks up to me, so maybe he'll listen."

"Everyone looks up to you," I say. "You're six foot two."

Margie gives me a mock glare. She snatches the cloche from the top of her bunk, plops it on her head, and grabs her purse.

"Anyway, I need to go burn the wires. I'll be back in time for rehearsal." She throws a "ta, ta" back over her shoulders and heads for the door.

"Good luck," I shout as it slams behind her.

"Come on," Doris says, putting her arm around my shoulder and pushing me forward. "I promised Lillian I would make you some tea before I left. I've never made tea before, so you'll have to be a mite forgiving."

I navigate the narrow hallway and try to avoid hitting anything harder than a mattress. I follow Doris to Lillian's makeshift kitchen. Each step feels a little easier to take. Maybe it is only a matter of time.

Surveying this former storage closet, it's hard to believe Lillian can coax the succulent things she serves us from using merely a dilapidated hotplate and miniscule refrigerator. Doris reaches out to the small sink, pours water into the kettle, sets it on the well scrubbed but banged up hotplate and plugs in the slightly frayed cord. I make a mental note to get Lillian a new hotplate for Christmas.

"Where is she?" I ask, leaning against the doorframe with my hip.

"She's getting Duane settled in Whitey's compartment. When Whitey heard some of the boys here didn't want to share their quarters with a Negro, he said he'd open one of the berths in his compartment for Duane to use until the boy has to go back to barracks. And he said if anybody doesn't like it, they can take it up with Emma. Whitey usually bunks alone and there are three unused bunks in there. But maybe you already know that?"

"You're fishing, Doris," I say. "I've never seen the inside of his compartment."

"Maybe when you're feeling better?" She smiles at me, revealing perfectly formed, white teeth. "It's a shame to let all those bunks go to waste."

I start to laugh and can't stop.

"What did I say, honey lamb? It wasn't that funny."

"Never mind, Doris. I've just got the giggles."

"Now you sit down over there, Sugar, and let me make you some tea. There isn't enough room for more than one person to move around in here, even when they know what they're doing."

I sit down at Lillian's table and watch the mile-high blonde go about the domesticity of making tea just like any other woman. Never thought she had it in her.

"You know, he is a wonderful man," she says suddenly. Holding two white cups in her hand, she turns to me.

"Duane?" I ask, deliberately misunderstanding her. I love putting Doris on.

"Whitey. He's a wonderful man, not that I'm interested. I've got Tony, if he behaves himself. But if I didn't, 'my, oh, my, what sparks would fly,' as my mama would say." Doris puts the cups down on the table with a bang and looks at me. "You think about that."

"I have thought about that. And you're right. Whitey is a wonderful man. I think he just might be the one for me."

Doris' eyes open wide and she bats mascara covered eyelashes at me. "Well! It's high time someone paid some attention to what I say. Tea's almost ready. Now where's that teapot got to?" For fifteen minutes Doris dithers in the small kitchen getting the tea made.

She sits down across from me and exhales enough air to have run up a flight of stairs. "How are you doing, Jeri? Really now, among best friends?"

I feel tears rush to my eyes. Doris leans across the table and strokes my shoulder but doesn't say anything. We sit like that for a full minute, me fighting for control, Doris stroking my shoulder.

Finally, I say, "I've got a lot on my mind, Doris. And I don't know what to do about... something."

She doesn't ask me any more questions but stands and looks down at me. "You take your time thinking, then. It will come to you. It always does. And you'll do the right thing. You always do. But let's go brush your teeth right now. You've got the breath of swamp water."

Afterwards, Doris helps me into a full-skirted dress I usually save for "good," a soft, green gabardine with buttons up the front. My bandages peeked out below on my legs and arms. Ten minutes later, she's off to rehearsal. Restless, I wander the lot for several minutes, listening to the music and noise coming from inside the Big Top, feeling odd not to be a part of it.

I find myself in the Big Cat section. Most of the cages are empty at this time of day. The cats are either outside being exercised in the main cage, sleeping on its many overhanging platforms, or performing. I don't think Old Kirby will be here but I'll look, anyway. I miss the old guy.

I approach the green and gold wagon and see Harold down on his hands and knees scrubbing the floor of the cage. Kirby sits in a corner, ears perked, watching him intently. Old Kirby seems to be back to his normal self.

I bend down and wave in Harold's face to attract his attention.

"Jeri! As I live and breathe," he says, obviously glad to see me. He pushes back on his haunches and throws the scrub brush into the sudsy pail with a kerplop. "I hear you had an exciting night." He looks me up and down. "But you look good. Can't say as I like your gloves and stockings," he says, with a wide grin, "But you're looking good."

I laugh at his joke about my bandages. That's how most circus people make it through the day, I've discovered. When things are so bad you could scream or cry or give up, you go for the joke. A sense of humor can lift the spirits and get you through almost anything.

"I came to see how Kirby is. He's looking good, too."

"Yeah," Harold answers, in a nonchalant manner, He picks up a bucket of clean water and throws it on the newly-washed spot. The water comes over the sides and down onto the base and wheels. "My boy's doing okay. The vet stopped by with a report. I never liked that man. Too glum." He turns to the lion. "Right, boy?"

"What report?" I ask. "What did it say?"

Before Harold answers, he reaches over for a clean rag, dries the floor, then spreads hay about. I wait.

"Ticker's not so good," Harold finally says. "What they call an enlarged heart. Vet said something like congestive heart failure. I got to keep him quiet. No more performing for my boy." Harold goes over and ruffles the lion's mane. The lion gently grabs the man's hand and they play together for a moment. Harold laughs and Kirby rubs his face against the man's body. I watch them share a fondness I rarely see shared between most people. I almost forget to breathe.

"I'm sorry to hear that, Harold," I whisper, holding onto the bars with my fingertips.

"What's that?" he shouts, arms wrapped around the big cat.

"I'm sorry," I mouth slowly.

"Psshaw," he exhales. "Old Kirby, he'll be all right, won't you, boy?" The lion half roars, half purrs at the man, in answer. Harold gets up and yanks down a chain collar and leather leash from a hook near the ceiling.

"My boy's got a lot of life left in him. Maybe another six months to a year." He puts the chain links around the lion's neck and snaps on the leash. "That's more notice than most folks get. We'll just make the best of what we got, won't we, boy?"

He opens the cage door and tugs at the leash. The lion obediently follows him out and down the steps. They pause, both looking at me. I come over, stand by the lion's side and stroke the coarse hair on his back with my fingertips, forcing a smile to my face.

"This collar and leash don't mean diddily," Harold pseudo-whispers to me, with a grin. "He could be free of it with one tug but it keeps the locals happy." Harold chortles. "Like that iddy-biddy chain on the elephant's foot, tied up to a stake. Like they couldn't break it, one, two, three, if'n they wanted." He sobers. "Sometimes I half wonder why they don't just pick up their foot and walk away."

"It's all in the mind, Harold," I say. "I think they stay where they want to be, like the rest of us."

"Maybe so. We're going over to the field behind the train. Kirby likes to sit in the grass in the sun. Maybe he pretends he's back on the plains of Africa like his ancestors. Don't know. But it makes him happy." He turns to Kirby. "Let's go, boy, time's a'wasting." The lanky man ambles away, followed by the rickety old lion. I watch them for a few minutes until they're on the other side of the train and out of sight.

"Jeri," I hear Tin Foot call. I turn around. He runs up and envelopes me in his arms, then breaks free. "I guess I should be more careful, with you hurt and all."

"I'm okay, Tin." I hug him back. "I won't be doing any web for a few weeks, but I'm fine." I look at the bandage on the side of his head and touch it carefully. "How are you?"

"Me?" he brushes it off. "Takes more than a conk on the head to bring me down."

"Thanks for saving my life, Tin."

He brushes that off, too. "I didn't do anything you wouldn't have done for me. Besides you already saved yourself. I just kept you company on the way down the ropes."

I can't speak. I can't say what I want or need to say. I just cover my face with my bandaged hands and try to keep from sobbing out loud.

"Jeri," I hear my friend say. "What is it? Are you all right?"

I let my hands down, look into his anxious face and nod.

"Let's sit down," he says. He guides me to the steps on Old Kirby's empty wagon, looks at the open cage door and then all around. "Where's the lion?"

"Sunbathing," I say, sitting down. Instead of sobbing, I laugh.

"You're sure you're all right?" He sits down beside me. "Shouldn't you be in bed?"

"No. I'm a little stiff and sore, but I'll be fine." I reach inside the purse on my waist gingerly, with the tips of my fingers, and pull out a small key. "Tin," I say reaching over to him, "while I'm thinking about it, try this key in the lock on the cage door."

Asking no questions, he takes it from my hand, stands and inserts the key in the lock. "Seems to work just fine." He looks down at me for an explanation.

"That's the key I found in Constantin's tent. I'm tying up loose ends." I reach out for the key.

"Why'd he do that?" asks Tin, putting it in my hand. "Why Old Kirby's cage?" He lowers down beside me.

"It was Constantin's warped sense of humor, I think. It was his last laugh on the boy. 'They gaped upon me with their mouths, as a ravening and a roaring lion.' That's another quote underlined in Constantin's Bible. I think he was in the process of putting Eddie inside the cage but got interrupted, maybe even by Catalena. We'll never know for sure why the body was left outside and Old Kirby's door open. Eddie, Catalena and Constantin are all dead and the lion's not talking."

"When did you suspect it was Constantin?"

"Pretty early on but it seemed so atypical for a parent to behave that way, I looked elsewhere. By the time I figured it out, he was dead."

"And by his own hand," Tin adds.

I'm silent.

"It seems only fitting after what he did to Eddie," Tin offers, his face thoughtful. "He destroyed three lives with that, Eddie, Catalena, and their baby."

Again, I don't say anything. Nobody knows the truth of what Constantin did to Catalena or whose baby it really was, except Doc and me. And it will stay that way.

"Ah, Jeri," Tin says then hesitates, looking down at his hands. We sit for a moment or two in silence. He looks troubled.

"What is it? You've got something on your mind."

He nods.

"Well, spill, as Margie would say."

"I got a letter from Ma a couple of days ago. I didn't get a chance to mention it to you, what with all that's been going on."

"Something's wrong." I reach out and touch him on the arm.

"Pop had a stroke."

"Oh, no," I gasp.

"Ma says he's going to be okay." He reaches inside the breast pocket of his shirt and pulls out a folded, two-page letter. "It happened a couple of weeks ago, but Ma didn't want to write me until they knew more. Already he can use his left hand, but she says he walks with a limp. He's got a cane. My pa with a cane." He shakes his head in disbelief.

"Oh, Tin, I'm so sorry."

He swallows hard, looking straight ahead. "I got to go home, Jeri. Ma says they need me. Pop can't run the farm anymore and Clayton's barely seventeen years old."

"Clayton's your youngest brother?"

"He's the only one left at home. The others are in the navy. The neighbors are helping out with the animals until I get there. I just talked to Tony. I leave next week."

I inhale a breath but it sounds more like a sob.

Tin never looks at me. "I've got to go, Jeri. They need me. Besides, this is my chance to go home."

"I know. I think somewhere inside, you've always wanted to go home. There are all those cows, just waiting to be milked." We laugh and I brush at my damp face. We still don't look at one another.

"I'll miss you." I reach out and touch his hand lightly with my gauze-covered one. "More than I can say. Nobody could have a better friend." We sit in silence for a moment.

"I always wanted to be more than a friend, Jeri. I guess you knew that."

I nod but don't speak.

Tin goes on, "I'd ask you to come with me, Jeri, marry me, help me milk those cows, but I don't see you ever leaving the circus. It's in your blood."

"Ninety-nine percent sawdust," I say. We both laugh, still not looking at one another.

I finally get the courage to look over at him. "In all honesty, Tin, can you see me as a farmer's wife?"

"In all honesty? No." Studying me, my carrot-topped friend smiles and his whole face lights up. "But I wish I did."

"Tin, I --"

"Jeri," he interrupts, "we've said it all. Time to get off the stage." He stands and hands me a carved cow painted white and black. "This is for you."

I turn the small statue over with my fingertips and consider the beauty of the workmanship through misty eyes. It's hard to believe it was just a lump of wood a few days ago. "It's beautiful. I'll treasure it always."

"I want you to have something to remember me by."

"I don't need anything to remember you by, Tin."

"Take it anyway. I'm heading for the real things soon enough." Tin Foot returns his mother's letter to his pocket. "I got to go and rehearse with the girl that's taking your place. Mitzi something or other."

"Mitzi Levine. First of May. This is a good opportunity for her. She's got promise."

"She's no Jerull Deane but she'll do," Tin says with a wink. "Rumor has it you're going to be taking over the center trapeze with the other featured performers when you're better."

I look up at Tin. "You mean I'll be taking Rosie's place?"

"That's what I hear."

"Boy, life doesn't miss a beat around here, does it?" I'm not sure how I feel about taking over for Rosie, wearing her costumes, sitting at her makeup table, doing her routines. Maybe I don't have to. Opportunities come, opportunities go. I want to be a star, but not this way.

"By the way," Tin says, "I seem to be spending my days telling you this, but Whitey's looking for you." He pauses. "I think he loves you, Jeri," Tin says, looking me in the eye. "And I think you love him, too, only you're too scared to admit it."

"I'm not so scared, anymore."

"Good."

I smile up into his face. "Don't you have some place to be?"

We both laugh and I watch my friend leave, wondering how I'll get through my days without him.

Chapter Thirty-one
9:50 am, Wednesday

I sit for a minute, then get up and make my way to Tony's office. People are running here and there, going about the business of the circus. Some wave at me, some stare, almost as if I'm an outsider. That's how I feel, not being a part of the routine. And I must look peculiar in my 'stockings and gloves,' as Harold would say.

I knock on Tony's door, uncertain of why I'm here. Do I want to find out about the rumors of me replacing Rosie? Or am I here to turn Doc in? Usually, I'm pretty sure about everything. I hear Tony's voice telling me to come in. When he sees me from behind his mammoth mahogany- carved desk, he jumps up and rushes to my side.

"Jeri, come in, come in. How are you doing? Are you all right? Doc says you're going to be all right and Doris says –"

"I'm fine, Tony, just fine."

"Sit down, sit down," he says, and guides me to a green, overstuffed chair in front of his desk. His voice is anxious and filled with what sounds like genuine concern and maybe more. Guilt?

"What can I do for you? Can I get you something?"

"I've heard a rumor that you want to replace Rosie with me. True or untrue?"

He returns to his desk, sits down and his face dons the Boss Man mask. "Untrue. We have no intention of putting you into that slot."

I am so relieved; I let out a long sigh of trapped air.

"Thank God. That's all I need in my life, following the ghost of Rosie around on a trapeze from town to town."

"I wouldn't do that to you, Jeri." He pauses, reaches for a small coffee pot on a hot plate and pours himself a cup. "Want some coffee?"

"I don't drink coffee, anymore. Makes me too jittery."

A fleeting smile crosses his face. "Strikes me that you've got nerves of steel."

I smile back. "Not really." I struggle out of the chair, still stiff and sore. "I'll get going now that I've got that one straight."

"Wait a minute. Sit down, Jeri. We do have another idea. Now that you're here, I'd like to run it by you, see what you think."

"Oh?" I sit down again and stare at him. "I think my nerves of steel may have just vanished. What is it?"

"I'm going to expand the Four Family Liroffs' act by adding the remaining two girls from the featured trapeze into their act. The girls need a place to go and the Liroffs need a bit of glamour. They're getting stale. They'll go in right after the spec."

I smile. "That sounds great. Everybody's happy. What do you want to run by me?"

He looks straight at me. "I'll just say it right out. We'd like to give you your own specialty trapeze act with Topsy."

"Topsy and I? On a trapeze?" I must look as shocked as I feel. For the first time in a while, Tony's laugh is genuine and warm, almost boyish.

"Not exactly. She'll stay on the ground. You'll be on the trapeze. What we're thinking of doing is combining your ability to work with her and your assets in the air. We'll pull the last two tricks you do with Topsy from the Dance of the Elephants, have you exit with everybody else instead of staying, and save those two bits for the opening act after intermission."

"So far, you sound nuts."

He ignores my comment. "You'll open your routine by coming in on Topsy. You'll do the underbelly trick, just the same, do the stand on her forehead trick, just the same. Only you won't get down. A rope will lower from the top of the center ring –"

"I'm in the center ring?"

"Yes, it's time for you to be there. We were thinking of putting you there even before all of this happened, Jeri. You haven't gone unnoticed." Tony smiles at me and sips his coffee. "Where was I? Oh, yes. Then a rope will lower, you'll grab it and you'll be lifted up in the air to a trapeze, maybe twelve, fifteen feet high. Not more than that because there won't be the traditional netting below, just a trampoline for safety. Once you're seated, you'll throw down a rope to Topsy and she'll pull you back and forth, just like the web sitters do."

"A pachyderm web sitter?"

"It won't take her long to learn how to do that trick plus a few other things that help you perform. Whitey's going to start working with her today on this."

"Whitey? He knows about this?"

"It was his idea about using you and Topsy together as an act." He looks at me. "You don't seem too happy. We thought you'd be pleased. Everyone knows how much you love Topsy."

"Of course, I love my girl. But it strikes me as a comedy act, where I'm to be laughed at, like the clowns."

"I see I haven't explained this well. There will be nothing to laugh at. Rather than using a catcher for you, which the other acts do, we thought you would perform by yourself on the bar, do some layovers, twists, balances, things like that -- what we've seen you do in practice -- peppered occasionally by Topsy helping out from the ground by pulling the swing back and forth. Your solo stuff is grand.

You have top-notch extensions and you're beautiful to watch, Jeri, glamorous and classy. That's where your strength lies. It's when you work with a catcher that it falls apart."

He stops speaking and studies me, trying to determine my reaction. He's measured out the truth in pretty strong doses, but truth it is and I have to admit it. I'm terrified of the swan dive and until I get over that, if ever, I'll never be able to work with others. Or be as good as I'd like. Tony watches the expression on my face as I think.

"Jeri, you've been with the Big Top for about two years, right?"

I nod.

"Do you realize how far you've come in such a short amount of time? You can do stuff people who've been in the circus all their lives can't do." He seems able to read my mind. "You'll get the swan, if that's what you want. It just takes more time. Meanwhile, do this act with Topsy. You two have magic together and the crowds love it. And we need it. We need more in the show. We're down two acts. You'll be doing management a favor and it'll be good for you. And I promise, you'll go as far as you want around here. You've got it all ahead of you. Don't rush it."

He smiles at me and I realize, once again, why he is a first rate Boss Man. He knows his performers inside and out and how to fit us into the show. With him, the Big Top always comes first. That's how it is with me, so I understand it. He crosses his legs, leans back in the chair and stares at me, a half-smile on his face.

I smile back. "Of course, I'll do it, Tony. But when did you and Whitey cook this up?"

"We were up half the night. We talked about that and…other things." I have an idea where he's going with this, so I sit back and wait. Now more unsure of himself, Tony tugs on his moustache before saying, "Jeri, he told me he told you about the hobo." He looks at me.

"Yes."

"He said you promised to keep it a secret, you wouldn't tell anyone."

"That was for him, not necessarily for you." My tone is light but I know my face conveys my intent. "It's better if you tell Doris, if she hears it from you, especially if you two are patching things up."

He shakes his head. "Never. It's in the past. I want to keep it that way. You know Jeri, the one good thing that's came out of that night was my winding up here. My father had been good friends with the circus owners, both in business and personally. He asked them to find a spot for me, initially as a bookkeeper, to keep me out of trouble." He laughs at the memory. "I've been hooked ever since I walked onto the lot. In eleven years I've worked my way up to Boss Man and it wasn't as easy as you might think. But the past is the past. Let's keep it that way."

"Tony, these things have a way of coming out, even long after you think they're dead and buried. Don't underestimate Doris' ability to understand and forgive."

He uncrosses his legs and leans forward, body tense and alert. "What are you saying? Are you going to tell her?" His eyes search mine for the answer.

"I'm just giving you some friendly advice. Think about it."

"Thank you." He relaxes again and smiles. "I know how to handle this."

I narrow my eyes on him and my voice carries a possibility that goes through me like a shock wave. "Is this why you said I can go as far as I want to? You think I might try to blackmail you with this?"

Now it's his turn to look shocked. "That hadn't even crossed my mind. You're not the type, Jeri, and I'm a good judge of character."

"No, I'm not the type. As you say, the past is the past. So for the moment, let's drop it."

"Gladly." He opens the top drawer of his desk. "I've had a check cut for you for five hundred dollars and one for Tin Foot, as promised. Constantin may have committed suicide, but that doesn't alter the fact that you knew it was him, and you were close on his heels. In fact, you may have been one of the factors that caused him to do what he did."

I stay motionless and look at him with what I hope is a blank face.

"Here you go." He leans forward with the two checks in his hand.

I take them from him, directing my eyes to the large checks with the circus name and logo written colorfully at the top. I push mine back across the desk. "I'll give Tin's to him but I want you to take my share and have a new check made out to Ioana Baboescu. I think she could use a leg up right about now. Tell her aunt it's a departing gift from the circus, anything, but don't tell her it's from me."

"That's pretty generous. Why? Why would you do this?"

"You ever read Virginia Wolff's A Room of One's Own?"

He shakes his head, puzzlement written all over his face.

"Then you might not understand, but do it, anyway."

He shrugs and picks up the check. "Whatever you say, Jeri." Looking down, he taps the check on the desk several times, leans back in his chair, and studies me.

"You're an old softy, you know that? You like to come across tougher than you are, but you always lead with your heart."

"I have to go," I say and get to my feet. "If you think I'm soft, you cross Doris. You'll see how soft I am." I walk awkward and stiff to the door, Tony's voice follows me every step of the way.

"I love her, Jeri. I would never hurt her. And I'm going to think seriously about what you said. Things do have a way of coming out when you least expect them to. For the record, I want to marry her."

I pivot around to see a pensive look on his face. His mood changes and he drops the subject.

"You start rehearsals in three weeks so you'd better be in shape. Don't spend that time laying around, reading those books you're so fond of. Keep in shape, you hear? And forget about all of this. The past is the past."

"Not always."

He flashes me a hesitant smile and waves. All in all, Tony is a good guy. I return his smile.

"Just see that Ioana gets that check," I say and close the door.

Chapter Thirty-two
10:45 am, Wednesday

Listening to the music coming from inside the Big Top, and John Murray Anderson's amplified commands, I head toward the First Aid Tent. My stride is slow, almost a saunter, so it's not so painful. Doc's voice keeps coming back to me, wrapping me in his words. Or smothering me; I can't tell.

'Do what your heart dictates.'

The words reverberate again and again inside me like the lyrics to a song I can't stop humming. I veer off, crossing the lot back toward the train. Not yet, I think, not yet.

I shade my eyes from the sun's reflection off the steel of the train, fifty-five cars gleaming like a giant's charm bracelet. A yellow and green taxicab speeds down a narrow path that runs beside it, bright and colorful against the silver backdrop of the train.

From the distance I can barely make out the words 'Sam's Taxi Service.' It stops at the "C" car. Suspecting I know what the cab is doing there and who it's taking away, I move closer, slowly at first and then as fast as I can.

The cabbie honks his horn twice, then twice again. A beautiful woman, tall and well dressed in a light gray suit, complete with hat and gloves, emerges from the train and comes down the platform stairs carrying a small suitcase. She's followed by Ioana, also carrying a small suitcase. I scoot behind one of the prop trucks and peek around the smoke stack that helps shield me from their sight.

Ioana wears a light blue frock, almost too small for her, and carries a pink and white striped giraffe, one of the stuffed animals I remember seeing on her bunk. She says something in Romanian, her face tear-stained but with a small light of happiness upon it.

The woman turns, bends over and hugs her. When she releases Ioana, she replies in a voice with a hint of an accent and fragrant with love,

"Ana, you must speak only English now. We are in America and soon you will be going to an American school with other American children. You will like that, yes?"

Ioana looks up with outright adoration and smiles. "Yes. I will have my own room and we will stay in one place all the time? No more traveling?"

Her aunt's laugh is low and musical. "Not unless you want to see Yellowstone Park next summer. Or the Grand Canyon. Wherever you'd like to go. You're going to be our daughter now, just like your mama would have wanted. Your Uncle Gerd said to tell you that he loves you very much."

She envelopes the girl again, one arm wrapping around the child's body while the other cradles the small head to her bosom. She rocks back and forth almost crooning.

"He would have been here with me but he needs to be at the factory. He has to be there every day to supervise, sometimes even at night and on the weekends. Otherwise, he would have come with me." She releases Ioana and touches her face, tracing a cheek with gloved fingers.

"That must be a very important job," says Ioana.

"It is and that is why you and I will be company for one another. Sometimes I get very lonely in that big house all by myself. Now I will have you to look out for and to take care of."

"I will take care of you, too, Aunt Flori. You wait and see," Ioana says solemnly.

"Yes, Ana. We will take care of each other," the woman agrees, standing tall and looking down at the girl.

Ioana looks up at her. "Do you think we could have a dog someday? They're good company, too."

The woman laughs just as the taxi driver, impatient to get going, toots his horn again. He gets out of the car, opens the trunk and put the two suitcases inside. Then he opens the back door of the cab and stands looking at his fares.

"We should go," says the woman. "It is time to go to the train. Do you have anyone you want to say goodbye to?"

Ioana thinks for a moment then shakes her head.

The aunt moves toward the door of the cab saying, "We already have a dog, Ana. You'll love her. Her name is Penny and she is a...."

The rest of her words are lost to me, as they move to the other side of the car. Ioana gets in first, followed by her aunt. The cabbie shuts the door, gets in himself, and starts the engine. I step out from behind the tractor and watch the brightly-colored car turn around on the narrow path, tires protesting with a crunching sound on the gravel. Ioana is now on the side of the car nearest me and sees me out of the corner of her eye. I lift a bandaged-covered hand and give a fleeting wave goodbye. Our eyes lock for a moment but neither of us smiles. She raises her hand in more of an acknowledgment than a wave, and the car darts off.

I hear a voice behind me say, "She'll be all right. That man her aunt married is rich. He's got the monopoly on all the buttons made for the army's uniforms. Runs two factories. They don't have any kids, either."

I turn to look at our reinstated general manager. "You missed your calling, Vince. You should have been a detective. You seem to know everything about everybody."

"Like they say, knowledge is power." A half-smile steals across his face. "Thanks for helping prove it wasn't me that killed Eddie. That could have followed me around for the rest of my life. I owe you."

"You don't owe me, Vince. But walk with me for a while. I'm on my way to have these bandages changed."

"Sure."

He falls in step and we stroll together in the sunlight, both silent, absorbing the sounds of the rehearsal inside the main tent, animal noises, and passersby. This is the most companionable I think I've ever been with him.

"I'm curious about something, Vince."

"How's that?"

"Why did you keep that empty envelope in Rosie's file, the one from Napa?" I stop walking and look at him.

He faces me, with a grimace. "The truth? Insurance. I knew she was a nut case from the beginning. Met a lot of people like her in Juvie Hall, just plain mean. She'd slice you open as soon as look at you if it served her purpose, pretty as she was. One day about three years ago, I saw her drop an envelope. She didn't know. I picked it up and gave it back to her the next day but I read the letter inside first." He look at me sheepishly. "I know, I know. I'm a nosy son of a bitch, so what else is new?"

"What did the letter say?"

"It was from an uncle of hers in the loony bin, writing to tell her about his shock treatments and how he hoped she didn't have to go through them when she was in the hospital. Anyway, I told her I was keeping the envelope and if she ever gave me any trouble, I was going straight to Tony with it and tell him what I knew. She stayed in line for me pretty good after that."

"It sounds like you've got yourself a dangerous hobby," I say. "Maybe you need to find a new one."

His voice falters. "Tony already told me to throw out anything in the files that isn't a clipping, brochure or legal document. No more personal comments, either, he said. Going to be pretty boring," He sounds more than a little sad.

"I'd follow his advice, if I were you."

"Got no choice. He's the Boss Man. Anything else?" he says, now impatient. I guess the camaraderie is over. "I got to see about two missing saddles. They're probably thrown under some bleachers, but I got to find them. Worth a lot of dough."

"There is one more thing that's nagging at me. Wally, the boy who found my watch the other day, what's going to happen to him if he's under sixteen, which I suspect he is? Will he have to go away? I hate to think of him ending up in --"

"Hey, you think I want any kid winding up like I almost did?" Vince smiles at me, relaxed again. "I got papers that say he's of age. I got them for all the boys. We take care of our own."

"Then I think that covers it, Vince. Thanks." I watch him scuttle away and wonder if he can kick the habit of nosing into other people's lives. I certainly haven't.

The Big Top has become quiet and subdued. Inside, everybody is probably on a break, sitting around alone or chatting in small groups, smoking, resting, doing all the things performers do with fifteen minutes to themselves.

The animals are low-keyed, too, no doubt fed and watered, waiting for the first show of the day. My shoes pad on the fresh sawdust. The sound of them seems to quiet me. A bird in one of the trees twitters a greeting as I pass. It's time, time to see Doc. I accept it.

I go inside the First Aid Tent, a tent which had seen so much action in the last three days, but now is empty and quiet, save for the nurse. In one of the back corners, Laverne is putting an assortment of bottles, scissors, a stethoscope and other items of her trade into a small bag. Her sad, round face looks up at me when I throw back the flap, but she gives me a faint smile and resumes her packing.

"Doc around?" I ask.

Laverne doesn't reply, but gestures with her head toward his office in the back of the tent.

I try to remain calm as I pass her with a nod; I rap on the pole and push back the flap. Doc is sitting at his desk, reading a magazine on medical equipment, and glances up with an easy smile.

"Good morning, Jeri. I've been expecting you." He dog-ears his page, closes the magazine and sets it down. "How are you feeling today?"

"Fine, better, sore. My hands and the inside of my legs hurt when I move but --"

"That will pass," he interrupts. "Is Laverne still out in the patient's area?"

I nod.

"She's leaving, retiring, giving up being a nurse, and going back to New Hampshire."

"She is? Why?"

Keeping his voice low, he says, "She said she can't continue nursing after what happened to Catalena. She blames herself. I spent hours trying to talk her out of it. I told her it was my fault, not hers. I told her the country needs good nurses but she says she's through. Damn shame, too, leaving a profession you've devoted thirty-five years of your life to in this way."

It hits me that what happens in our lives can affect many others. I never gave a thought to the nurse and here her life has been completely changed, if not ruined, by the events of the past few days.

"Oh, Doc, I'm so sorry," I murmur. I look at him. "Do you think if I had a talk with her, it would it help?"

He doesn't reply but shakes his head, grim lines taking hold of his mouth. He gestures for me to sit down, which I do, and he begins to unwrap the bandages on my hands.

There's a faint rap on the wooden pole. "Doctor Williams?"

Doc's head jerks up. "Yes?"

"I'm leaving now," Laverne says through the canvas. "I've left the name of my replacement and an address where you can mail anything I've forgotten."

He doesn't stir, but looks in the direction of her voice. His tone is careful and professional. "Very well, Laverne. Thank you for everything. Have a safe trip."

"Goodbye, Doctor Williams." She hesitates. "Take care of yourself."

I hear her exit then wait a beat before turning to him. In a low voice I ask, "Does she know?"

"Nobody does but you, Jeri." He smiles at me. "You're my own personal whispering tree." I look at him bewildered. "That's a tree with a small hollow in it, a hollow you can go and tell all your secrets, knowing full-well your words will never go any further."

"Some secrets aren't meant to be kept, though."

"That's true," he says. "As I told you last night, a person has to do what their heart dictates."

He applies the ointment and bandages while I sit still. My eyes begin to tear and I brush at them with the back of a newly bandaged hand.

"Doc," I say, in more of a croak than a whisper, when he was done. He looks up at me. I clear my throat and go on.

"May I come and see you? When you go to the hospital? I could bring you some Tootsie Rolls. I'm willing to share." I give him a shy smile.

"Nothing would give me greater pleasure, Jeri. It will be something to look forward to." He kisses me on the forehead. This time I don't pull back. Doc gets up and pats me on the head, before crossing to his desk.

"I've got to go," I say brusquely. "I'll see you this evening to change the bandages."

"This evening, Jeri. See you then." He turns back to me and says in a louder voice, "Have you read Dante's Inferno?"

"Most of it."

"I'm rereading it now. Food for thought, don't you think?"

"Not really. It's just one man's opinion, Doc."

A broad grin creases his face. "Ever the pragmatist, Jeri, that's what I love about you."

Chapter Thirty-three
11:30 a.m., Wednesday

I leave the First Aid Tent needing time to myself. I don't want to do anything. I don't want to talk, listen, feel, mourn, but mainly, I don't want to think.

I cross the lot and go between two of the railway cars, into the large and open field. I can hear the breeze rustling through the tall weeds nurtured by the sun and recent rains. Some are two or three feet high, now beautiful in their mature grace, unfettered by interfering, human hands.

I feel more at peace than I have in three days. My lungs rake in great gobs of air; my heart rate slows to normal.

Near a clump of trees at the far end of the field, I notice Harold and Old Kirby. Backs to me, the man sits in the grass, the big cat lying down beside him, each leaning against the other. Harold has one arm around the lion's bulky neck and shoulders in a companionable, protective, friend-for-life way.

They are so still, it might have been a photograph. Not even the cat's tail flicks the air, as they so often do. You can tell a lot about relationships, I muse, by how the captured subjects are touching one another.

A realization slams itself into me, so intense it's as if someone punched me in the stomach. I physically double over, then fall to my knees on the hard ground, jarring my injuries. The pain is excruciating, but nothing like the pain of seeing the truth that was staring me in the face since the beginning.

Why hadn't I seen it? I should have suspected Constantin's abnormal feelings for Catalena from the crumpled photo I returned to him. He was holding her more like a possessive lover than a doting father. The photo bothered me from the first, but I never saw why until now.

My mind goes back to the locked door between the two compartments. On the day I stole into them searching for Catalena's diary, the first thing Constantin did when he returned was to try the connecting door. I thought it was odd, but still wasn't suspicious. And the isolation in which he held the two girls, almost prison-like. Why didn't I see this? There were signs everywhere and I overlooked them all.

I find myself bawling like a baby into my bandaged hands, sobs so deep I feel them wrack throughout my body, so loud, I don't hear Whitey calling my name until he is upon me.

"Jeri, Jeri, darling!" He also drops to his knees and puts his arms around me. "Oh, my God. What is it? What's happened now?" He cradles me to his chest and tries to comfort me, much as Ioana's aunt did to her.

"Whitey, I failed her." I can barely talk but I force the words out. "Catalena is dead because I didn't see the truth."

"Shhhh," he says, rocking me back and forth. I can feel him enclose me, almost wrapping his body around me.

"It's all right. It's going to be all right. I don't know what you're talking about, but it's going to be all right."

I cling to him, wondering how I can keep the truth from him. I'm tired of keeping secrets. There are so many and they eat at me like a cancer.

I'll tell him. I'll tell him. But not today.

Whitey loosens his hold and looks down into my face, his startling blue eyes filled with love and worry. He brushes the hair from my forehead saying, "This will get better, darling. It will. Give it time. You'll see."

Whitey kisses one eye, then other, and embraces me again. "But if it makes you feel better, you go on crying until you're cried out. I know what it's like to need to do that." And so I do.

Several minutes later he gives me a handkerchief to wipe my face and never once asks me any questions. I love him for it.

"You know what I think?" he says after awhile. "I think you ask too much of yourself. I'm not sure why, but you do."

I let out a tight laugh. "Oh, Jesus, you must be kidding. All my life, Whitey, whatever I've been, it's never enough," I say, paraphrasing Doc's words. "Not for my father, not for my family, not for me. I've never been enough."

"Jeri," he says, taking my fingertips in his hand and stroking them. "There are a lot of people that think who you are is exactly enough. But you need to believe it yourself or you're never going to be happy. I've learned that the hard way."

We're both silent, lost in our own thoughts. When I steal a glance at him, his eyes are glazed over and far away, maybe in a small roadster, careening down a darkened road of long ago.

"You know the hell of it, Whitey?" I fold his handkerchief and hand it to him. He says nothing, waiting for me to go on.

"I'll never know if I had just lain down in the bank if that little boy might still be alive. And I'll never know if I'd seen the truth in the photo, Catalena might still --" I break off. "I'll never know."

"No, you never will."

"And I have to live with that every day of my life."

"'For of all sad words of tongue or pen, the saddest are these: 'It might have been!' John Whittier. Smart guy."

Whitey looks at me, rises and stretches out a strong hand. I grab onto it with both of mine, push up and into his arms.

About Heather Haven

After studying drama at the University of Miami in Florida, Heather went to Manhattan to pursue a career. There she wrote short stories, novels, comedy acts, television treatments, ad copy, commercials, and two one-act plays, which were produced at several places, including Playwrights Horizon. Once, she even ghostwrote a book on how to run an employment agency. She was unemployed at the time.

One of her first paying jobs was writing a love story for a book published by Bantam called *Moments of Love*. She had a deadline of one week but promptly came down with the flu. Heather wrote "The Sands of Time" with a raging temperature, and delivered some pretty hot stuff because of it. Her stint at New York City's No Soap Radio - where she wrote comedic ad copy – helped develop her long-time love affair with comedy.

Her first novel of the Alvarez Family Murder Mysteries, *Murder is a Family Business*, won the Single Titles Reviewers' Choice Award 2011, and the second, *A Wedding to Die For*, received the 2012 finalist nods from both Global and EPIC for Best eBook Mystery of the Year. The third of the series, *Death Runs in the Family*, has already received rave reviews and is a finalist in the EPIC Best eBook Mystery of 2013.

Stand-alone noir mystery, *Death of a Clown*, is steeped in Heather's family history. She is the daughter of real-life Ringling Brothers and Barnum and Bailey Circus folk. Her mother was a trapeze artist/performer and father, an elephant trainer. Heather brings the daily existence of the Big Top to life during World War II, embellished by her own murderous imagination.

Death of a Clown is published by The Wives of Bath Press, March 1, 2013.

The Wives of Bath Press

The Wife of Bath was a woman of a certain
age, with opinions, who's on a journey.
Heather Haven and Baird Nuckolls are
modern day Wives of Bath.
www.thewivesofbath.com

Made in the USA
Charleston, SC
27 July 2013